THE

James Hannay (George A. Bir_____
1865, and educated in England and at Trinity College, Dublin. Like his father, the young Hannay became a clergyman, first as a curate in County Wicklow, and from 1892 as rector of Westport, County Mayo. His first novel, *The Seething Pot* (1905), was written in an attempt to alleviate financial hardship, but it had the unintentional effect of enraging many of his parishioners with its irreverent depiction of the Church. Hannay was denounced, ostracised, and forced to withdraw from the Gaelic League, of which he was a leading member.

Real success came with the publication of *Spanish Gold* in 1908. The book was reprinted thirty-one times in the next twenty-seven years, and established Hannay as one of the most popular comic writers of his day. He also gained a reputation as a dramatist, his play *General John Regan* (later adapted as a novel) being produced in London and New York in 1913. After a performance in Westport, however, Hannay was burned in effigy, and the play condemned as 'an insult to Irish womanhood'.

From 1915, Hannay spent two years as a commissioned army chaplain in France. After the war he accepted a small parish in the Curragh, County Kildare, then spent two years attempting to revive the Church of England in Budapest. He returned to Ireland to take up the living at Mells. His final clerical appointment was as vicar of Holy Trinity, Kensington. He died in 1950.

As George A. Birmingham, Hannay was the author of over fifty novels, including *The Search Party* (1909), *Found Money* (1923) and *The Grand Duchess* (1924). He also published a collection of essays, *Spillikins*, and other works of non-fiction including *Children, Can You Answer This?*, *Do You Know Your Bible?* and *God's Iron: The Life of Jeremiah*.

SPANISH GOLD

George A. Birmingham

*New Introduction by
Terence de Vere White*

THE HOGARTH PRESS
LONDON

To
Theodosia and Althea,
who asked me to write a story
about treasure buried
on an island

Published in 1989 by
The Hogarth Press
30 Bedford Square
London WC1B 3SG

First published in Great Britain by Methuen & Co. 1908

All rights reserved. No part of this publication may be reproduced, stored in a retrieval system, or transmitted in any form, or by any means, electronic, mechanical, photocopying, recording or otherwise, without the prior permission of the publisher.

A CIP catalogue record for this book is available from the British Library.

ISBN 0 7012 0787 6

Copyright © Althea C. Hannay and Susan Harper 1908
Introduction copyright © Terence de Vere White 1989

Printed in Great Britain by
Cox & Wyman Ltd
Reading, Berkshire

INTRODUCTION

George A. Birmingham, one of the most talented comic writers of his day, was the pseudonym of Canon James Owen Hannay. The clergyman son of a clergyman, he was born in Belfast on 16 July 1865. He was proud of his origins, although he admitted in his memoirs: 'The rest of the world has not nearly such a high opinion of Belfast as Belfast has of itself'. He was inclined to underrate his own abilities and achievements, but he claimed to be able to complete any poem in Palgrave's *Golden Treasury* if given the first line. He grew up in a household where literature was respected – his father was a keen student of Milton. In Belfast rectories in those days it counted as iniquity to go to the theatre, but young James was granted permission provided he did nothing to draw attention to himself.

None of his early writing was fiction, but as a young curate in Delgany, County Wicklow, he wrote a short story and submitted it to *Temple Bar*, a reputable London magazine. He only did so to pay a pressing debt of ten pounds, but when the story was accepted and publication was followed by an invitation from a publisher to write a novel, he began one at once. After a conference with his wife – they were inseparable – he decided that novel-writing would interfere with parish duties and began instead a study of monasticism. To do that properly meant learning German. In the long winter evenings his wife sat with a German book on her lap and he sat at her feet with a dictionary in his hands.

In 1892 he became rector of Westport in County Mayo, a large scattered parish in which Protestants were thin on the ground and Dublin, on the other side of Ireland, was the most accessible city. He was very hard-up, but the scenery was matchless and there were admirable facilities for boating, Hannay's chief amusement since boyhood. With children to be educated, and wanting his sons to go, as he had, to a public school, he overcame his conscientious objections, and tried his hand at a novel. The result – *The Seething Pot* – was accepted by Edward Arnold after eleven refusals and published in 1905. Sales were modest, but there were some encouraging reviews. The parish priest in Westport took offence on the grounds that he was caricatured in the book. Hannay insisted in vain that he hadn't met the priest until after the book was written. There was nearly a riot in Westport, where Hannay was denounced, ostracised, and told to retire from committees, including the Gaelic League. He was physically threatened, and at this stage questions were asked in the House of Commons, where the matter, as Hannay would have wished, was not taken tragically. In 1914, after he had left Westport, there was an alarming scene when his play *General John Regan* was acted by a touring company in the town. Hannay was burnt in effigy.

He had been in trouble with his own flock since shortly after his arrival in the parish, having drawn attention to himself by defending Douglas Hyde in the letter columns of the *Church of Ireland Gazette*. Hyde was the leading spirit behind the founding of the Gaelic League to revive Irish as the spoken language of the people. The controversy that arose turned on the question of whether, as Hyde claimed, this could be brought about without a political entanglement. Hannay had written to say that it could be, and was at once taken on to the governing body. Many of Hannay's parishioners looked askance at these activities, and worse was to come when at a reading club he had formed in the parish Mrs Hannay delivered a paper about the Young Irelanders, as the poets and rebels of 1848 were called. An ardent nationalist who was present took the opportunity to deliver a speech in their favour. Distress and disapproval among the audience was not allayed when Hannay recited 'Oh, my dark Rosaleen' to soothe the ruffled feathers. No wonder he left Westport in 1913 when the success of *General John Regan* in London and New York made him financially independent at last. *Spanish Gold* had paved the way. First published in 1908, the thirty-first edition came out in 1935. In the author's own words, it was 'the first book of mine which won me anything more than a semi-political reputation'.

After that school fees presented no problems, and the rectory for the first time had a 'sufficient staff' of maids. Best of all, the Hannays could afford a good boat. They called it (and its two successors) *Mary Kate*, after the little girl in *Spanish Gold*. A simple act of gratitude, Hannay records, 'for it was that child, with her ragged frock and her silences, who earned us the money with which we bought the boat'. She was indeed an attractive creation, but, surely, the book's greatest triumph is the Reverend Joseph John Meldon. Eloquent, argumentative, persuasive, resourceful, he reconciles an uninhibited readiness to lie himself out of a tight corner with the doctrines of pragmatism. For sheer gusto, Shaw's Broadbent is the only fictional character of the time he can be compared with. Shaw is relevant here. He wrote about 'a certain humorous blackguardism ... which suits the flexibility of the Irish mind very well'.

The novel is dedicated to the Hannays' two daughters. They had asked their father to write a book about treasure buried on an island. He met the challenge in high good humour. The subject appealed to him (he would return to it in *Found Money*). It gave scope to his passion for boats and for the unmatched Westport scenery with its magic carpet of offshore islands.

Meldon's exuberance is given the foil of Major Kent's monumental impassivity. A slow-moving, slow-thinking sceptic, he has an unshakeable suspicion of Meldon's enthusiasms and stratagems. Those were the days when Holmes and Watson were flourishing. Here was another such incongruous but inseparable pair. The plot didn't matter very much, keeping up the pace was the challenge. It never slackens. Ireland and her political problems were Hannay's absorbing interest, as he acknowledged. Up to now they had given a serious or satirical spine to his novels. On this occasion he gave himself a holiday and discovered that his true gift was as an entertainer. His imagination was a happy one. The qualities which made him beloved in later years by the distinguished men and women who sought him out included a certain boyishness which neither his calling nor his serious interests ever seem to have succeeded in wholly suppressing. All children like tall stories, and Hannay shared that taste. There is a sort of blessed innocence about his blackguards, among whom Meldon stands supreme.

Hannay made *Spanish Gold* into a play, but his friend in the Haymarket Theatre who encouraged him to write it turned the apprentice effort down. Success on the stage had to wait for *General John Regan*, written in three days for Charles Hawtrey, a master of light comedy. Golding Bright, the dramatic agent who organised the production, told Hannay that English audiences would not accept a clergyman like Meldon on the stage, as he would give offence.

If politics as such play no part in *Spanish Gold*, the book does show Inishgowlan, the treasure island, enjoying the efforts made in the early years of the century 'to kill Home Rule by kindness'. Higginbotham, who represents the Congested Districts Board, and is marking out economic holdings for the few residents, turns out unexpectedly to have been one of Meldon's Trinity College contemporaries. He is extremely gullible, a perfect victim for Meldon's brilliant lies. Indeed, all the local inhabitants have to be lied to, to explain the presence of the Major's yacht and to give Meldon the freedom to search for the treasure. Any lie that seems not to be working has to be scrapped and replaced. In the middle of all this preliminary work the Chief Secretary, the Member of Parliament responsible for the government of Ireland, turns up unannounced on an unofficial visit. When confronted by the eminent visitor Meldon is abashed not a whit and helps himself to one of his special cigars.

'If you'd been familiar with the pragmatist philosophy it would have saved time. As you're not – though as Chief Secretary for Ireland I think you ought to be – I'll have to explain. Pragmatism may be described as the secularising of the Ritschilian system of theological thought. You understand the Ritschilian theory of value judgments, of course?'

The Chief Secretary doesn't, and goes down before the confident flow, like everyone else. Before they part he offers to recommend Meldon to his friend Lord Cumberley, who is looking for a suitable candidate for one of the livings in Nottingham that are in his gift. 'He never goes near the parish himself. He lives miles away and detests the place.'

Hannay, with a wide audience, especially in England, concentrated on amusing his readers. His output was remarkable, at least one novel a year, more often two, sometimes four. Considering his output he kept up a civilised standard. Looking for a comparison to his light touch, Compton Mackenzie – when in farcical vein – springs to mind. But the most obvious rival is that gifted pair, Somerville and Ross. Hannay could not have written their masterpiece *The Real Charlotte*. It evokes ambitious comparisons. Nor does he often get their consistent richness of phrase. His use of the vernacular is more superficial. There are exceptions, as when Mary Kate, his little heroine, on hearing that her grandfather Thomas O'Flaherty Pat has been thrown into a hole by the rival treasure hunters, exclaims: 'The Lord save us. They've took him at the latter end.'

Pomposity was his principal target, and his flippancy must have anguished solemn persons. He laid down the axiom that 'public business ought never to be taken seriously. It is always comic and should be treated as a joke.' His own experience on relief committees had taught him that. He recalled an applicant who used to place her hand on the minute book and preface her statements with a kind of oath until one member of the committee turned on her and said: 'Arra, woman, will you leave the name of God alone for one minute and tell the truth.'

For all his incursions into national controversies – even though he remained an outsider – Hannay was true to his origins. He had no desire to change the social hierarchy. In *Benedict Kavanagh*, published in 1913, he had this to say:

'In Ireland a curious national history has created a class distinction which almost exactly corresponds to the lines of political and religious cleavage. Men of one particular party claim – have indeed been almost forced to claim – a position of social superiority to everyone else in the country...'

(He was convinced that the clear implication that he was not a gentleman lay behind the anger of Westport's parish priest over *The Seething Pot*.) Hannay's Irish heroes tend to come from good families. The leader of the rival search party in *Spanish Gold* has a title. This – it may now seem – snobbish tendency may well have been a ploy for English readers, the sort of comfortable person who read the excellent *Strand Magazine* in its heyday and expected to be amused on the basis of certain social assumptions. Hannay, like most of his Irish literary contemporaries, was a member of the Protestant Ascendancy, but he saw the peasantry from outside, he did not look for material among them as Synge and Lady Gregory did, following the example of Douglas Hyde. Of Irish writers now living Hannay bears most resemblance to Molly Keane. Her satirical teeth are sharper, but both authors are accessible to English audiences.

Hannay gradually became disillusioned with the Irish scene. He broke with nationalist friends who saw the outbreak of war in 1914 as an opportunity to embarrass England. Though he was 50 in 1915 he asked for a commission as a chaplain and was in France for two years. After the war he accepted a small parish near the Curragh in Kildare, where the horse is the principal object of worship. When the La Touches, who had invited him, died within two years and Ireland was in the misery of guerrilla war, he resigned, not before he had been lucky to avoid the nervous revolver of a Black and Tan. There followed a year of recuperation in Dinard and two years trying to reorganise the English church in Budapest. He was there when a letter came from Sir John Horner, a total stranger, offering him the living at Mells. His reputation as a delightful acquaintance had travelled so far. He had by then broken his connection with the Church of Ireland. There followed happy years in a charmed circle, although he missed the scenery of North Antrim where he had holidayed as a boy, and Westport with the magnificent coastline of Mayo, and the Mayo people, with their

'grave courtesy ... We had been accustomed all our lives to the exquisite manners of the Irish people ... But at their worst English manners are not meant to be either rude or insulting ... We very soon discovered that the English – I think of every class – almost invariably tell the truth. They have made a habit of it and the effect on a stranger is startling at first.'

Terence de Vere White, London 1988

I

Moy Bay is full of islands, inhabited and uninhabited, and has many smaller bays leading from its main waters far inland. If it were anywhere but in Connacht it would be the haunt of yachtsmen. Being where it is, a pleasure boat rarely sails on it. At the south-eastern corner of the bay stands the town of Ballymoy. It is rich, like most West of Ireland towns, in public-houses and ecclesiastical buildings. It is rich in nothing else. Westwards, along the shore of the bay, runs the road which connects the town with the farmhouses of the neighbourhood and at last with the poverty-stricken villages which are scattered over the great bog. On this road there is a great deal of traffic. Country carts, droves of cattle, donkeys laden with panniers of turf and Major Kent's smart dogcart come into the town along it on market days and fair days. Therefore during nine-tenths of the year it is extremely muddy. When it is not muddy the dust blows in great clouds over it, to the discomfort of wayfarers who are accustomed to wet feet and mud-clogged boots, but hate to feel limestone grit between their teeth and in their eyes.

The Rev. Joseph John Meldon bicycled along this road one afternoon near the end of May. The day was very hot and the little wind there was blew against him as he rode. The dust had powdered his black clothes till they looked grey, and lay thick in the creases of his trousers, which were bound round his ankles by thin steel clasps. He rode rapidly and was most uncomfortably hot. His hands were red and moist. Every now and then a drop of sweat gathered beside his nose, trickled down and lodged among the hairs of his thick red moustache.

A soft felt hat, grey with dust like his clothes, was pushed back from his glistening forehead.

There was no reason why Mr Meldon, curate of Ballymoy, should have ridden fast on such a day. He was out upon no desperate enterprise, rode no race against death or misfortune, would win no bet by arriving anywhere at any specified time. His day's work, not a very arduous one—for members of the Church of Ireland are few in Ballymoy—was done. He might have ridden slowly if he liked, might have walked, need not have travelled the road at all unless he chose. The afternoon and evening were before him, and he proposed to spend them with Major Kent at Portsmouth Lodge. It made no difference when he arrived there. Four o'clock, five o'clock, six o'clock, any hour up to seven o'clock, when he dined, would be the same to Major Kent, who was one of those fortunate gentlemen who have nothing particular to do in life. Mr Meldon rode fast and got hot, when he might have ridden slowly and been no more than warm, because he was a young man of impetuous energy and liked going as quickly as he could on all occasions.

'I hope,' he murmured, conscious of his heat while he enjoyed increasing it, 'that old Kent will give me a proper drink when I arrive. I could do nicely this minute with a lemon squash.'

Another man, while dwelling with pleasure on the expectation of a drink, would have also wished for a wash and the use of a clothes brush. The ideal curate, the 'dilettante, delicate-handed priest' of Tennyson's poems, the beloved of ladies in English country towns, would have wished first to be clean and then desired some mild refreshment—tea, perhaps, served in an old china cup. But Mr Meldon was no such curate. Indeed, those who knew him well wondered at his being a curate at all. He was more at his ease in a smoking-room than a drawing-room, and preferred a gun to a Sunday-school roll-book. He cared very little about his personal appearance, and considered that he paid sufficient respect to the virtue of cleanliness if he washed every morning. He was physically strong, played most games well, had been distinguished as an athlete in college, smoked black tobacco, and was engaged to be married. Also, though no one ever gave him credit for being studious, he read a great many books.

'A dash of whisky,' he murmured again, 'would improve that lemon squash. To do the Major justice, he's free with his drinks. A fellow has to be careful of himself with that old boy.'

A dogcart approached him, driven towards Ballymoy. The driver was a stout, fair man. Beside him, wrapped in a shabby, fur-lined coat, sat a thin, sallow youth.

'Hullo, Doyle,' shouted Meldon, 'what brings you out here?'

He dismounted from his bicycle and stood in the middle of the road. He recognised that the sallow youth in the fur coat was a stranger in Ballymoy. Meldon wanted to find out something about him—all about him if possible. Ballymoy is situated in a district not frequented by tourists. Therefore strangers are rare and objects of great curiosity to the regular inhabitants. There are, broadly speaking, just two classes of strangers to be met in West of Ireland towns which lie off the tourist track. There are gentlemen connected with the Government, the engineers, surveyors, and inspectors of our various benevolent boards; Members of Parliament on tour, and journalists despatched by editors to report on the state of Ireland, who are regarded by the people of Ballymoy as more or less connected with the Government, a sort of camp followers. This class of strangers is only moderately interesting. In Connacht we are getting quite familiar with the Government, and familiarity breeds, if not actual contempt, at all events a lack of curiosity. The second class consists of men who have come to grief somewhere else, through wine, women, or one of the other usual causes of disgrace, and are seeking seclusion till the memory of their misdeeds has faded from the minds of relatives and friends. Respectable relatives and friends, English for the most part, have apparently come to the conclusion that the pastures of the West of Ireland are peculiarly suitable to black sheep. This class is smaller than the other, but much more interesting. The stories of the exile's misdeeds, when we get to know them, as we always do in the end, are frequently most diverting.

Meldon leaped to the conclusion that Mr Doyle's companion belonged to the class of scandalous livers. He had not the look of benevolent intelligence which is always to be found on the faces of men connected with the Government, and he wore a fur coat, whereas officials, Members of Parliament, and journalists always wear brown tweed suits and disdain luxurious overcoats when they wander in wild places. Besides, Mr Doyle, the owner of the principal inn in Ballymoy, was likely to have a stranger of the second class under his care, while anyone connected with the Government would prefer to go round the country with a priest or a policeman. Meldon wondered whether it was love, or debt, or whisky, which had brought this prodigal to Ballymoy.

Mr Doyle pulled up his horse and greeted the curate.

'Good-evening to you, Mr Meldon. A warm evening for the end of May. I'd rather be driving, than riding that machine of yours today. On your way to see the Major, eh? You'll find him at home. We've just been out at his place.'

'Oh, have you? Wanting to buy the chestnut filly? Take my advice and don't do it. She wouldn't suit your work at all. She's cut out for a polo pony, that one. You're too fat to start polo, Doyle. It wouldn't agree with you at your time of life. You may take my word for that.'

Doyle grinned.

'It wasn't the filly I was after. The fact is that this gentleman, Mr Langley——'

'Langton,' said the stranger.

'That this gentleman,' said Doyle, avoiding a second attempt at the name, 'wants to hire a yacht, and I thought the Major might let him have the *Spindrift*. She's the best boat about these parts, though there's others, of course—plenty of others.'

'I have one myself,' said Meldon.

'You have,' said Doyle, 'and I was intending to take the gentleman round to your place this evening. Your boat would just suit him.'

'What sort of a boat does he want?' said Meldon.

'I'm looking out for a small yacht,' said Langton, 'anything from ten tons down to five would do. I and a friend intend to take a little cruise together, and we want something that we can work without professional assistance.'

'The Major didn't see his way to hiring him,' said Doyle.

Meldon eyed the stranger and thought that the Major was quite right in refusing to trust the smart, well found *Spindrift* to Mr Langton. The man didn't look as if he ought to go to sea without professional assistance. He looked like a man who might make a wreck of a boat through incapacity to manage her. Meldon's own boat was neither smart nor well found. He had got her cheap because her hull was rotten and most of her rigging untrustworthy. It was one thing to hire the trim *Spindrift* to a chance stranger, who might knock the bottom out of her or ruin her sails; it was quite a different thing to bargain for the use of his own *Aureole*, which no amount of battering could make much worse than she was. Like everyone else in the West of Ireland, cleric or layman, Meldon had a keen taste for making money out of a stranger. He looked at Langton and hoped that it was love or whisky, not debt, which had driven him to Ballymoy.

'There's more boats in the country than the Major's,' he said.

'That's what I'm just after telling the gentleman,' said Doyle, 'there's yours.'

'I'm wanting her for my own use.'

'She's a good boat,' said Doyle.

'I must be getting along,' said Meldon. 'Good-evening to you, Doyle. Good-evening, Mr Langton.'

'You wouldn't be wanting to hire her?' said Doyle, unimpressed by the curate's farewell. 'It's not often you take her out.'

'How long would your friend require her for?'

'One month,' said Langton. 'My friend and I want to have a cruise on your charming coast, to take a pleasure trip. To find repose from the tumult of the world on the bosom of the Atlantic.'

Doyle winked at the curate. Meldon, reflecting that a man who talked in such a way in broad daylight must be a fool about money, determined to hire the *Aureole* to the stranger.

'I can't wait now,' he said, 'but I'll call round at your place tonight, Doyle. Don't go to bed till I come. We'll talk the matter over.'

He mounted his bicycle and rode on towards Portsmouth Lodge.

Kent is an English name. The traveller meets it in Connacht with surprise; perhaps, if he is an amateur of local colour, with disgust. An inhabitant of Mayo or Galway ought to have a name beginning with O', a name with several apparently unnecessary letters in it. He has no business to sign himself John Kent. Still less has a house in the West of Ireland any right to a name like Portsmouth Lodge. It raises thoughts of merry England, of the concreted parade of some naval town. It is incongruous. It meets the sentimental traveller, who expects the Celtic glamour, Tir-na-noge, and fairy lore, like a slap in the face. Yet it never occurred to the Major to alter one name or the other. He was born too early to come under the spell of the Gaelic revival, and never felt the slightest inclination to write himself Seaghen Ceannt, or to translate his address into Béal an Chuain. He had inherited both names from his grandfather, an English sailor, the first of his family to settle in Ireland.

The Major himself had served for many consecutive years in a line regiment. The drill, to which he took naturally, being the kind of man who enjoys drill, had straightened his back, and it continued to be straight long after his retirement from military life. The feeling in favour of smartness of attire which prevails among men holding His Majesty's commission remained with Major Kent and distinguished him among the small landholders and professional men of the Ballymoy district. They preferred comfort to neatness. Major Kent, at great sacrifice of leisure, creased his trousers and dressed for dinner every night. He had a taste for discipline which he carried into the management of his small estate and into the business of the petty sessions court. He annoyed both his tenants and his neighbours by his fads, but was a popular man because of the real goodness of his heart. He was an excellent shot, a good amateur yachtsman, a regular subscriber to the funds of the church, and a bachelor. He had formed a friendship with the Rev. Joseph John Meldon in spite of the curate's free-and-easy manners, habitual unpunctuality, and incurable untidiness. It is said that men are attracted to those who differ from them, that like does not readily mate with like. If this is a law of nature, the friendship between Major Kent and the curate formed a fine example of its working.

Meldon entered the dining-room of Portsmouth Lodge and found the Major at the writing-table with a pile of papers and parchments beside him. Papers of any kind, except *The Times*, which the Major read regularly, were rare in Portsmouth Lodge. To see his friend occupied with what looked like legal documents was unprecedented in Meldon's experience. He stood amazed at the sight. The Major looked up.

'Who the devil's disturbing me now? Oh, it's you, J. J. I beg your reverence's pardon for swearing, but this is the fourth time I've been interrupted this afternoon already. First there was James Fintan, the publican from Ballyglunin, wanting an occasional licence for the day of the races, the old reprobate. He'll poison half the county with the stuff he sells as whisky in those tents of his. Then nothing would do the chestnut filly but to cut her near hind leg on the barbed wire, and she had to be seen to. Then Jemmy Doyle came over with some stranger who wanted to hire the *Spindrift*. As if I'd lend my boat to a man I've never set eyes on before—a fellow in a fur coat, who most likely knows no more about sailing than I do about midwifery. And now it's you, J. J. But sit down and light your pipe. I suppose you want a drink. There's whisky and a syphon of soda on the sideboard.'

'I want a lemon,' said the curate, 'and a big tumbler.'

'Well, then, you'll have to ring the bell. The housekeeper will get them for you. When you've settled yourself you may as well give me a hand with the job I'm at.'

'I'll go out to the kitchen and get what I want,' said Meldon. 'That'll be quicker and easier than ringing bells.'

He secured his lemon and concocted for himself the drink he desired. With the tumbler on the floor beside him, he stretched himself in a deep chair and lit his pipe.

'Now, Major,' he said, 'I'm ready. What can I do for you?'

'Can you read Latin and Greek?' said the Major.

'Of course I can. I'm a B.A. of Trinity College, Dublin, and that means that I've read a heap of Latin and Greek in my day. At the same time, Major, I warn you fairly, that if you want me to sit here translating Plato or Aristotle to you all the evening, I'm not on. The weather's too hot.'

'What are you talking about?' said the Major. 'Who wants you to translate Plato? When I asked if you could read Latin and Greek what I meant was, can you read lawyer's English?'

'Oh, you meant that, did you? Well, I can read lawyer's English or any other kind of English for that matter. I tell you, Major, a man who has been through the Divinity School of T.C.D. and read Pearson on the Creed isn't likely to be beaten by anything a lawyer could write. What's your difficulty?'

'Old Sir Giles Buckley's dead,' said the Major.

'I know that. The rector's in a fine fizz over losing his subscription to the church. The old boy hasn't been near the place this twenty years, but he paid up like a man. Now the property has gone to a nephew, who means to sell it, I hear, as soon as he can, and who doesn't care a rap about the church. By the way, isn't there a son somewhere?'

'There is. A bad lot—and always was a bad lot. Cards, women, horses, and the devil. The Lord alone knows where he is now. He got the baronetcy, of course, and the house and demesne, which were entailed. But that's all. Old Sir Giles didn't leave him a penny nor an acre more than he could help. But that's no affair of mine. The point for me is this. My grandfather got the land I hold now from old Sir Giles's father. He got it for services rendered in '98, when the French landed at Killala. He was a sailor, a naval man——'

'I know,' said Meldon. ' "Hearts of oak are our ships, hearts of oak are our men," and all that sort of thing.'

'The Sir Giles of that day got into a panic when the French landed. It appears that he wasn't particularly popular in the county, and he didn't feel quite sure what the people might do to him.'

'They might have done several things. They might, for instance, have hanged him.'

'So he seemed to think. Well, my grandfather took him off in his sloop, which happened to be lying in the bay at the time, and kept him safe till the business was over. In return he got the land out of old Buckley, and here we are, father and son, three generations of us, ever since, the Kents of Portsmouth Lodge. Now that this new man is going to sell the estate, the question comes up what kind of title have I?'

'That'll be all right,' said Meldon. 'Don't you worry about the matter. I'll see you through. Just you hand me over those papers. You trot off and do anything you think you have to do before dinner. I'll get the meaning out of the papers for you and have a clear statement of the case ready when you get back. Give me the whole bundle. There's a little brown book left on your desk. Hand it over with the rest.'

'It's of no importance.'

'Is it private? No? Then pass it over. What you think of no importance is just as likely as not to be the vital document. It's always the papers that seem unimportant to the mere amateur which turn out to contain the clue in these cases of disputed inheritance, and so forth. You don't read many novels, I know, Major, but you must have noticed that fact.'

'But this little book is nothing but an old diary of my grandfather's.'

'Quite so,' said Meldon. 'That's just the sort of thing I want to get at. Now do you be off and leave me in peace.'

'I'll go down and have a look at the *Spindrift*,' said the Major. 'I'm having her overhauled and fitted out for a cruise. What do you say, J. J.? Will you come with me for a week? We might go off to Inishgowlan and shoot seals.'

'Are there seals on Inishgowlan?'

'There are, I believe. When do you get your holiday?'

'June,' said Meldon. 'The rector's taking July and a bit of August. I don't care to put off till September. But I can't go with you. I'm booked. I promised to spend a week with my old governor and the rest of the time with my little girl in Rathmines.'

'Bother your little girl.'

'You wouldn't say that if you saw her. She's a remarkably nice little girl, nicer than any you've ever seen. I have her photo here——' He put his hand into his breast pocket.

'Thanks,' said the Major. 'You've shown me her photo before.'

'This is a different photo. It's a new one, done by a first-rate man. Look here.'

'Keep it till after dinner. I must be off to take a look at the *Spindrift*.'

'Very well then, go. But you may whistle for the photo after dinner. I won't show it to you. No man shall say I rammed my little girl down his throat. You may be a callous old mysogynist, Major——'

'A what? I wish you wouldn't use that sort of language out of the pulpit, J. J.'

'A mysogynist. It means a sort of curmudgeon who doesn't care to look at the photo of a pretty girl when he gets the chance.'

'A mysogynist shows some sense then,' chuckled the Major.

'You may think so; but I can tell you a mysogynist is the exact opposite kind of man to what Solomon was, and he is generally given credit for not being quite a fool.'

2

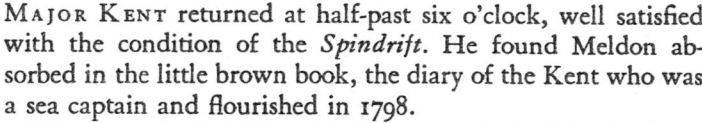

MAJOR KENT returned at half-past six o'clock, well satisfied with the condition of the *Spindrift*. He found Meldon absorbed in the little brown book, the diary of the Kent who was a sea captain and flourished in 1798.

'Have you worked through the papers?' asked the Major.

'Haven't looked at one of them,' said Meldon, 'and don't mean to. I've got something here worth Portsmouth Lodge and your whole footy little property along with it.'

'I don't believe you.'

'Very well, then, don't. Be an incredulous Jew, if you like. But I can tell you you'll open your eyes when you hear what I've found.'

'Hurry up, then, and tell me. It's time for me to go and dress for dinner.'

'Go on. Get into your starched shirt and your silk-lined coat. After dinner I'll tell you all about it.'

'Wouldn't you like a wash yourself J. J.?'

'No,' said the curate, 'I'm a busy man. I can't spend hours and hours every day washing and dressing myself. I've something else to do. At present I have to run through this log of your grandfather's again and copy out a few of the most important bits.'

Major Kent dressed quietly. He dined with a good appetite and without hurry. Meldon seemed excited and eager to get dinner over. Contrary to his usual custom, he ate very little. He kept the old diary beside his plate, and every now and then stroked it affectionately.

At last the meal came to an end. The servant, after leaving coffee on the table, finally withdrew. Major Kent lit a pipe and lay back in a comfortable chair, Meldon stood with his back against the chimneypiece.

'I'm coming with you on your cruise to Inishgowlan,' he said.

'What about your poor old governor and the little girl in Rathmines?'

'Never you mind about them. When I've explained things to you a bit you'll see that it'll be a jolly sight better both for my governor and for my little girl if I go with you.'

'You mean to shoot seals and to make muffs out of their skins for the little girl.'

'No, I don't. I know well enough that the seals off this coast don't have the proper sort of skins for muffs. I mean to go to Inishgowlan and bring back a whole pot of money, thousands and thousands of pounds. I'll rig my little girl out in proper furs when I get back. She shall have silk dresses and real lace and a motor-car, and I'll drive her up and down Grafton Street and buy her any mortal thing she chooses. I'll take my poor old governor out of that beastly dispensary, where he's slaving away doctoring people who neither pay nor say "Thank you." I'll set him up in a jolly little house down near Kingstown with a couple of daily papers, a bottle of good whisky, and as much tobacco as he cares to smoke. I'll give the rector a couple of hundred or so for the church, and make his mind easy about the loss of Sir Giles's subscription. I'll——'

'Perhaps you'll tell me,' said the Major, 'where this enormous fortune is to come from.'

'Out of Inishgowlan.'

'Oh! out of Inishgowlan. I see. But how?'

'Look here, Major. Your grandfather went to that Island in 1798 with Sir Giles and Lady Buckley. He anchored his sloop in the bay, and, naturally, as they were there nearly six weeks, they occasionally went on shore.'

'I shouldn't wonder if they did.'

'Very well. The people of Inishgowlan in those days talked

nothing but Irish, and so naturally your grandfather and Sir Giles couldn't understand them. But Lady Buckley could.'

'I know what you're at now,' said the Major. 'I've read that diary or log or whatever the old man called it. You've got a hold of that cock-and-bull story about the Spanish Armada shipwreck and the lost treasure.'

'Do you mean to deny,' said Meldon, 'that a Spanish ship was wrecked on Inishgowlan?'

'No, I don't. I daresay there was one wrecked there. That Armada seems to have piled up ships all round this coast. My grandfather brought back an old iron chest from Inishgowlan which is in the house this minute. I always heard it was an Armada chest.'

'So far, so good. You give in to the shipwreck. Now it appears that Lady Buckley didn't say a word to her husband or your grandfather at the time about what she heard from the island people. But when she came home she told them a long story. All the people believed then that there was a pile of gold hidden somewhere on the island. They said that the Spanish captain left the island with the remains of his crew in two of their curraghs, or rather their great-grandfather's curraghs, and didn't, in fact couldn't, take anything with him except some papers and arms. That's the story Lady Buckley heard.'

'I don't think much of it,' said the Major. 'I don't see where the treasure comes in.'

'Well, you must be uncommonly thick-headed if you don't. If the Spanish captain didn't carry off the treasure, he must have left it on the island. You follow that reasoning, I suppose?'

'I do, of course, but——'

'Well, if the treasure had been found anytime between the shipwreck and 1798 the people would have known about it, wouldn't they? And they wouldn't have told Lady Buckley it was still on the island. Therefore the treasure was still there in 1798. See?'

'But——'

'Wait a moment. If the treasure was discovered since 1798 we'd have heard of it. Those Inishgowlan men come in here to Ballymoy to do their marketing. Now suppose they'd taken to offering the shopkeepers hundreds and thousands of Spanish gold coins any time during the last century, do you suppose we shouldn't have heard of it? Why, man, the whole country would be full of stories of their find. But nobody in their neighbourhood has ever so much as seen a Spanish coin, therefore the Inishgowlan people can't have found the treasure. Therefore it's on the island still.'

Meldon paused triumphantly. His chain of reasoning was complete.

'That's all right,' said the Major, 'supposing there ever was any treasure to find.'

'My dear Major, do try to be sensible. Further on in the log-book, which you say you've read, I find that old Sir Giles and your grandfather, having heard Lady Buckley's story, made another expedition to the island to look for the treasure.'

'They did, and brought back the old iron chest that's in my bedroom this minute.'

'Now I ask you,' said Meldon, 'were your grandfather and old Sir Giles the kind of men to go off on a wild-goose chase after treasure which didn't exist? They weren't that kind of men at all, either of them. They were shrewd, hard-headed men who thought things out carefully before they acted. If they had a fault, it was that they were a bit too keen about money.'

'How do you know all that?'

'It stands to common sense,' said Meldon. 'People who keep their property safe, as the Buckley's did, all through the eighteenth century in Ireland, must have been pretty sharp business men. Besides, I always heard that the first Buckley came over from Scotland. And the Scots, as we all know, don't waste their time fooling after treasure which doesn't exist. You may take my word for it, Major, that those two old gentlemen knew what they were about.'

'They didn't find it.'

'No, they didn't. That's where we come in. If they'd found it, it wouldn't be there for us, would it?'

'I don't see that you've proved yet that there was any treasure to find. The ship, supposing there was a ship wrecked there, mightn't have had treasure in her.'

'That's where your want of a proper education tells against you, Major. If you'd read history you'd know that all those Spanish ships were full of treasure. Take Kingsley's "Westward Ho!" for instance. You may have read that perhaps.'

'That's only a novel.'

'Well, I can't help quoting novels to you when you've read nothing else, and very few of them. If you'd read other books I'd refer you to them. But "Westward Ho!" will show you that the Spaniards never went to sea without a good supply of gold in the holds of their ships, besides silver cups and any amount of ecclesiastical robes, copes, and mitres and things, simply studded with gems. That's the kind of men the Spaniards were.'

'I suppose you think you're going to find all this wonderful treasure yourself.'

'Of course I am. It only wants a little intelligence.'

'You said just now that old Sir Giles and my grandfather were intelligent men, and they didn't find it.'

'They hadn't the advantages we have now,' said Meldon. 'I don't deny their intelligence, but they didn't know, they couldn't know, how to go about the business. The discovery of buried treasure hadn't become an exact science in their time. Edgar Allen Poe hadn't written his stories. The art of the detective hadn't been developed. They hadn't so much as heard of Sherlock Holmes. They had about as much chance of finding that treasure as Galileo with his old-fashioned telescope had of discovering a disease germ. Now we are in quite a different position. We start with all the methods of highly-trained intellects ready to our hand, so to speak. There's only one thing I'm sorry for, and that is that there isn't a cryptogram. I'm particularly good at cryptograms.'

'How do you mean to start?'

'It would have been easier,' said Meldon, 'if there had been a cryptogram. However, there isn't. Or, if there is, we haven't got it. As it is, we've got to do without it. The first thing is to put ourselves in the place of the Spanish captain. That's the way great detectives always begin. They put themselves in the other fellow's place and think what they'd have done if they'd been him. Now, supposing you'd been the Spanish captain and found that you couldn't carry off your treasure, what would you have done with it?'

'I suppose I'd have dug a hole and buried it.'

'No, you wouldn't. Not unless you'd been a perfect fool. If you'd been the Spanish captain you'd have had more sense than you appear to have now.'

'Then it wouldn't have been me.'

'It would, because we started with the supposition that you were the Spanish captain, and he must have had some sense. You don't suppose the Spaniards, the greatest nation on earth at the time, would have started off a thing like that Armada without seeing that the captains of the ships were sensible men. Of course they wouldn't.'

'But if the captain had sense and I haven't——'

'There's no use arguing round a subject in that way. Put it like this. Suppose I was the Spanish captain, what would I have done? I wouldn't have dug a hole, because I would have known that the people of the island would have watched me dig it. Even if I'd dug it at night they'd have seen the marks next morning, and the moment my back was turned they'd have dug the treasure up again. You must give the captain credit for being a reasonable man.'

'Well, now you've barred burying the treasure, which I still think was the obvious thing——'

'Too obvious. That's my point.'

'What would you do? There aren't any caves on the island that ever I heard of.'

'I shouldn't have put it into a cave in any case. A cave is exactly the place the amateur treasure-seeker always looks for first. No. If I were the Spanish captain I should have picked out an unobtrusive-looking hole or cleft in the rocks, just above high-water mark, and dumped my stuff down there. What we have to do is to find that hole or cleft.'

'That will be a longish job,' said the Major. 'I should guess the island to be about two miles around. It will take some time to poke into every hole in two miles of rough rocks.'

'We shan't do that. We shall proceed on a carefully reasoned, scientific plan, which I shall think out and explain to you when we get there.'

Meldon lit his pipe, which he had hitherto neglected, poured himself out a cup of coffee, and sat down. He remained silent, and it was evident that he was thinking out the scientific plan. The Major took up his *Times* and began to read a leading article on the appallingly lawless condition of Ireland. At the end of a quarter of an hour Meldon spoke.

'Have you a map of the island?'

'No. I have a chart and the sailing directions, but they are on board the *Spindrift*.'

Again Meldon remained silent for a time. Then he asked—

'Are there many people on the island?'

'Ten families, I believe,' said the Major. 'All cousins of each other.'

'I ask,' said Meldon, 'because if there are people there we may find it necessary to adopt some disguise.'

'If you imagine for a moment that I'm going to wander round that island, or any other, dressed up in a false beard and blue spectacles——'

'I don't imagine anything of the kind. When I said that we must adopt some disguise, I meant that we must be able to give a reasonable account of our proceedings to the natives. If we let them know we're after their treasure there may be trouble. They will naturally want to go shares in our find.'

'I'd take half a crown,' said the Major, 'for all I find.'

Meldon knocked the ashes out of his pipe and rose.

'I must be off,' he said. 'I've got to see Doyle and that fellow Langton tonight about hiring my boat to them. I was thinking of asking £30 for the month.'

'The boat's not worth it to buy,' said the Major. 'You only gave £25 for her.'

'Well, I said I'd ask £30. I'm quite prepared to take £25. That will simply be getting my money back, with no profit on the business at all.'

'You'll have the boat at the end of the month.'

'Will I? Unless the friend he talks about is a different sort of man from what Langton looks there'll be precious little of the *Aureole* left at the end of the month.'

'All right,' said the Major. 'Get what you can. If the man is fool enough to hire your *Aureole* for £25 he's certainly fool enough to smash her up. But I advise you to see the colour of his money before you hand over the boat.'

Meldon winked.

'In any case,' said the Major, 'he'd be a fool to go to sea in her. She's rotten.'

'I don't expect he wants to go to sea,' said Meldon. 'He'll just potter about among the islands in the bay. Anyway, he's got to take my boat if he wants one at all. You won't hire yours, and there's no other. Doyle said this afternoon that there were plenty, but that was only to encourage Langton to stay on at the hotel. There's nothing else that could be called a yacht within fifty miles of Ballymoy. But I must be off. Let me see, is there anything else we have to settle?'

'You might fix a day for starting,' said the Major.

'Monday next. I'll see the rector tomorrow and arrange about it. I could start on Sunday night if you like. It's my turn to preach in the evening and I'd cut it a bit short, so as to be out here with you by half-past seven.'

'No, thanks. Monday morning will be time enough for me. But we'll get off early. You'd better come out and sleep here or on the boat. I'm glad you're coming, J. J. We'll have a jolly cruise. We'll spend a couple of days on the small island and then run across to the big one.'

'We'll do nothing of the sort. I can't give more than a week altogether, and it will take us all that time to get the treasure.'

'You don't mean to say that you really expect to get that treasure?'

'I do, of course. I tell you, Major, I've all my life had a taste for treasure-seeking. Next to piracy or being wrecked on a desert island, there's nothing in the world I'm so keen on as hidden treasure. I'm pretty sure that I have a special talent for finding it. Do you suppose I'm going to miss my chance now I've got it? Not likely.'

'J. J.,' said the Major solemnly, 'you're a bigger fool than any one would take you for by your looks.'

'All right. Just you wait till we're coming home again, and see who is the fool then.'

3

Meldon mounted his bicycle and rode towards Ballymoy even more rapidly than he had ridden out in the afternoon. It was a moonless night and the road in some places was difficult to see. About three miles from the town Meldon ran into a donkey, which, after a fashion common among donkeys in Connacht, was lying asleep in the middle of the road. The creature was greatly startled but not much hurt. It floundered over the bank into the nearest field as quickly as its hobbled forelegs allowed it. Meldon was pitched over his handle-bars and cut the palms of both his hands. He picked himself up and found that the front forks of his bicycle were badly bent. It was impossible to ride and almost impossible to wheel the machine. With the perfect confidence in everybody's honesty which residence in the West of Ireland begets in a man, he laid the machine in a ditch and walked on. His card was in the tool-bag, and he felt sure that some carter would bring the thing into the town in the morning. He whistled cheerfully as he tramped along. The Rev. J. J. Meldon had an excellent temper. It took more than a trifling accident and a few cuts to upset it. He didn't even use unkind language about the donkey.

It was late when he arrived in Ballymoy. The windows of most of the houses were dark and the people were in bed. A light still burned in an upper window of Mr Doyle's hotel. Before the days of the Land League it had been called the 'Buckley Arms'. Mr Doyle's father, recognising the fact that politicians and farmers were his best customers, had taken down the old sign, which might have been offensive, and put up in large gilt letters, 'The Imperial Hotel'. Some day, perhaps, if patriotism becomes the motive power of Irish agitation, another Doyle will change the name again and call his house 'The National'. In the meanwhile 'The Imperial' is a good name. It suggests a certain spacious sumptuousness and justifies the price which Mr Doyle charges for beds, dinners, and breakfasts.

The prospect of the large fortune which he expected to get on Inishgowlan Island did not in the least modify Meldon's eagerness to make the best possible bargain with the stranger. Even if he had actually secured all the Spanish gold, he would still have been keenly anxious to get the most he could for his boat. Like all Irishmen, he found a pleasure in bargaining, and haggled for shillings without being particularly covetous, in the spirit of the sportsman who hunts foxes which he doesn't want to eat. Meldon looked forward to being able to brag afterwards of having got the better of a stranger. That, and the delight of proving himself the better man, were the attractive things, not the mere acquisition of a pound or two.

He entered the hotel and found Mr Langton sitting in lonely splendour in a room called the drawing-room. There was a bottle of whisky on a table before him and a jug of water. But Mr Langton, perhaps because the visitor he expected was a clergyman, had drunk very little. The bottle was almost full. The carpet was littered with tobacco ash and the ends of cigarettes. All the books which usually adorned Mr Doyle's solitary bookshelf were on the floor. Mr Langton had been trying to read them and had failed. There were four sixpenny novels, three biographies of saints with gilt tops to their leaves, a prayer-book with an imitation ivory cross on its cover, a copy of Moore's 'Melodies' with the music, and several very old magazines. There was also a tattered book called 'Speeches from the Dock', which Mr Langton seemed to have found more interesting than the others, for he held it in his hand.

'Good-evening to you, sir,' said Meldon. 'I called with reference to the boat about which we were speaking this afternoon.'

'Quite so. I'm glad to see you. Sit down. Do you mind if I ring the bell for Mr Doyle? He kindly promised to give me the benefit of his advice.'

'I don't believe that bell acts,' said Meldon, as Langton tugged at a knob beside the chimneypiece. 'For the matter of that I don't know a bell in Ballymoy that does act, barring, of course, the church bell and the chapel bell, which are different.'

'Stupid of me,' said Langton. 'I ought to have guessed that, except those of the various churches, which are, as you say, different, the bells in this country wouldn't be meant to ring. It is, if I may say so, characteristic of Ireland that they don't.'

Meldon looked at the man in front of him. It crossed his mind that the stranger might possibly be poking fun at him. He dismissed the idea at once as absurd.

'If you want Doyle,' he said, 'the best thing to do is to go to the top of the stairs and shout. I told him not to go to bed till after I'd called.'

Langton shouted as he was bidden, and in a few minutes Doyle entered the room.

'Good-evening to you, Mr Meldon,' he said. 'I suppose now you didn't succeed in persuading the Major to change his mind about the boat.'

'I did not,' said Meldon.

'I wouldn't wonder now if you didn't try very hard.' Doyle cast a knowing look at Langton out of the corners of his eyes as he spoke. 'Nor it couldn't be expected that you would, seeing as how you have a boat of your own that might suit.'

'I don't know yet that she would suit,' said Meldon. 'What do you want her for?'

'My friend and I want to cruise about your bay,' said Langton. 'We are spending our holiday here.'

'She's a good boat,' said Doyle. 'And what's more than that, she's a safe boat. I never heard tell yet of any man being drownded out of her, long as I'm living here; and there's many a boat you couldn't say that for.'

'Is she for hire,' said Langton, 'and at what price?'

But this direct method of arriving at the point of the negotiation did not commend itself either to Doyle or Meldon.

'I mind well,' said Doyle, 'when old Tommy Devoren used to be sailing her for the R.M. that was in it them times, he'd say how divil a safer nor a drier boat for a lady ever he come across, and him taking the R.M.'s two daughters out in her maybe as often as twice in a week.'

'Is there a cabin in the boat,' asked Langton, 'in which my friend and I could sleep?'

'Cabin! What would hinder there to be a cabin? Tell the gentleman what kind of a cabin there is in her, Mr Meldon. Sure you know it better than me.'

'There is a cockpit and a small cabin,' said Meldon. 'She's a five-ton boat.'

'That would suit. Now what do you want for her by the month?'

'Can you sail a boat?' said Meldon. 'I don't want to be giving my *Aureole* to a man that would knock the bottom out of her on some rock. And let me tell you there are plenty of rocks in this bay.'

'Sail her!' said Doyle. 'Why wouldn't he be able to sail her? Is it likely now, Mr Meldon—I put it to you as a gentleman who knows a boat when he sees one—is it likely that

Mr Langton would come all the way to Ballymoy to look for a boat if he couldn't sail her when he got her? Sail her! I'll answer for it he can sail her right enough.'

Mr Doyle was anxious to preserve an air of fine impartiality. He praised Mr Langton's seamanship, of which he knew nothing, with an air of profound conviction, just as he praised Meldon's boat, of which he knew all there was to know. His argument was powerful and unanswerable. Why should a man travel all the way to Ballymoy, which is twenty miles from the nearest railway station, to look for a boat, unless he felt himself able to make some use of her?

'I'm not much of a sailor myself,' said Langton, 'but my friend is. I give you my word that he's well able to look after your boat.'

'Who is your friend?' said Meldon.

'I don't see what business that is of yours,' said Langton, displaying a certain irritation for the first time. 'If you won't hire your boat without seeing our baptismal certificates and our mothers' marriage lines you may keep her. I'm prepared to pay for what I want, and nothing else matters to you.'

'Good-evening,' said Meldon, rising.

'Gentlemen,' said Doyle, 'gentlemen both, this is no way to do business. Mr Meldon, you've no right to be asking the gentleman questions about his mother. Isn't his money just as good if he never had a mother at all? Mr Langton, sir, you'll excuse me, but Mr Meldon is a clergyman, and it's only right that he shouldn't want his boat to fall into bad hands.'

'Will you hire the boat or not?' asked Langton.

'You can have her for a month,' said Meldon, still standing hat in hand, 'for thirty pounds, money down in advance, and I'll have no more talk about the matter. You may take it or leave it.'

'Thirty pounds!' said Doyle. 'Come now, Mr Meldon, it's joking you are.'

'Considering the risk I run, I'll not take a penny less.'

'Thirty pounds!' said Doyle, 'is a big lump of money.'

'Take it or leave it.'

'I don't deny that she's a good boat and well suited to what Mr Langton wants her for. But thirty pounds! Come now. The gentleman here is a friend of mine. You mustn't be hard on him. Say twenty pounds.'

'Thirty,' said Meldon. 'After all, I don't want to let the boat at all. I'd just as soon keep her for my own use.'

Like every one else in Ballymoy, Doyle knew exactly what Meldon had paid for the boat, and was very well aware of the rottenness of her hull and the dilapidated condition of her rigging.

'You're a hard man, so you are,' he said. 'I never knew priest nor parson yet but was desperate hard to get the better of in a matter of money. I'll tell you now what you ought to do. Split the differ and say twenty-five pounds.'

'Well, rather than stop here all night talking about it,' said Meldon, 'I'll call it twenty-five pounds.'

'And a pound back out of that for luck,' said Doyle.

'No, not a penny back. Twenty-five, money down.'

Doyle drew his chair over to Langton and whispered.

'It's a fair offer. You'll find it hard to better it. The Major now would have asked fifty for his old *Spindrift*. It's my advice to you, Mr Langton, to close on it this minute before he has time to sleep on the offer. Maybe tomorrow morning he might be asking the advice of some one that would be for putting up the price on you. What do you say now?'

'I'll give it,' said Langton, 'on your assurance that the boat is as represented.'

'The gentleman takes your offer, Mr Meldon,' said Doyle. 'Twenty-five pounds down and the boat to be returned in good condition, all damages to be made good. What do you say now to a drop of something to wet the bargain?'

But Meldon would not drink. He went home to his lodgings and meditated, as he smoked a final pipe, on the glories and splendours which would be his when he had found the treasure on Inishgowlan. His conscience was quite untroubled by the thought of his bargain with Langton. The boat was rotten—so rotten that a man who knew anything about boats would hesitate to go to sea in her. If Langton's friend knew no more about boats than Langton did, some kind of accident was certain to happen. Meldon consoled himself with the thought that it would happen before they got far enough away from land to run any serious risk of drowning. Moy Bay was full of islands, and the water was always calm in summer time inside the bay. If the *Aureole* did go to pieces Langton and his friend could row to one of the islands in the punt. Meldon's punt was a good one.

4

THE *Spindrift*, close hauled, thrashed her way out towards Inishgowlan against a south-westerly breeze. The coast to the east, a low dark line, lay almost hidden in the haze. The entrance to Moy Bay was scarcely distinguishable. Major Kent, in an oilskin coat, sat at the tiller. The Rev. J. J. Meldon, most unclerically clad in a blue fisherman's jersey, old grey tweed trousers, and a pair of sea-boots, sprawled on the deck near the mast. He was apparently indifferent to the sheets of spray which broke over the bow of the boat now and then, when she struck one of the short seas which happened to be a little larger than its fellows. His red hair was a tangle of thick wet curls. His face and the backs of his hands were speckled with white where the salt had dried on them. The skin of his nose, under the influence of bright sunshine and sea-water, already showed signs of beginning to peel off. He had a pair of field-glasses in his hand, which he polished occasionally with a red cotton pocket-handkerchief, and through which he gazed at the island in front of him. To the south lay Inishmore, the larger of the two islands. Dead ahead was Inishgowlan, a long green bank as it seemed, sloping down eastward, dotted over with small white cabins, and divided into tiny fields of the most irregular shapes imaginable.

'In another half-hour,' said the Major, 'we'll be well under the lee of the island and the water will be a bit calmer. Then we'll have something to eat.'

'I suppose we anchor in that bay,' said Meldon, pointing forward.

He was more interested in the island and in the adventure before him than in the prospect of luncheon.

'Yes. It's a fine, safe bay, good bottom, perfect shelter from the west, south, and north, and deep water up to the very shore. You could anchor a man-of-war in that bay and lie snug the whole winter through.'

'I thought you told me,' said Meldon, a few minutes later, 'that there was nobody upon the island except natives.'

'No more there is. At least, there wasn't last time I was there five years ago.'

'And that they live in thatched cabins.'

'Yes.'

'Well, they don't. There's a galvanised iron hut on the grass just above the shore of the bay.'

'Nonsense! There can't be such a thing on Inishgowlan. Why would the people fetch a galvanised iron house out from the mainland when they can build anything they like out of stones ready to their hands?'

'I don't know. But the thing's there.'

'Do you take the tiller for a minute,' said the Major, 'and give me the glasses.'

He gazed at the island.

'You're right enough,' he said. 'The thing's there. It's exactly like the one the engineers lived in when they were making the railway down to Achill. Now I wonder who the deuce put a thing like that on Inishgowlan?'

'They couldn't be building a railway on the island, could they?'

'No, they couldn't. Who'd build a railway on an island a mile long?'

'The Government would,' said Meldon, 'if the fancy struck them. But it's more likely to be a pier, and the Board of Works engineer will be living in that hut.'

'It can't be a pier. They built a pier there only three years ago. You can see it, if you look, on the south side of the bay.'

'That wouldn't stop them building another,' said Meldon. 'I dare say you've observed, Major, how singularly little originality there is about Chief Secretaries. One of them, whose name is lost in the mists of antiquity, thought of piers and seed potatoes, and since then all his successors have gone on building piers and giving out seed potatoes. They never hit on anything original. Now if I was a Chief Secretary I'd strike out a line of my own. When I found I had to build something I'd run up a few round towers.'

'I dare say you would.'

'Of course there would be difficulties in the way. A pier is a comparatively simple thing to build, because part of it must be in the sea and the rest on some beach which nobody in particular owns. Whereas I should have to get a site in somebody's field for my round tower, and I should probably have the League denouncing me for land grabbing.'

The Major took the tiller again, and Meldon resumed his inspection of the island through the glasses.

'Do you know,' he said after a while, 'if there is a Government official of any kind in that iron hut it may turn out awkward for us.'

'How?'

'I'm not quite sure of the law on the subject, but I've always understood that the Government sets up to have a claim to all treasure that's found buried or hidden anywhere. It won't do to let this fellow, whoever he is, find out what we're after.'

Major Kent, who had never taken the treasure-seeking very seriously, made no reply to this remark.

'We'll have to adopt a disguise,' said Meldon. 'I told you all along that we probably would.'

'I won't——'

'Now don't make that remark about the false beard again. What we have to do is invent some plausible excuse for spending a week on the island.'

'Tell him we're out trawling.'

'That won't do. In the first place we shan't trawl; in the second place he'd ask where our nets were. Those fellows who spend their lives watching other people doing things develop an unholy curiosity about everybody else's business. We must hit on something more likely than that. Suppose we told him we were out to learn Irish?'

'Stuff!' said the Major; 'you wouldn't take in a newspaper correspondent with that tale. Just look at me. I've turned fifty, and I'm developing an elderly spread. Do I look like the kind of man who would go off to a desert island to learn Irish?'

'Oh, well, there may not be an engineer there after all. It'll be time enough to think of what we'll say when we see him.'

'Besides,' continued the Major, in whose mind the idea of learning Irish seemed to rankle, 'the fool will very likely be learning Irish himself. Lots of those fellows do, I'm told. Then he'd want us to join him, and it might end in our having to learn Irish, whether we liked it or not. Here, take the tiller, and I'll go below and get some grub up on deck.'

Still grumbling at the idea of learning Irish, the Major fetched some cold meat, bread, and a bottle of whisky from the cabin. The *Spindrift* was in calmer water, and Meldon was able to give both hands to the task of feeding himself, steadying the tiller by hooking a leg over it. The boat raced into the shelter of the bay, and the Major, having stowed away the remainder of the food in the cabin, busied himself in getting ready the anchor.

'The inhabitants,' said Meldon, 'are turning out *en masse* to welcome us. They are all down on the end of the pier—

> ' "Old men and babes and loving friends,
>   And youth and maidens gay." '

And there is an engineer there. At least, if he isn't an engineer, he's mighty like one. He's dressed in grey tweed knickers and brown boots, and I think he has spectacles. There isn't a doctor on the island by any chance?'

'There is not, nor ever was. Cock the likes of those fellows up with a doctor!'

'Well, then, he's an engineer. He couldn't be anything else. Pass the glasses aft till I get a good look at him.'

'He is wearing spectacles,' said Meldon, staring through the glasses. 'And I fancy I know him. He's a fellow called Higginbotham; he was in my class in college. We went in for our Little-Go together. I heard he had got a job under the Congested Districts Board. Now could the Congested Districts Board have a man out here?'

'They might; there's no saying where you'd run across one of their officials. The less likely the place is the more certain you are to meet one of them. Round her up into the wind, J. J.; we're near enough to the shore.'

The boat edged up into the wind; the jib and the mainsail flapped furiously. The anchor splashed into the water and the chain rattled out. Meldon ran forward and slacked the jib halyards. The Major gathered in the sail.

'If that's Higginbotham,' said Meldon a few minutes later, when he and the Major were making up the mainsail, 'it's all right. There'll be no difficulty whatever in dealing with Higginbotham. In the first place he's a thoroughly decent sort, and I don't believe he'd want to meddle with the treasure; in the second place he's quite an easy man to deceive. He always took what's called an intelligent interest in his work when he was in college, and never paid the least attention to anything else. If they've sent him to cover the whole island over with galvanised iron sheds, he'll do it quietly. He'll talk and think of nothing else till it's done. Any lie will do for Higginbotham; he'll believe whatever I tell him.'

'If you are going to stuff him up with any cock-and-bull story,' said the Major, 'you may go and do it by yourself. I'll stay here and tidy up. You take the punt and go ashore to your long-lost friend. But, mind now, if you say a word about learning Irish, I'll go back on you straight away.'

A collapsible canvas punt lay folded amidships. Meldon stretched her out, fixed the seat, and lowered her carefully into the water. He seated himself in her with the utmost caution, complaining that he was quite unused to a boat of the kind, and paddled towards the pier. In a few minutes he was shaking hands with Higginbotham in the middle of a group of admiring islanders.

'Well, now,' he said, 'isn't the world small? Last time I saw you was at the winter commencements in old Trinity, when we took our degrees together. Fancy meeting you here of all places!'

'I'm very glad to see you,' said Higginbotham, blinking benignantly through his large round-glassed spectacles. 'I find it lonely here, with nobody to speak to. But I thought you were a parson, J. J.?'

He eyed Meldon's collarless neck, the blue jersey, the shabby trousers and sea-boots, dubiously. Higginbotham himself was a young man who took care to be faultlessly attired on all occasions. Even on Inishgowlan he wore a clean collar, a light blue tie, and a well-cut Norfolk jacket. He carried his affection for civilised usage so far as to change his shirt and wear a smoking jacket every evening in his iron hut.

'So I am,' said Meldon; 'but you can't expect me to wear a dog-collar and a black coat on a ten tonner. Tell me, now—what brings you to this island?'

'The Board has bought the island, and I'm here stripping it. You know what I mean, don't you? I'm dividing it up into proper-sized, compact farms, building fences and walls, so that the people won't be holding it, as they do at present, in little bits and scraps, and not knowing properly what belongs to each of them.'

'Will you soon be done?'

'I would be done very soon,' said Higginbotham, 'only for one old fellow who's blocking the whole business. He refuses to stir from a wretched little field, right in the middle of the island, and the most miserable, tumble-down shed of a house you ever saw—a place you'd be sorry to put a pig into.'

'I wouldn't; I hate pigs. Pigs and cats—I'd put them anywhere.'

'There's a hole in the middle of his field, too,' said Higginbotham, in an aggrieved voice, 'a hole that a heifer once fell into and got killed, and he won't so much as let me near it to put up a fence.'

'Why don't you reason with him, and show him that you're acting for his own good? You are acting for his good, aren't you? You haven't any little game on of your own, I suppose?'

'I try to reason with him, but he doesn't understand English. He speaks nothing but Irish himself.'

'Well, why don't you tackle him in Irish? Do you mean to tell me, Higginbotham, that you can't talk Irish? You ought to be ashamed of yourself.'

'I'm trying to learn,' said Higginbotham. 'In fact, I'm determined to master the language. I've got a grammar and a dictionary up in my house now. I'll talk to that old man in a way that he'll understand before I've done with him.'

'Quite right. I'd offer to help you myself, only that I'm afraid I shan't have time.'

'Are you going off tomorrow? I'm sorry. I hoped you might have been here for a few days.'

'We shall be here for a week at least,' said Meldon, 'but I shan't have time to teach you Irish. We shall be frightfully busy.'

'Busy! What are you going to do?'

'I'm here with my friend, Major Kent. He's been sent to make a geological survey of the island.'

'Really! I never heard anything about that. The Board ought to have let me know.'

'He isn't acting for the Board. It was the Lord-Lieutenant and the Chief Secretary who sent him here. The fact is, Higginbotham, that the Major's business is of rather a private nature. I don't mind telling you, but it mustn't go any further, that an important syndicate has made the Government an offer for the mining rights of this island.'

'Over the head of the Board?'

'Oh, I know nothing about that. In fact, neither the Major nor I knew anything about the Board having bought the island when we came here. You know the way these Government departments overlap each other, and none of them know what the others are doing. I shouldn't wonder a bit if the Estates Commissioners turned up before long and said the island was theirs. However, you can understand that the Chief Secretary wasn't going to sell the mining rights of the place without finding out what they were worth. He sent out Major Kent to make a report.'

'But—but—there must be some mistake. Can you have come to the wrong island?'

'Certainly not,' said Meldon. 'You ought to know me better than that, Higginbotham. Am I the sort of man who comes to a wrong island?'

'Of course not. But there must be some mistake. There are no minerals on the island at all. The whole place is nothing but pliocene clay.'

'You may be right or you may be wrong. My friend Major Kent will find that out for himself. I'm not a mining expert, so I don't offer an opinion; but I'll just say this, speaking as a man with no special knowledge of geology, but still with a good general education—it doesn't *look* to me like pliocene clay, not in the least.'

'I assure you, J. J., the geological map——'

'I'm not an expert, Higginbotham, and I don't propose to start an argument with you on the subject. What's more, I don't advise you to try to argue with the Major. He's a good-natured man and easy to get on with so long as you don't touch his own particular subject. But he's as snappy as a fox in a trap if any one starts talking geology to him. You know what these experts are. It's the artistic temperament. You wouldn't like it yourself if some outsider began laying down the law to you about galvanised iron sheds.'

'Still, I'd like to tell him——'

'Take my advice and don't. If you so much as mention pliocene clay, or tertiary deposits, or auriferous reefs, or anything of that kind to the Major, you'll be sorry afterwards. The best thing for you is not to let on that you know what he's here for at all.'

'I won't, of course, if you say I'm not to, but——'

'That's right. It's better not, for your own sake. And besides, you'd only get me into a mess. I'd no business to tell you about the matter. The Major is frightfully particular about official reticence and all that kind of thing. He's a man of violent temper if he's roused. He'd do anything when his blood's up. In fact, they say that his career in the army was cut short on account of his smashing up a man who insisted on asking him questions he didn't want to answer. The man recovered more or less in the end and the thing was hushed up, but the Major had to resign. Of course I can't be sure of the truth of that story. I only heard it at third hand. It may be nothing but gossip. But any way, don't you worry the Major. Let him potter about the island tapping rocks if he likes. He won't do you any harm.'

'All right, old man. And look here, you and the Major had better come and feed with me tonight. I can't call it dinner, but I'll do the best I can. I've got a tinned tongue and a lobster.'

'Delighted. I'll answer for the Major. And we'll subscribe to the feast. On a desert island every shipwrecked mariner brings what he can to the common store. We'll contribute some corned beef and a tin of sardines. What time?'

'I've a little writing to do,' said Higginbotham. 'Shall we say 7.30? Of course you needn't dress.'

'Thanks,' said Meldon, with a grin; 'we won't, if you're sure you don't mind. I'll take a stroll round the island and then go and fetch the Major.'

5

The island of Inishgowlan is formed on a simple plan, common among islands off the west coast of Ireland. The western side consists of a series of bluffs, rising occasionally to the dignity of cliffs. At the base of these the Atlantic rollers break themselves, carving out narrow gullies wherever they find a suitably soft place. From these bluffs the island slopes gradually down to its eastern coast.

Meldon, after leaving Higginbotham, walked to the top of the western ridge, climbing a number of loose stone walls on his way. He made his way to the highest point of the island, and from it surveyed the whole coast line. Then he sat down and thought. He was working out a plan for discovering the treasure, which, as he believed, lay concealed somewhere. After smoking two pipes he went down again to the pier, embarked in the collapsible punt, and paddled off to the *Spindrift*. The Major was sound asleep in the little cabin. Meldon woke him.

'It's all right,' he said. 'I've put Higginbotham completely off the scent. We can go where we like and do what we like and he'll ask no questions. We're to dine with him tonight. I hope you won't mind. I promised to bring along your corned beef and some sardines. Higginbotham doesn't seem to have anything except a tinned tongue and a lobster. I don't know how you feel, but I fancy I could account for the whole tongue myself without spoiling my appetite for the lobster.'

'You're quite right,' said the Major. 'But what about drink? Shall we bring some whisky?'

'It might be just as well. Higginbotham wasn't a teetotaller when I knew him in college, but he may be now—you never can tell what fads a man will take up. He told me he was learning Irish.'

'We'll take the whisky, then,' said the Major.

The beef, the sardines, and the bottle were stowed in the bow of the punt. The Major seated himself in the stern. Meldon took the paddles.

'By the way,' said Meldon, when about half the journey was accomplished, 'what is pliocene clay?'

'I don't know. How could I know a thing like that? I never heard of the stuff before. Is there any of it on the island?'

'According to Higginbotham the whole island consists of nothing else.'

'Let it. It makes no odds to us what it consists of.'

'It may make a great deal of odds to you, Major.'

Meldon had stopped paddling and sat looking at his friend. A smile lurked under his moustache; his eyes twinkled. A feeling of uneasiness, a premonition of coming evil, a sudden suspicion, took possession of the Major's mind.

'J. J.,' he said solemnly, 'tell me the truth. What did you say to that Congested Districts friend of yours? What did you tell him we were here for?'

'I told him that you were a mining expert and that you'd been sent by the Lord-Lieutenant and the Chief Secretary to make a geological survey of the island.'

'Great Scott!'

The Major started so violently that the punt rocked from side to side. The water lipped in first over one gunwhale, then over the other.

'Sit still,' said Meldon. 'This is no place to be giving way to strong emotion. Remember that you are floating about in a beastly umbrella turned upside down, a thing that might shut up under you at any moment. It may not matter to you whether you are drowned or not, but I want to see my little girl again before I die.'

'But—but—gracious Heavens, J. J.——'

'He believed it all right in the end,' said Meldon. 'He seemed a bit surprised at first, but I put it to him in a convincing way and I think he believed me. That was how we got on the subject of pliocene clay.'

'Turn round,' said the Major sternly, 'and row back to the *Spindrift*. I'll up anchor and leave this place tonight! I'm not going ashore to be made a fool of by your abominable inventions.'

'It's all right. You won't be made a fool of. Higginbotham will respect you all the more for being an expert. He's just the sort of man who looks up to experts. And he won't bother you with questions. I told him you were a man of violent temper and couldn't bear being worried about your work.'

Meldon began to paddle towards the pier. The Major sat limp in the stern of the punt. A sweat had broken out on his forehead.

'What else did you tell him? Let me have the whole of it.'

'Oh, nothing else. I never say a word more than is necessary. There's no commoner mistake than overdoing one's disguise.'

'That's all well enough, but why couldn't you have put the disguise, as you call it, on yourself instead of me? Why didn't you say that you were a mining expert?'

'He wouldn't have believed that. I simply couldn't have made him believe that I know anything about pliocene clay.'

'Well, you might have told him something else about yourself, something he would have believed. I hate being dragged into these entanglements.'

'There's no entanglement that I can see,' said Meldon. 'But I'm sorry now that I mentioned you at all. If I'd known the way you'd feel about it, I wouldn't. I tell you what it is, Major, I'll take the very first opportunity of telling him something about myself. I'll shift the whole business off your shoulders. Higginbotham will forget all about you. Come, now, I can't do more than that. I don't say it will be easy to get him to swallow a second story immediately on top of the first, but for your sake, Major, I'm willing to try.'

The spirit of Higginbotham's hospitality was all that could be desired. His means of making his guests comfortable were limited. He had only two plates in his establishment. They were given to Meldon and Major Kent. Higginbotham himself ate off a saucer. The tongue was placed on the table in its tin, and morsels were dug out of it with a knife. There was no dish for the corned beef, so Meldon laid it on a drawing board with a newspaper underneath it. There was one tumbler, a cup, and a sugar-basin to drink out of. Higginbotham turned out not to be a teetotaller. He provided bottled stout for his guests. The lobster, when it came to the time for eating it, was torn in pieces by Meldon and then taken outside to have its shell broken with stones. Major Kent was accommodated with a hammock chair, from which he reached his food with great difficulty. Meldon had a wooden stool. Higginbotham sat on a corner of his bed, which he dragged into the middle of the room.

When the meal was over the three men went out of doors and smoked. The evening was beautifully fine. The breeze which blew earlier in the day had died away. The water of the bay was motionless. The *Spindrift* lay at her anchor, a double boat, every spar and rope, every detail of her hull, reflected beneath her. On the beach near the pier lay two canvas curraghs, turned upside down, their gunwales resting on little piles of stones. Some children played round them. On the pier stood a group of five or six men, who smoked, gazed at the *Spindrift*, and occasionally made a remark to each other. The hammock chair was brought out for Major Kent, and he lay back in it luxuriously. Meldon and Higginbotham sprawled on the grass. When the dew made it uncomfortably wet, Meldon fetched a blanket off Higginbotham's bed and spread it for himself. Higginbotham perched, stiffly, on a stone.

For a long time the conversation kept on perfectly safe topics. Higginbotham described the operations of the Congested Districts Board on Inishgowlan and elsewhere. He waxed enthusiastic over the social and material regeneration of the islanders; he spoke with pitying contempt of their original way of living. They grew, it appeared, wretched potato crops in fields so badly fenced that stray cattle wandered in and trampled the young plants at critical stages of their growth. The people lived in ill-lighted, ill-ventilated, and, according to modern ideas, wholly insanitary cabins. Their system of land tenure was extraordinarily complicated and inconvenient. The holdings were inextricable mixed up, so that hardly any one could walk through his own fields without trespassing on his neighbour's.

'You'll hardly believe me,' said Higginbotham, 'but sometimes a man holds a bit of land not much larger than a decent table-cloth, entirely surrounded by a field belonging to some one else.'

This evil condition of things Higginbotham, at the bidding of his Board, had undertaken to remedy. He brought out from his hut a map of the island, and showed how he proposed to divide it into parallel strips. He explained that each strip was to be bounded by a fence six feet high; that good wooden gates were to be erected; that a house was to be built at the top of each strip—a house with a slated roof, three rooms, and a concrete floor in the kitchen. He displayed with great pride a picture, curiously wanting in perspective, of a whole row of singularly ugly houses perched along the western ridge of the island.

The Major yawned without an attempt to hide the fact that he was bored. He had no taste whatever for philanthropy, and hated what he called Government meddling. Higginbotham continued to display plans and elevations with unabated enthusiasm. He was, as Meldon had said, a young man who took a real interest in his work. His eyes, behind his spectacles, beamed with benignant satisfaction while he described the earthly paradise he meant to create. Suddenly his face clouded and the joy died out of it.

'But the whole thing is blocked,' he said, 'by the pig-headed stupidity of one old man.'

'Tell the Major about him,' said Meldon.

'They call him the king of the island,' said Higginbotham, 'but of course he's not really a king any more than I am myself.'

'Not nearly so much,' said Meldon. 'From all you've told us I should say you are what's called a benevolent despot.'

'He's simply a sort of head of the family,' said Higginbotham. 'They are all brothers and sisters and cousins on the island. His name is Thomas O'Flaherty Pat. At least, that's what the people call him. I don't see much sense myself in sticking in the Pat at the end.'

'No more do I,' said Meldon. 'Thomas O'Flaherty ought to be name enough for any king.'

'Of course, there are three other Thomas O'Flahertys on the island, and it might be difficult to distinguish them. There's Thomas O'Flaherty Tom, and Thomas——'

The Major yawned more obviously than ever. He had spent a long day on the sea; he had eaten with a good appetite; he had smoked a satisfying quantity of tobacco. He was totally uninterested in the family of the O'Flahertys. Higginbotham became aware that he was boring his principal guest. Inspired, perhaps, by some malignant spirit, he changed the subject of the conversation to one more likely to hold the attention of Major Kent.

'I'm afraid you won't find Inishgowlan very interesting, Major, from your point of view.'

'My point of view?'

'I mean as a scientific man.'

The Major woke up and scowled at Meldon.

'The geological formation——' said Higginbotham.

'Oh, that's all right,' said Meldon, cheerfully. 'As a matter of fact the Major's tremendously interested in pliocene clay. It has been a hobby of his from his childhood. You'd be surprised all there is to know about pliocene clay. The Major has quite a library of books on the subject, and he tells me that it isn't by any means fully investigated yet.'

As he spoke he leaned forward from his blanket and pinched the calf of Higginbotham's leg severely.

'All right,' said his victim, 'I'll drop the subject if you like; but I was going to say——'

'I took a walk before dinner,' said Meldon, 'and had a look

at the island. I came to the conclusion that we couldn't find a better place for the school——'

'What school?' said Higginbotham.

'The school I was telling you about this afternoon. But perhaps I forgot to mention it.'

The scowl on the Major's face deepened. He realised that Meldon, in fulfilment of his promise, was going to shift the burden of the disguise to his own shoulders.

'I never heard anything about a school,' said Higginbotham.

'I wonder you didn't. But I dare say the post is rather irregular here. The fact is that the Board—not your Board, you know, but the Board of National Education—has determined to build a school on the island and asked me to run across and look out for a site.'

The Major with a struggle sat upright in his hammock chair. His mouth opened. He made an effort to speak.

'It's all right,' said Meldon soothingly. 'I know what you are going to say—official reticence, and that sort of thing. But it doesn't matter mentioning these things to Higginbotham. He's in the Government service himself.'

The Major opened his mouth again, but his thoughts failed to express themselves. Meldon felt the necessity of modifying his statement.

'Of course the Board didn't actually send me here specially for the purpose. They heard I was coming here with the Major, and just dropped me a line to say that I may keep my eyes open and let them know if there was a suitable site for a school.'

Higginbotham stared in blank amazement. As an official he knew something of the ways of Irish Governments and was seldom astonished at their doings. He had swallowed, with some little misgiving, the story of Major Kent's mission. It was just possible that a Lord-Lieutenant and a Chief Secretary, in a moment of temporary insanity brought on by overwork and much anxiety, might have sent an expert to make a geological survey of Inishgowlan. It was quite incredible that the National Board of Education could, of its own free will, intend to build a school. Meldon was unpleasantly conscious of having aroused scepticism. He nerved himself to reduce Higginbotham to a condition of passive belief.

'The Board has heard of all you're doing here,' he said, 'and naturally wants to put a finishing touch to the work by providing for the education of the children. After all you've done in the way of improving the material conditions of life, the Commissioners feel that it would be a national disgrace if the rising generation is left in a condition of barbaric ignorance. You recollect what the hymn says:

> ' "Every prospect pleases
> And only man is vile."

That's how the Commissioners feel, and you can't blame them.'

'But there are only nine children on the whole island,' said Higginbotham.

'Still there are nine. Why should nine children go ignorant to their graves? It isn't the fault of the nine that there aren't more. Besides, there may be more. That's what the Board of Education feels—there may be more. The Commissioners are long-headed men, Higginbotham; not a cuter lot on any Board in Ireland. They look to the future. They see before them generations of Thomas O'Flahertys yet unborn, little toddlers coming out of those slated houses of yours with copy-books in their chubby fists, all of them filled with a desire for knowledge. I tell you what, it's an inspiring picture, say what you like.'

'Where,' said Higginbotham, overwhelmed by this vision of the future, 'where do you propose to build the school?'

'There's a house,' said Meldon, 'if you can call it a house, at the end of a particularly abominable bohireen. The thatch, what there is of it, is tied on with straw ropes, and there's only one small window to it that I could see. It's just under the brow of the hill above the place we're sitting now. It's bang in the middle of the island, and it's just the place for a school.'

'That's the very cabin we've been talking about,' said

Higginbotham. 'That's Thomas O'Flaherty Pat's—the place he won't give up.'

'Oh, I'll manage him,' said Meldon. 'Don't you worry. Give me a week and I'll talk the old boy round. And now I think the Major and I had better be getting back to our floating home. We've got to navigate the bay in a punt that's more like the half of the cover of a football than anything else, and I don't much fancy doing it in the dark.'

The Major remained obstinately silent while Meldon paddled him home. Nor did he make any reply to Meldon's remarks while undressing to go to bed. Half an hour later he put his head over the side of his bunk and said:

'I'm not going to stand this, J. J. It's all very fine. I don't deny that you're a fluent liar, but I'm not going to be made a fool of. I won't stand it. Either you tell Higginbotham to-morrow that you've been pulling his leg, or I leave the island. Do you hear me? Why, man, we might get into serious trouble if these stories of yours ever came out. Are you listening to me?'

'More or less,' said Meldon sleepily. 'Don't you worry. Leave it to me! I'll manage all right. Good-night, Major. Don't you get dreaming of pliocene clay.'

6

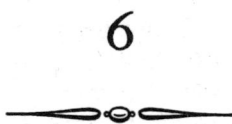

MELDON woke early next morning. At six o'clock he plunged overboard and swam delightedly round the yacht. Treasure or no treasure, he intended to enjoy his holiday, and the June weather was as good as could be wished for—better than any reasonable man would dare to hope. Half an hour later he roused Major Kent, and then set to work to light the stove in the galley. Every now and then he poked his head up and shouted a remark to the Major, who was making his toilet on deck.

'We'll go ashore directly after breakfast and set to work. Have you any plan of operation in your mind?'

The Major stopped shaving and, razor in hand, looked over to the place from which the red head of the curate had already disappeared.

'I have not,' he shouted. 'I left that to you. I took it for granted that you would know the exact spot where the treasure lies, and that I would have nothing to do but walk there and put the gold into a hand-bag.'

The Major, though not intellectually nimble, prided himself on his power of polished sarcasm. He was disappointed to find that his taunt had apparently failed to reach the curate. He received no reply; but a noise of frizzling and a pleasant smell of bacon melting on a frying-pan reached him from the fore hatch. Then Meldon's voice, this time without the appearance of his head, reached him again:—

'There are only six eggs. I suppose I may as well fry them all.'

'Yes, and some ham along with them.'

'It's bacon I have on the pan, but I'll do a slice or two of ham for you, if you like.'

Half of Meldon's body emerged from the hatchway, and the shells of six eggs were pitched overboard.

'It was full tide at six this morning,' he said, returning to the subject of the treasure hunt; 'I expect by eight o'clock we ought to be able to make our way round the base of the cliffs on the west side of the island. We'll be all right there till one or two o'clock, any way. What do you say?'

The Major finished shaving and proceeded to fill a tin basin with water.

'What do you expect to take by doing that?' he said.

He got no answer for a time. The frying-pan demanded

Meldon's whole attention. The noise of frizzling increased rapidly. The Major balanced his basin on the cabin skylight and scrubbed himself vigorously. On the deck beside him lay a cake of soap, a towel, and a small piece of pumice-stone. They who go down to the sea in ships are apt to get tarry substances stuck on their hands, and the Major was a man who liked to be clean once a day at least. Beside the basin on the skylight lay his tooth-brush and a box of carbolic powder, but he did not get a chance of enjoying these.

'Breakfast's ready,' shouted Meldon. 'Shall I drag it all up on deck? The air's pleasant.'

'No, let's be as civilised as we can and eat in the cabin.'

Realising that the curate's appetite would not endure much delay and that his own chance of securing a fair share of the six eggs depended on his promptitude, the Major slipped on the jacket of his pyjamas and went below. The eggs, bacon, and ham steamed together in a heap on a dish. Plates, knives, and forks were set out. The teapot and a tin of condensed milk stood at the end of the table.

'I call this jolly,' said Meldon. 'I only wish my little girl was here to take a share with us.'

'God forbid!' said the Major, with pious gravity. 'How can you wish for such a thing, J. J.? Just fancy a woman on a boat like this.'

'You don't know her. She wouldn't mind a bit. In fact she'd enjoy roughing it. It would be the greatest fun out of her.'

'Well, it wouldn't be any fun for me,' said the Major. 'But tell me, what's this plan of yours about scrambling about among the rocks?'

'I've given a lot of serious thought to the subject of the treasure,' said Meldon. 'I sat for nearly an hour on the top of this island yesterday afternoon, and, as the hymn says, "I viewed the landscape o'er." The result is that I've picked out the scene of the shipwreck.'

'Oh, have you? You're quite certain you're right, of course.'

'Not quite certain—tolerably certain. It's this way. The galleon——'

'The what?'

'The galleon. I wish you'd try not to interrupt me so often. All Spanish ships were galleons if they were big and caraques if they were small. Our one was big, therefore she must have been a galleon. We may just as well call things by their right names and go to work in a business-like way. The galleon was wrecked. Very well. Where was she likely to be wrecked? On the west coast of the island.'

'I don't see why.'

'Because of course if she'd got to the east side she'd have been in calm water under the lee of the land, and she wouldn't have been wrecked.'

'That doesn't follow. The wind might have been nor'-east.'

'I'm pretty sure it wasn't,' said Meldon, 'because it hardly ever is. Even nowadays, with all the improvements there are in things, there's hardly ever a nor'-east wind on this coast, and in those days—two hundred years and more ago—I expect the wind just shifted about through three points of the compass, nor'-west, west, and sou'-west. However, if you like, I'll argue out the other possibilities afterwards. For the present we'll say the galleon was most likely wrecked on the west side of the island. Now, put yourself in the place of the Spanish captain.'

'I've done that before,' said the Major, 'and it was no good.'

'I remember now; it wasn't. But anyhow we came to the conclusion that he stored his treasure in some hole in the rocks. Obviously, on account of the weight of the treasure and the difficulty of carrying large quantities of loose coin, he'd choose a hole as near the scene of the shipwreck as possible. Having fixed the scene of the shipwreck——'

'You haven't explained how you fixed that.'

'I can't either till I show you the place. Once you've seen it you'll admit that it is by far the likeliest place for a thing of the kind. In fact it's the only really suitable place I saw. What we've got to do is to search the rocks in the immediate neighbourhood for the hole that caught the eye of the Spanish captain.'

'That's all well enough. But the treasure, if there ever was any treasure, was hidden more than two hundred years ago. The place must be entirely altered since then. I understand that the whole island is made up of pliocene clay.'

'What's that got to do with it?'

'Of course,' said the Major, 'I don't know what pliocene clay is. But if it's like any other kind of clay it'll be soft stuff, and any hole there might have been two hundred years ago will be all washed away or covered up now.'

'In the first place,' said Meldon, 'we've only got Higginbotham's word for it that the island is pliocene clay, and in the next place I don't believe pliocene clay is that kind of stuff at all. It stands to reason that it can't be. Why, man, if it was anything like common clay the whole island would be gone ages ago. You take my word for it, pliocene clay is some uncommonly hard substance that doesn't melt anything worth speaking of in a couple of centuries.'

'Then why is it called pliocene clay?'

'Oh, that's the sort of way those scientific Johnnies talk. I believe they do it just to deceive the general public. You know they speak about lunacy, although they know jolly well it hasn't got anything to do with the moon. What they like is to get a hold of a name which is sure to deceive plain, straightforward men like you and me, and then when we take it at its face value, put the obvious meaning on to one of their own words, they make us look like fools for not knowing any better. It's just the same with typhoid fever. I was talking to a doctor once, not a common castor-oil and linseed-poultice doctor, but one of the sort that runs to germs and microscopes and things, and he told me—I forget exactly how he put it, but it amounted to this: that any one who went by the name typhoid would get on a wrong track altogether—wouldn't, in fact, have proper typhoid but something else. I think he said he'd have something like typhus, which is an entirely different disease; beastly infectious, for one thing, whereas the real typhoid, the thing that the name doesn't mean, if you understand me, isn't catching at all. Which just shows how much trust you can put in scientific names. No, Major, you take my word for it, pliocene clay is some jolly hard kind of rock—igneous, I expect—and this island is pretty much as old Don What's-his-name found it when he scrambled on shore out of that galleon.'

'Very well,' said the Major, 'but I believe we're on a fool's errand. I doubt very much if there's any treasure there at all. And I'm sure we won't find it.'

'Don't croak,' said Meldon. 'You get into your duds and light your pipe. I'll wash up and get out the punt. It's getting on for eight o'clock and we ought to be off.'

An elderly man and five out of the nine children resident on the island stood on the end of the pier when Meldon and the Major landed. The man was clad in a very dirty white flannel jacket and a pair of yellowish flannel trousers, which hung in a tattered fringe round his naked feet and ankles. He had a long white beard and grey hair, long as a woman's, drawn straight back from his forehead. The hair and beard were both unkempt and matted. But the man held himself erect and looked straight at the strangers through great dark eyes. His hands, though battered and scarred with toil, were long and shapely. His face had a look of dignity, of a certain calm and satisfied superiority. Men of this kind are to be met with here and there among the Connacht peasantry. They are in reality children of a vanishing race, of a lost civilisation, a bygone culture. They watch the encroachments of another race and new ideas with a sort of sorrowful contempt. It is as if, understanding and despising what they see around them, they do not consider it worth while to try and explain themselves; as if, possessing a wisdom of their own, and æsthetic joy of which the modern world knows nothing, they are content to let both die with them rather than attempt to teach them to men of a wholly different outlook upon life.

'I shouldn't wonder,' said Meldon to the Major, 'if that was old Thomas O'Flaherty Pat himself. He has a royal look about him, hasn't he? But I can't say much for his robes of state. I wonder if he'd talk to us.' He approached the old man.

'Good-morning to you. Glorious weather we're having. Looks as if it meant to hold up, too.'

'Ní Beurla agam' ('I have no English'), said the old man.

'Come now,' said Meldon cheerfully, 'you needn't play that game off on me. I can understand your doing it to Higginbotham. He's a Government official, and naturally you distrust him; but I'm a private man, I don't want to turn you out of your house, and I won't give you away.'

'Ní Beurla agam air bith. Ní aon focal' ('I have no English at all, not one word'), said the old man.

Meldon turned to the five children, and singled out a little girl who stood staring open-mouth at him.

'Molly O'Flaherty,' he said, 'come here.'

The children, holding on to each other, edged away doubtfully.

'Bridgy O'Flaherty,' said Meldon, 'if you're not Molly I suppose you're sure to be Bridgy. Tell me what the old gentleman's name is.'

He stepped forward suddenly and seized the child by the arm. She struggled for a minute and then began to cry.

'There now,' said Meldon soothingly, 'don't cry; I'm not going to hurt you. Major, give me a penny. You haven't got one? Never mind, a sixpence will do quite as well. Here now, Nora Acushla, look at the pretty silver sixpence. That's for you. Stretch out your hand and take it, and I'll tell your mammy what a good girl you are.'

The child seized the sixpence, stopped crying, and looked up timidly to Meldon's face.

'That's right,' he said, patting her head. 'Now we're friends again. Tell me now, Nora—is it Nora they call you?'

'It is not,' said the child. 'It's Mary Kate.'

'There now. I might have guessed it. Sorra a prettier name there is in the whole province of Connacht than Mary Kate, nor a prettier little girl than yourself. I've a little girl of my own away in Dublin, and they call her Gladys Muriel, but I declare I think Mary Kate's a nicer name. Tell me now, Mary

Kate, is Thomas O'Flaherty Pat the name they have on the old man there?'

'It might,' said Mary Kate.

'Off with you then,' said Meldon. 'Have you got the sixpence safe? Take it up to the gentleman that lives in the new iron house, the gentleman from the Board—you know who I mean.'

Mary Kate grinned.

'Is it the man that does be measuring out the land?'

'It is,' said Meldon. 'That exact man. Do you take your sixpence up to him and ask him to give you the worth of it in sugar candy. Don't be put off if he tells you he hasn't got any. He has sacks and sacks of it stored away there in the house, and he does be eating it himself whenever he thinks there's nobody looking at him.'

'Do we go round the north or the south side of the island,' said the Major, as he and Meldon left the pier, 'to reach this treasure-cave of yours?'

'The scene of the shipwreck,' said Meldon severely, 'is about the middle of the west coast. We'd get to it just as quick one way as the other, but I think we'll go by the north. Higginbotham's house is to the south of us, and there is no use passing his door oftener than we can help; especially just now when Mary Kate is approaching him on the subject of sugar candy.'

Walking in Inishgowlan is slow work because there are no regular roads, and because the whole island is laced with loose stone walls which have to be climbed. These are built not so much to separate the fields from each other, as with a view to collecting into manageable heaps the stones of which the walls consist. Originally the stones lay scattered over the grass in such numbers that ploughing and even digging were difficult. Here and there, where it is evidently impossible to pile any more stones on the walls without making them dangerously top-heavy, cairns have been built in the middle of the fields and the superfluous metal got rid of in that way. This superabundance of stones was a serious trouble to Higginbotham. He had devised a plan for building a very high wall, a solid structure with mortar in its joints, along the western ridge of the island. He represented to his Board that such a wall would form a splendid shelter for the whole island from the westerly gales and would prevent careless sheep from falling over into the sea. The Board was still deliberating on the scheme.

Major Kent grumbled a good deal at having to climb so many walls; but Meldon, generally a field in front of him, encouraged him with false promises of easier walking further on. Thomas O'Flaherty Pat followed them at a distance. Meldon stopped to light his pipe, and allowed the Major to overtake him.

'I rather think,' he said, looking back, 'that the old chappie in the ragged clothes is tracking us.'

'Let him,' said the Major, who was rather out of breath and disinclined for discussion. 'He can't do us any harm.'

'He might not, but all the same I'd like to know what he has in his mind. I wish now that I'd brought Mary Kate along with me. She'd have come for another sixpence, I expect.'

'Another of my sixpences.'

'Oh, well, you needn't grumble. What's sixpence here or there compared to the pile of gold that we're going to take home with us? Think of it, Major, great fat doubloons, no wretched little slips of coins like our modern sovereigns, but thick, round chunks, weighing, maybe, as much as an ounce or an ounce and a half each, solid gold! And very likely there'll be gems, golden goblets with precious stones stuck in them. Those Spaniards were awful dogs for luxury.'

'You don't really expect to find diamonds and emeralds, do you, J. J.?'

'Of course I do. What else have I come for if it isn't to find every kind of treasure? But here we are, Major, at the other end of nowhere. We've got to scramble round now.'

The cliffs on the western coast of Inishgowlan are not very lofty, nor, except in odd places, are they really precipitous. Here and there the sea at high tide washes against their bases.

Elsewhere there are long shelves of rock which are never more than half-covered by the waves, and wildernesses of huge boulders, worn into all sorts of fantastic shapes, among which on calm days the sea winds itself into curiously fascinating pools and channels, where in storms there is a welter of foam and spray and angry water.

Meldon, keeping a few paces in front of the Major, scrambled along with the greatest activity. He scaled apparently impossible rocks, and seemed actually to enjoy slipping and stumbling among the pools. After an hour's hard work, with scratched hands and a large rent in the knee of his trousers, he reached the mouth of a little bay. There, seated on a large stone at the bottom of the cliff, was Thomas O'Flaherty Pat.

A few hundred yards from the north end of the island there is a break in the line of cliffs. A narrow path, very steep and rough, has been made from the top of the ridge to the beach below. It is used during the kelp-burning season by men and girls, who climb down it, gather sea wrack among the rocks, and toilsomely ascend again with dripping creels on their backs and soaked garments flapping round their legs. Old Thomas O'Flaherty Pat had used this path as a short-cut, and intercepted the men he was following.

Meldon waited for the Major, who was some distance behind.

'Look here,' he said, 'there's that old gentleman, Higginbotham's favourite enemy, waiting for us again. Now, what on earth does he want?'

'I don't know, and what's more, I don't care. But I see the path he came by, and I vote we take it as the shortest way home. I've had enough of this ridiculous expedition.'

'Nonsense, Major. You can't go back now. We've hours before us still. But we'll recollect that path. It'll save us going the whole way back to the north point of the island when we've done. I wish I knew what T. O'Flaherty Pat supposes he's doing. It's perfectly ridiculous not being able to get him to talk. I can't imagine why he keeps up the pretence of not knowing English with me.'

'Perhaps he doesn't know any.'

'Rot! Excuse my putting it plainly, but that's simple rot. Of course he knows English. Everybody must know English.'

'Well, there's no use standing here and staring at him. We shan't find out anything that way. Let's go on if you're bent on going.'

'I shouldn't wonder,' said Meldon, 'if he had some kind of inkling of what we're after. Your great aunt said in her diary——'

'My grandfather. I never had a great aunt that I know of.'

'Well, your grandfather. It's all the same. He said anyhow that the natives here knew about the treasure in his day. Now that's just the kind of information that would be handed down from father to son, and old T. O. P. is just the sort of man——'

'Who's T. O. P.?'

'T. O. P.? Oh, Thomas O'Flaherty Pat, of course. You can't expect me to say that whole name over again each time. Our friend Tommy is just the kind of elderly ass who'd be sure to remember the story even if everybody else had forgotten it. You back he's gone treasure-hunting on his own every fine day for the last fifty years, and now when he sees we're after it and going about the job in a jolly sight more intelligent way than ever he did, he thinks he's nothing to do but hang on to us till we find it, and then chip in and claim a share. I'll tell you what it is, Major. It's absolutely necessary to put him off the scent.'

'How will you do that when you can't talk to him?'

'Oh, I'll manage. Mind you, he can understand every word we say. Come along, now. I'm going to pretend to be a bug hunter, an entomologist, one of the fellows who look for marine monsters of unusual kinds in little pools. I wish to goodness I'd thought of bringing a butterfly net with me; a nice green butterfly net would have completed the disguise. Come along, Major. Take my arm and try and look affectionate. Put on the sort of expression you'd wear if we were scientific pals out of the same laboratory in London. Do your best to display an intelligent interest in what I say.'

Stumbling among the stones, but walking arm-in-arm, they approached Thomas O'Flaherty Pat.

'Major,' whispered Meldon, 'do you happen to recollect the name of any insect?'

'The flea,' said the Major promptly.

'The scientific name,' said Meldon. 'What good are fleas? He knows what fleas are well enough, and is probably much better acquainted with their habits than we are. He knows that we wouldn't come here to look for fleas. Tell me a scientific name. I can't think of one myself, except "fritillary". Well never mind. If you can't, you can't. Now, listen.'

In a clear, loud voice, calculated to carry some distance, he said—

'I hope, Professor, that our long journey has not been in vain; I hope, I trust, not. This place, the rocks and pools beyond us, seems to me a likely habitat for the *Athalonia miserabilis*, the marvellous sea-beetle, found nowhere but on these western shores.'

He cast a rapid glance at Thomas O'Flaherty Pat. The old man appeared wholly unimpressed, and sat gazing with wide, dreamy eyes past the strangers straight out to sea. But Meldon was not the man to be baffled by any affectation of indifference and inattention. Convinced that the old man understood English, and was keenly interested in what he heard, he took the Major slowly across the beach, climbed a neighbouring ledge of rock, and stooped down as if to make a minute examination of a weedy pool. Looking up, he was gratified to see the eyes of Thomas O'Flaherty Pat fixed on him.

'I thought I'd rouse him,' he said to the Major. 'Now I'll make him quite sure that I'm after nothing more thrilling than the corpse of an *Athalonia miserabilis*.'

With every appearance of intense excitement, Meldon dropped on his knees beside the pool. He took off his coat and rolled up one of his shirt sleeves; he lay flat on his stomach; he plunged his bare arm deep into the water. Then he rose and looked round to see how Thomas O'Flaherty Pat was taking the performance. The old man had left the stone on which he sat, and was approaching the pool.

'I thought I'd draw him,' said Meldon.

After examining minutely some shreds of green seaweed which he had dredged from the depths of the pool, he plunged his arm in again. Thomas O'Flaherty Pat came quite close, looked at the curate with an expression of some wonder, and passed on. Reaching the edge of the sea, he too, lay flat down, bared his arm and plunged it into the water. Meldon, rising to his knees, looked at him.

'What's the old boy at now?' he said.

'Looks very much,' said the Major, 'as if he was trying to catch a Paphlagonia What's-it's-name, too.'

'*Athalonia miserabilis*,' said Meldon. 'Do try to get things right, Major. You set up to be a tidy man and take it on yourself to lecture me every now and then for getting things into wrong places, but you're the most untidy person I ever met in conversation. You never get a name right.'

'Well, Athalonia whatever you like. Anyhow, he's trying to catch one.'

'He can't be, can't possibly be. There's no such creature, so far as I know.'

'Well, he's catching something, and what's more he's caught it and he's bringing it over to you.'

Thomas O'Flaherty Pat came towards them, and certainly carried booty of some sort in his hand. With a dignified and gracious bow, he presented Meldon with a large red crab.

'Good Lord!' said Major Kent.

The curate took the creature carefully, and bowed politely in return.

'Thanks awfully,' he said. 'I mean to say, of course, *merci beaucoup*.'

'Ní Beurla agam,' said the old man.

'Oh, never mind about the Beurla. What I want you to know is this, I'm greatly obliged to you for the crab. So's the professor here. We weren't exactly looking for crabs. We were looking for an *Athalonia miserabilis*, but we're just as much pleased as if you brought us one. The fact is we're both passionately fond of crab, dressed with breadcrumbs and pepper, you know. And in London, where we come from, the chief city of the Sassenach—you know the place I mean—crabs are too expensive for poor men like us to buy. You can't pick them up there the way you do here. You'd hardly believe the price a fishmonger would charge for a crab like this.'

Thomas O'Flaherty Pat shook his head solemnly.

'Ní Beurla agam air bith,' he said.

'All right,' said Meldon. 'Goodbye for the present. So long, old boy. We oughtn't to be taking up your valuable time. I really believe he doesn't know a word I'm saying. Look here——'

He seized the old man's hand and shook it heartily.

'Céud mile failte—there, that's all the Irish I know, and if that doesn't send you off home I can do no more.'

This hearty welcome produced the effect intended. Thomas O'Flaherty Pat, after a courteous salutation, turned and climbed slowly up the path which led to the top of the cliff.

'I hope,' said the Major, 'that that will be a lesson to you, J. J.'

'A lesson about what?'

'About telling lies. You see the trouble they get you into.'

'I see nothing of the sort. My lies, as you call them, got rid of that troublesome old fool, who might have gone on following us all day. Also they secured us this excellent crab, which I shall cook for supper tonight. And anyhow, they aren't lies. They are what is called diplomacy, and that's an art practised by the most honourable men—lords and marquises, and kings, and people of that kind. Do you suppose that the Prime Minister, when he thinks he'll have to go to war with Germany, tells the literal truth? Does he go and ask to have the first battle put off for a week because he's short of cartridges? Of course he doesn't. He gives the Germans to understand that England is chock full of cartridges of all sizes. The fewer he really has the more he says he has. That's diplomacy, and it's reckoned to be a very noble line of life. Well, the principle applies to treasure-seeking just as much as to international politics. No treasure would ever have been found if the people who were on the track of it went telling all they knew to every chance acquaintance. They simply have to put the general public—people like Higginbotham and Thomas O'Flaherty Pat—off the scent, and there's no way of doing that except the one. Besides, it wouldn't be the slightest use telling the literal truth. People wouldn't believe you. Suppose I went up to Higginbotham and said that you and I were here on a treasure hunt. Do you think he'd believe it? Not he. He'd laugh. He hasn't got enough imagination to believe the truth if you hung it up before him. His mind isn't fit for it. If you knew any theology, Major, you'd understand that economy, as it's called, consists of dealing out to the average man just the amount of truth he's fit to receive, and no more. The Church has always gone on that principle, and I'm acting in the same way towards Higginbotham and Thomas O'Flaherty.'

7

MELDON, encouraging the reluctant Major by example and exhortation, continued to scramble southwards along the base of the cliffs. It grew very hot. Now and then Major Kent sat down, mopped his face, and declared that he would go no further. On such occasions Meldon lit his pipe and argued with his friend. It always ended in the Major going on, slipping, staggering, clutching. At last he sat down with an air of great determination.

'J. J.,' he said, 'the tide has turned. I'm going back. We've passed some nasty corners, places we couldn't get round at half-tide. I've no fancy for being drowned. You know I can't swim.'

'All right,' said Meldon, 'trust me. I'll pull you through.'

'If you mean that you propose to save my life in a heroic manner and get credit and perhaps medals for it afterwards, I tell you plainly that I don't mean to give you the chance. I'm going home the way I came, partly on my two feet, partly on my hands and knees. I'm not going to be towed about the sea to gratify your vanity.'

'The place I'm going to is just ahead of us. It's the very next promontory. We've time enough to get round it. You'll be sorry, Major, if you go back now.'

The Major rose with a sigh, and followed Meldon to a headland which jutted further out into the sea than any they had passed. It was very difficult to get round it. The sea washed almost against the base of the precipitous rocks. There was no more than a narrow ledge, three or four feet above the level of the water, along which it was possible to walk; and even there it was necessary to press close to the side of the cliff. Once round the point, a long, narrow inlet opened before them. It was, even at the entrance, not more than thirty feet across, and it narrowed as it reached inland. On the south side of the channel the rocks rose sheer out of the water to a height of thirty or forty feet. Above them was a steep slope of short, wiry grass. On the north side, where Meldon and the Major stood, the cliff rose less precipitously, and it was possible to scramble along for a short distance. The tide was almost at dead ebb, and at the end of the channel the water lapped on a tiny beach, surrounded closely on three sides by cliffs. At the shoreward end of the beach, a few feet from the water, was a small hole, hardly to be dignified by the name of cave. It was evident that when the tide rose a little the water would reach the hole, and that at half-tide the entrance to it would be entirely covered.

Meldon gazed down the channel and saw the hole in the cliff. His face wore a look of intense satisfaction. Major Kent also seemed pleased. He gave a sigh expressive of relief.

'Now,' he said, 'we're stuck and we can't go any further. We've reached the last rock on which it is possible to climb, and I can neither swim nor fly. Suppose we start to go back?'

Meldon sat down and began to take off his boots.

'This,' he said, 'is the scene of the shipwreck, and in that hole the Spanish captain concealed his treasure. Reconstruct the scene for yourself, Major. The galleon, partially disabled by the loss of one or more of her masts, comes driving down on the island before a nor'-westerly gale. I gave you my reasons for saying the wind was nor'-west, so we needn't go into that again. Where does she strike? On the point we've just passed. It's the furthest sticking-out point there is, so of course she struck on it. You follow me so far? What happens next?'

Meldon, having got rid of his boots and socks, stood up while he took off his coat and waistcoat.

'What are you going to do?' said the Major.

'Swim to the end of the channel, of course, and see what's inside that hole. You can stay here and mind my clothes. But to go on where you interrupted me. Where was I? Oh yes. The galleon had just struck on the point. What happens next? A great sea lifts her stern and slews it round. Her bow slips off the ledge of rock over which we walked—it would be about half-tide when the thing happened—and the galleon drifts stern foremost into this channel and sticks fast just where we're standing now. You follow me all right, don't you?'

'It's very interesting,' said the Major, 'but I don't suppose for a moment it's true.'

'Of course it's true. It's what must have happened. Don't you see that under the circumstances nothing else could happen? Tell me this, now—if a wave, with a nor'-west wind, lifted the stern of the galleon round in the way I have described, what could the old hooker do but go stern first along this channel until she stuck?'

'Oh, I dare say that's right enough, but there's such a lot went before that.'

'Have you any other hypothesis which meets the facts of the case better? No. Very well, then, accept mine. That's the way all scientific advance is made. Some Johnny with brains produces a hypothesis. Everybody calls him a rotter at first. But he remains calm in the face of opprobrium.'

'I'm the opprobrium, I suppose,' said the Major.

'Well, in this case you represent the opprobrient. But to go on. What does the scientific Johnny do next?'

'You needn't go on.'

'Oh, but I will. I read the whole thing up at college in Mill's Logic when I was thinking of going in for honours. I was young then. The scientific Johnny says, "Take my hypothesis. If it doesn't account for the facts give it the chuck out; but if it does, then stop scoffing and get ready a statue to erect in my honour." Now, what I say is this, Does my hypothesis cover the facts? There now, you've kicked one of my socks into a pool. I do wish you wouldn't fidget in a place like this. There isn't room for a display of temper.'

Meldon got his shirt off and stood poised on the edge of the rock for his plunge. 'I'll finish explaining what happened when I get back,' he said. 'I won't be long. Hallo! Who's that? Oh, Great Scott!'

He pointed with his finger to the top of the grassy slope which crowned the cliff opposite him. The Major looked upwards and saw, seated above the hole, Thomas O'Flaherty Pat. The old man, his hair and beard blown in picturesque wisps by the sea-breeze, was watching Meldon with a calm, disinterested gaze.

'What are you going to do now?' asked the Major.

'I'm going home again for today,' said Meldon, clutching at his shirt. 'I'm not going on with that old boy watching me. I tell you he knows what we are after. He can't have believed that story about the *Athalonia miserabilis*. What horrid sceptics these unsophisticated-looking people are in their hearts!'

'He'd have been a precious ass if he had believed it. You give nobody credit for any intelligence, J. J. You invent stories which wouldn't deceive a babe in arms, and then expect people to be taken in by them.'

'Well,' said Meldon, 'Higginbotham believed much taller stories than that one.'

'I knew you were going too far with that sea-insect of yours. Why couldn't you have invented something more likely if you had to invent?'

'Oh, well, if we're going to enter upon a course of mutual recrimination, why couldn't you have refrained from kicking my sock into a pool?'

Meldon was pulling his boot over the damp garment, and spoke feelingly.

'But never mind, Major, I'm not by any means at the end of my tether yet. Tomorrow we'll come back here at low tide and I'll swim to the hole then.'

'What about Thomas O'Flaherty Pat? He'll follow us again.'

'Oh no, he won't. I'll manage him.'

'How?'

'That'll be all right, Major. You leave it to me. If I say I'll manage him, you may take it as a fixed thing that he'll be managed. I can't tell you just this moment how I'm going to do it. I shall have to think the matter out by myself. But you may feel perfectly certain that it'll be all right. I've not done badly so far, have I?'

'In the matter of lies,' said the Major, 'you've shown an inventive power which has surprised me.'

'Don't call them lies; call them disguises. Nine fellows out of every ten who go out treasure-seeking have to adopt some sort of disguise, and it's always considered quite right. Now, what's the difference, the moral difference, between a detective——'

'We're not detectives.'

'The principle is exactly the same—between the detective getting himself up as a dock labourer in order to deceive the wily criminal, and our saying that we're bug hunters in order to put old T. O. P. off the scent? There's no earthly difference that I can see; so there's no use being offensive and talking about lies. Come on, now. I'm dressed, and we ought to be getting back before the tide rises.'

'I said so an hour ago.'

'Apart altogether from the disguises that we've been compelled to adopt,' said Meldon, when they had scrambled round the point and conversation became possible again, 'I maintain that I've done pretty well so far.'

'I don't see that you've done anything except cut a hole in the knee of your best trousers.'

'They're not my best; they're the oldest pair I have. I bought them two years before I was ordained. That's how they come to be the colour they are.'

Mr Meldon meant that the date of their purchase explained their having once been light grey. It also explained the fact that they were now considerably faded and mottled with a fine variety of stains.

'But leaving my trousers out of the question,' he went on, 'I think I've done a good deal. I've located to a certainty the exact scene of the wreck; I've reconstructed the catastrophe precisely as it happened, and I'm practically sure I know where the treasure was hidden.'

'Oh, you're sure of that, are you?'

'Practically sure, is what I said. I don't set up to be infallible. The best men may make mistakes. Listen to me, now, till I explain. The galleon is lying jammed in that channel. The water is, of course, comparatively calm there on account of the shelter of the headland. The Spanish captain, not being a fool—we agreed from the first, you remember, that the Spanish captain wasn't an absolute fool—sees that there is no immediate danger of the galleon breaking up. These Spanish galleons were all pretty tough. You remember the one that came ashore on Robinson Crusoe's island. It was pretty tough, and so was our one. Well, what does the Spanish captain do? He lowers his one remaining boat over the stern of the galleon and ferries his treasure into the mouth of the hole in the cliff. Then he drags it inland as far as the hole goes, maybe twenty yards or so. Afterwards he and the survivors of the crew landed just where we were standing, scrambled round the rocks—by that time it would be dead low water—very likely go up the same path that Thomas O'Flaherty Pat came down to meet us. Now what do you say to that?'

'I don't say anything,' said the Major.

'No, you don't. You save yourself up so as to say, "I told you so," in case there happens to be any trifling miscalculation. Or if, as is far more likely, I turn out to be perfectly right, then you're in a position to pretend you agreed with me all along. But it's waste of breath talking to you.'

'It is,' said the Major.

'I'm glad you agree with me there, anyhow. Here's Thomas O'Flaherty Pat's path. Let's go up it and get back to the *Spindrift*. I'm as hungry as a wolf. That's the worst of breakfasting so early. By the way, where's the crab?'

'What crab?'

'The large red crab that old Tommy Pat caught and gave to me. Major, have you left it behind?'

'I never had it. If anybody's left it behind it was you. You were carrying it.'

'But I told you to mind it while I swam up the channel.'

'You did not.'

'Well, I meant to, and anyway you ought to have known. How was I to go swimming with a large crab in my hand? Of course you ought to have minded it.'

'I'm sorry,' said the Major.

'Oh, well, it doesn't much matter. I don't so much care about the crab itself. I dare say we shouldn't have been able to cook it properly even if we had it. What I'm thinking of is poor old T. O. P.'s feelings. I'm afraid he'll be hurt if he sees us coming back without his crab.'

'I shouldn't fret about that if I were you.'

'Oh, but I do. It's not altogether Patsy Tom O'Flaherty's feelings that I mind. But on these occasions you ought always to try to win the goodwill and the confidence of the natives.'

'You go a queer way about it, then, if that's what you want.'

'Any book of travel,' said Meldon, ignoring the Major's last remark, 'will tell you that the really important thing is to get the natives to trust you thoroughly from the start.'

'That's why you told that yarn about the sea insect, I suppose?'

'Look here, Major, what's the good of rubbing it in about the *Athalonia miserabilis?* I've owned up that that was a slip. I can't do more, can I? I don't keep harping on to you about the way you put my sock into the pool and forgot the crab, and those are a jolly sight worse things than any I've done.'

'I wouldn't care much,' said the Major, as they neared the top of the steep and slippery pathway, 'to be climbing up this five or six times a day with a creel of seaweed on my back.'

'No more would I,' said the curate. 'Seaweed's poor stuff, but I wouldn't mind doing it that number of times and more with a parcel of doubloons slung over my shoulder; gold, Major, good solid gold. It's this way that we'll have to bring it up from that hole. I've been reckoning out how many journeys we'll have to make with it. Supposing, now, that there's——'

'Do shut up, J. J.! What on earth's the use of talking like that? You know as well as I do that there's not the smallest likelihood of our getting any gold out of your hole.'

'Oh, I'll shut up if you like. But I'll just say this: it's a good job for you, Major, that you have a man with you who has a little foresight, who figures things out beforehand and lays his plans in advance. You'd be particularly helpless if you were left to yourself.'

They reached the top of the cliff. In front of them lay the long, green slope of the island, a patchwork of ridiculous little fields seamed with an intolerable complexity of grey stone walls. Below, near the further sea, were the cabins of the people, little whitewashed buildings, thatched with half-rotten straw. On the roofs of many of them long grass grew. From a chimney here and there a thin column of smoke was blown eastwards and vanished in the clear air a few yards from the hole from which it emerged. Gaunt cattle, dejected creatures, stood here and there idle, as if the task of seeking for grass long enough to lick up had grown too hard for them. In the muddy bohireens long, lean sows, creatures more like hounds of some grotesque, antique breed than modern domestic swine, roamed and rooted. Now and then a woman emerged from a door with a pot or dish in her hands, and fowls, fearfully excited, gathered from the dungheaps to her petticoats. Men, leaning heavily on their loys, or digging sullenly and slowly, were casting earth upon the wide potato ridges. Apart from the other habitations stood Higginbotham's egregious iron hut; the very type of a hideous, utilitarian, utterly self-sufficient civilisation thrust in upon a picturesque dilapidation. It gave to the island an air of half-comic vulgarity, much such an air as Thomas O'Flaherty Pat might have worn if some one had added to his customary garments a new silk hat. Beyond all lay the bay, round which the island folded its arms, a sheet of glancing, glittering water with darker sea behind it, and far away the dim outline of the mainland coast.

The *Spindrift* lay at her moorings, and beyond her another boat, cutter rigged also, which had just dropped anchor. Her jib was stowed; her mainsail shook in the breeze. Two men were to be seen casting loose the halyards. Soon the sail was down, and the men were gathering the folds of it in their hands and lashing the gaff to the boom. Major Kent and Meldon stared at the boat in surprise. For a time neither of them spoke. Then, taking his companion by the arm, the Major said—

'What boat's that?'

'She looks to me,' said Meldon, 'uncommonly like my old *Aureole*.'

'I just thought she did. Now what brings her here?'

'I don't know.'

'Look here, J. J., you go in for being clever; you've been

swaggering all day about the way you understand everything and get the hang of whatever happens, even if it's two hundred years ago; just set your great mind to work on that boat and tell me what she's doing out there.'

Stirred by the taunt, Meldon spoke with some appearance of recovering self-confidence.

'It's the *Aureole* right enough. I hired her to a man in a mangy fur coat, who said he didn't know anything about boats but had a friend who did. Now I'll tell you this, Major, to start with. Either that friend knows nothing about boats either, or else he has some pretty strong reason for wishing to get to this island. Nobody but a fool, or a man who was prepared to take big risks, would have ventured out here in her. Why, every rope in her rigging is as rotten as a bad banana. If there'd come on the least bit of a blow that fellow in the fur coat and the other play boy, whoever he is, would have been at the bottom of the briny sea.'

'Well, they're not,' said the Major, 'so their deaths are not on your conscience.'

'They wouldn't have been in any case,' said Meldon. 'I never thought they'd go outside Moy Bay, or I wouldn't have hired the boat to them. Who'd expect a seedy individual in a fur coat, a fellow that looked sodden with drink, to take a boat out on to the broad Atlantic? At the same time the other fellow can't be altogether a fool. He must know something about sailing, otherwise he wouldn't have fetched up here at all. Now, what on earth brings him out here?'

'Maybe he's a tourist looking out for scenery.'

'He is not, then. There isn't any scenery here, not what tourists call scenery. And there's not a guide-book in the world that so much as mentions Inishgowlan. The place isn't even marked on most maps. Whatever else he is, he's not a tourist.'

'He might be a journalist.'

'He might,' said Meldon. 'And yet I don't think he is. It's quite true that a journalist might come to see Higginbotham. Higginbotham is the sort of man a journalist would fasten on at once. A really smart man at his trade would scent Higginbotham from miles and miles away, and would track him over land and sea. Higginbotham would talk all day long if he got any encouragement. He'd pour out just the sort of sentimental rot about improving the conditions of the people's life that the plump, kind-hearted Englishman loves to read. There's a good deal to be said for that journalist hypothesis of yours, Major, but there are serious objections to it too.'

Major Kent did not answer; he was not really much interested in the strangers. Meldon went on—

'In the first place, if he was a journalist, or if he was any kind of inspector, the Congested Districts Board would bring him round in their own steamer. They always take care to do a journalist middling well when they catch him, and they keep their eye on him. They don't let him off by himself in a boat to pry into all sorts of things which he has no business to see. That's one objection. The second is this: if he is a journalist, who is the other chappie, the one in the fur coat? Journalists never go about in couples. It would ruin their business if they did. No, on the whole I think we may decide that he's not a journalist. There's only one other thing he can be—a Member of Parliament, one of the conscientious, inquiring kind, who wants to look into the condition of Ireland for himself before he commits himself to an opinion on Home Rule.'

'I hope,' said the Major anxiously, 'that his coming won't make it necessary for you to tell any more—I mean to say to adopt any more disguises.'

'I expect I shall have to.'

'Well, now, J. J., like a good fellow, draw it mild this time. Remember, if he's a Member of Parliament he'll see through the ordinary disguise at once.'

'That's just it,' said Meldon gloomily. 'If he's an M.P. he's sure to have made inquiries about our educational system and he'll never believe that story about the National Board wanting to build a school.'

'He certainly won't believe about my geological survey.'

'You mean on account of the pliocene clay? I don't expect

he knows much about clay—not enough to make him sceptical, anyhow.'

'I wasn't thinking of the pliocene clay. What I had in my mind was the inherent absurdity of the whole story.'

'I don't see that at all,' said Meldon. 'On the contrary, I'm inclined to think that he will believe that story. Anyhow, he'll ask a question in the House of Commons about it.'

'I hope to God he won't! I should look a nice fool if that story ever got into the papers.'

'You'd do worse than look a fool. You'd probably be called to the bar of the house, or be sent to jail for contempt of the Chief Secretary. I'll tell you what it is, Major, if that M.P. gets hold of the story you'd better sail straight to America.'

'But it's not my story, it's yours.'

'It's you they'd prosecute, though. That's the beauty of Ireland. The clergy are perfectly safe. Even the Chief Secretary daren't proceed against me; but he would be against you, like a shot. He might set a Royal Commission on you.'

'Don't be an ass, J. J.'

'I'm not being an ass. I'm looking facts straight in the face and drawing conclusions. It's my opinion that if that man in my boat turns out to be a Member of Parliament—I say if—we shall have to adopt some fresh disguise.'

'I can't stand another, J. J. I can't be four things at once. My brain won't stand it.'

'It'll have to.'

'What do you mean to tell him?'

'I don't know yet. I must be guided by circumstances. But you leave it to me, Major, and you'll find it'll pan out all right. I'm not by any means such a fool as people are inclined to take me for. After all, what's a Member of Parliament?'

The Major's spirits sank as Meldon's revived. He was a plain man with an immense dislike of complications, and he foresaw bewildering confusion before him.

'J. J.,' he said solemnly, 'I'm Major Kent, I'm also a mining expert in the pay of the Lord-Lieutenant and the Chief Secretary.

I'm also a professor of sea-serpents and things of that sort. I can't and won't set up to be anything else on this trip.'

'Oh, we're done with the sea-serpent. You can get that off your mind as soon as you like. That was only temporary. Remember, Major, what Shakespeare said, or if it wasn't Shakespeare it was some one else—"One man in his time plays many parts." You're a man, aren't you? Well, there you are. You can't go behind Shakespeare in a matter of this kind. As soon as we've had a bite to eat I'll paddle across to the *Aureole* and call on the Member of Parliament.'

'You will not,' said the Major. 'What's the use of running unnecessary risks? You leave him alone unless he goes for you in any way.'

'That's the very worst possible policy to pursue,' said Meldon. 'He'll be off to collogue with Higginbotham straight away if I don't stop him; and it's ten to one he'll hear about the school or the geological survey. No, no. I'll take him in hand. If necessary I'll trot him round myself. How would it be now, if I dropped a hint that we were members of the Irish Lights Commission going about inspecting lighthouses? He might believe that, and it wouldn't interest him enough to set him asking more questions.'

'But there's no lighthouse here.'

'That's true, of course. Still, we might be thinking of building one. But anyhow, it's time enough to think about that. I can't possibly tell what the best thing to say is till I see the man. In the meanwhile let's go and get our dinner. I was hungry before; I'm simply ravenous now.'

'My appetite is pretty well gone,' said the Major.

'Rot! What is there to affect your appetite? Why, man, we're getting on swimmingly, far better than I expected. You can't go out treasure-seeking without meeting an occasional difficulty. That's where the sport comes in. And listen to me, Major, it doesn't in the least matter what I tell the Member of Parliament or what he hears from Higginbotham. The old *Aureole* is absolutely certain to drown him on his way home, and anything he happens to have learned will go to the bottom of the sea with him. It's nothing short of a miracle that he got here safe.'

8

HAVING paddled the Major out to the *Spindrift*, Meldon suggested that they should dine on tinned brawn and bread-and-butter. It would, as he pointed out, take a long time to light the galley stove and boil potatoes, and every moment was of value now that the strangers on the *Aureole* had arrived and might go on shore to interview Higginbotham. It is likely also that extreme hunger made the prospect of an hour's delay very unpleasant. The Major, in spite of the anxiety which affected his appetite, agreed to dine at once. A tin was opened and a loaf of bread taken from the locker.

'Last loaf but one,' said the Major, as he set it on the table. 'Tomorrow we shall be reduced to biscuits.'

'Not at all,' said Meldon. 'I'll make a point of seeing Mary Kate's mother this evening and getting her to make us a loaf of soda bread. There's nothing so good as one of those pot-oven loaves, baked over a turf fire, and Mary Kate's mother is just the woman to do it well.'

'You know nothing about the woman. You've never seen her. How do you know whether she can bake or not?'

'I've seen Mary Kate, and that's enough. You're very unobservant, Major. It's a great fault in you. And when by any chance you do observe anything, you fail to draw the most obvious inference. Now I know all about Mary Kate's mother by looking at Mary Kate. She's a plump, well-nourished little girl, comparatively clean, with a nice, comfortable, red petticoat on her, therefore—observe the simple nature of the inference—therefore Mary Kate's mother is a competent woman. Is it likely that a woman who couldn't make an ordinary loaf would have reared a child like Mary Kate?'

'She may not have a mother at all,' said the Major. 'It might be her grandmother or her aunt that reared her.'

'There you are again. That's your wretched, niggling, Anglo-Saxon way of grubbing about at details instead of grasping the broad principles of things. It doesn't matter to us whether Mary Kate has a mother or not. The point is that somewhere behind Mary Kate there's a competent woman, a grandmother, or an aunt, or a deceased wife's sister—it doesn't in the least matter which. Whoever she is she can bake. But I'll tell you what it is, Major, if we had my little girl here on board, we shouldn't be going on our bended knees to strange women for the want of a bit of bread. We'd be sitting down now to a good dish of steaming hot potatoes, with their skins just beginning to peel off them. In fact, I shouldn't wonder if she had them fried for us. Think of that!'

'I'd rather——'

The Major's remark was interrupted by a heavy bump on the side of the yacht. It was clear from the sound of scraping that followed that a boat had come alongside.

'That fellow, whoever he is,' said the Major, 'will have all the paint off us before he's done.'

'It must be the Member of Parliament off the *Aureole*,' said Meldon. 'I call this most fortunate.'

He sprang up and climbed on deck. The moment afterwards he thrust his head into the cabin again and said—

'It's not the Member of Parliament after all. It's only Higginbotham.'

He plunged forward as he spoke until his body hung down the ladder.

'Best thing that could have happened,' he whispered. 'So long as Higginbotham is here we are safe, and the Member of Parliament can't get at him. I'll bring him down and give him a bit of brawn. We can open another tin if he seems hungry.'

With a violent wriggle Meldon got his head and shoulders on deck again. He welcomed Higginbotham with effusive hospitality, and warmly invited him to go below and have some dinner. It appeared, however, that Higginbotham was not hungry. His face wore a look of perplexity and irritation. There was evidently something troubling him which he was anxious to have cleared up.

'I saw you leave the shore,' he said, 'and I got young Jamesy O'Flaherty to put me off. I hope you don't mind?'

'Not a bit,' said Meldon. 'We're delighted to see you. You say you won't have any brawn. Well, try a slice of bread-and-jam. Major, get out the strawberry jam; it's in the locker under you.'

'No, thanks. The fact is I only came out for a few minutes' conversation with you. I——'

'If you like,' said Meldon, 'I'll light the galley fire and make you a cup of tea.'

'No, thanks. I want to speak to you for a few minutes and then I'll go back to my work. I've been rather annoyed this morning. I'm sure there's some ridiculous mistake which can be cleared up in ten minutes. I thought it better to come straight to you.'

'Quite right,' said Meldon; 'if the thing is clearable at all, I'll clear it. I'm rather good at clearing things up. Ask the Major if I'm not. Just you make a clean breast of whatever the trouble is. You won't mind our eating while you talk.'

'It's about sugar candy,' said Higginbotham.

'Great Scott!' said Meldon. 'Mary Kate!'

'I don't know anything about Mary Kate, but all the children on the island have been following me about and bothering the life out of me for sugar candy. They say you set them on.'

'Look here, Higginbotham,' said Meldon severely. 'The Major and I are busy men, whatever you may be. If you're in any real trouble we're quite ready to do our best to pull you through, but I don't think it's fair of you to come here wasting our time over some trumpery business about sugar candy.'

'But the children said you sent them to me.'

'It's all well enough for you to be fussing and agitating in this way about mere trifles, but I have serious matters on my mind. I simply haven't time to waste over sugar candy. If the children have taken your sugar candy, see their parents about it and get them properly whipped. You can't expect us to go about taking sticky stuff out of their mouths to gratify you.'

'I didn't say they'd stolen my sugar candy. They haven't. What I said——'

'Very well, then, what are you making all this row about? Do you mean to suggest that we took your sugar candy? Neither the Major nor I ever eat sugar candy. If you set half a pound of it down on this table now, and invited us to gorge, we simply wouldn't touch it. Look here, Higginbotham, you and I are old friends, and you often used to go up to Rathmines with me to see my little girl, so I'll just give you a word of advice that I wouldn't give to a stranger—if you want to get on with the people on this island, don't go quarrelling with their children. There's old Thomas O'Flaherty Pat, for instance, as decent an old fellow as I ever met, and quite easy to make friends with. He went out today, quite off his own bat, without so much as a hint from me, and caught a crab and gave it to me. Any one with a grain of tact could get on with poor Thomas O'Flaherty Pat. As quiet a man as you'd see anywhere. But you go and rub him up the wrong way, get his back up, and generally play old hokey with his temper by nagging at his granddaughter about some barley sugar.'

'It was sugar candy,' said Higginbotham, feebly; 'and besides——'

'Well, sugar candy, then—it's all the same. It wouldn't make any difference if it was peppermint lozenges. You worry and threaten the poor child about a pennyworth of some ridiculous sweetmeat, and then you profess to be astonished that the old man won't give up his house to you. I'd have been very much surprised indeed if he did under the circumstances. No man likes to have his grandchildren ragged. You wouldn't like it yourself if you had any. And a little girl, too! Higginbotham, you ought to be ashamed of yourself.'

'If you'd let me speak for a moment,' said Higginbotham, 'I'd explain.'

'You're far too fond of speaking,' said Meldon. 'Half your troubles come from talking too much.'

'But you've taken the thing up wrong. I'm not blaming you. There's a mistake somewhere, I know. I wish you'd let me say one word.'

'I can't and won't spend the rest of the day arguing with you about sugar candy. It wouldn't be for your own good if I did. Are you aware, Higginbotham, that there are two English Members of Parliament in that boat, anchored a few yards away, and that they've come here expressly to see how you are getting on?'

'How do you know that?'

'Well, I don't absolutely know it. But I can't imagine what would bring a Member of Parliament to this island if it wasn't to inspect your work. They don't come here for the salmon fishing; you may bet your hat on that. Now, if you'll take my advice you would seize the earliest opportunity of smoothing down old Thomas O'Flaherty Pat before they get listening to his story.'

'But the old man can only talk Irish.'

'Don't you trust too much to that, Higginbotham. In the first place I strongly suspect that he can talk English just as well as you can; and besides, you can't be sure that the Members of Parliament don't know Irish. I can tell you there are some mighty smart men in Parliament now. It just happens, Higginbotham, that this morning, while you were chasing and ballyragging that unfortunate little Mary Kate round and round the island for the sake of a bit of sugar candy, I was having a quiet chat with Thomas O'Flaherty Pat. It just shows me the kind of fellow you are. You don't hesitate to come here bothering the Major and me with your wretched little grievances while I've been doing you a good turn in a really important matter.'

'What?' said Higginbotham.

'I've a very good mind not to tell you after the way you've behaved. But I'll just say this much. You want old Thomas O'Flaherty Pat's house and bit of land, don't you? Very well, you go up there tomorrow at half-past eight and talk to him about it.'

'Have you persuaded him to give it up?'

'I won't say another word. Just go up and see for yourself.'

'I'm awfully obliged to you, Meldon; I really am. I'm sorry for bothering you about the sugar candy. I wouldn't have mentioned the matter to you only——'

'All right,' said Meldon graciously. 'Don't trouble to apologise. The Major and I don't mind a bit. But I'll tell you what you can do now. I have to go and call on the Members of Parliament. Will you——?'

'There's no use doing that,' said Higginbotham. 'I saw them going ashore in their punt as I came off to you.'

'All the same, I'll look them up,' said Meldon. 'I'm sure to find them somewhere about on the island. What I want you to do is to stay here and play chess with the Major till I get back.'

He winked fiercely at Major Kent as he spoke.

'I know you play, Higginbotham, for you were a member of the chess club in college. You'll enjoy having a go at the Major. He's a perfect whale at the Muzio gambit. Very few men know the ins and outs of it as he does.'

'I don't,' said the Major sulkily; 'and anyway, there isn't a chessboard on the yacht.'

Meldon winked again, this time with fervent appeal.

'It's all right about the board,' he said. 'I saw one in Higginbotham's house last night. I'll go ashore in your curragh, Higginbotham, and send it off to you. Good-bye. Oh! Before I go, Major, you might as well give me another sixpence in case I meet Mary Kate again. You may as well give it to me as be losing it to Higginbotham, making bets as to how one of your gambits will turn out.'

There was no one on the little pier when Meldon reached it.

He supposed, quite rightly, that those of the inhabitants of the island who were interested in strangers had gone after the M.P.'s. It seemed likely that Mary Kate had followed them. She was a child of inquisitive mind. He walked up to Higginbotham's house, obtained the chessboard, and sent it off in the curragh to the yacht. Then he made his way to the nearest cottage, knocked at the door, and entered. A young woman, bare-armed, with a thick stick in her hands, was pounding a mass of potatoes and turnips in a large tub.

'Good-evening to you,' said Meldon cheerfully. 'Getting the food ready for the pigs? That's right. Feed your pigs well. There's nothing like it. Here, give me a turn at that stick. You look as if you were getting hot.'

'It isn't the like of this work that you'd be used to,' said the woman smiling.

'Oh, but I can do it,' said Meldon, taking the stick from her. He pounded vigorously at the unsavory mess for a while. Then he said, 'Are you the woman of the house?'

'I am, your honour.'

'Well, then, where's Mary Kate this afternoon?'

'Is it Michael O'Flaherty Tom's Mary Kate you'll be wanting?'

'How many more Mary Kates are there?'

'There's ne'er another in it only herself.'

'Well, then, it's her I want. Where have you her?'

'She's no child of mine,' said the woman. 'I haven't but the one, and he's beyond there in the cradle. If she was letting on to your honour that she belonged to me she was just deceiving you. Faith, and it's not the only time the same little lady was at them sort of tricks. I hear that herself and the rest of the children had the life fair bothered out of the gentleman that does be measuring out the land, about sugar candy or some such talk.'

'I wouldn't wonder at her,' said Meldon; 'but where would she be now, do you think?'

'She might be off chasing home the brown cow and the little heifer for her da.'

'And where would the brown cow be?'

'Faith, that same cow is mighty fond of roaming where she's no call to go.'

The woman stepped outside her cottage door and peered up and down. 'Come here now, your honour, and leave off mashing them turnips. If that isn't herself with the brown cow in front of her and the little heifer beyond there over by the wall, it's mighty like her.'

'I'm much obliged to you,' said Meldon. 'Good evening.'

He crossed two stone walls, waded through a boggy field, and came within hail of the child who drove the cattle.

'Mary Kate!' he shouted. 'Hullo, there, Mary Kate O'Flaherty!'

She turned and looked at him in wonder. Then, recognising the giver of the sixpence in the morning, grinned shyly.

'Mary Kate,' shouted Meldon again, 'will you come over here and speak to me? Leave those cows alone and come here. Do you think I've nothing to do only to be running about the island chasing little girleens like yourself?'

But Mary Kate had no intention of leaving the cow and the heifer. With a devotion to the pure instinct of duty which would have excited the admiration of any Englishman and a Casabianca-like determination to abide by her father's word, she began driving the cattle towards Meldon. Four fields, one of them boggy, and five loose stone walls lay between her and the curate. There were no gates. Such obstacles might have daunted an older herd. They didn't trouble Mary Kate in the least. Reaching the first wall she deliberately toppled stone after stone off it until she had made a practicable gap.

The cow and the heifer, understanding what was expected of them, stalked into the field beyond, picking their steps with an ease which told of long practice, among the scattered *débris* of the broken wall. Meldon, with a courteous desire to save the child extra trouble, crossed the wall nearest him. Mary Kate dealt with a second obstacle as she had with the first and reached the boggy field. The cattle, encouraged by her shouts, floundered through, drawing their hoofs out of the deep mud with evident exertion. Mary Kate, light as she was, sank to her ankles in places and splashed the calves of her legs with slime. Meldon, who wore boots and had to be careful where he walked, waited for her on dry ground.

'Well, Mary Kate,' he said. 'Here you are at last. A nice chase I had after you. Tell me this now, did you see the two strange gentlemen that came off the other boat?'

'I did.'

'Did either of them give you a sixpence the same as I did this morning?'

'They did not.'

'Didn't they now? I'd hardly call them gentlemen at all then, would you?'

Mary Kate grinned. Her first shyness was disappearing. She began to find Meldon a companionable person.

'Where did they go when they came ashore? Was it up to the iron house of the gentleman that does be measuring out the land?'

Meldon had gathered from the woman whom he had interviewed on his way that this was the proper description of Higginbotham.

Mary Kate understood him at once.

'They did not then.'

'Well, and if they didn't go there, where did they go?'

'Back west.'

'Do you mean up the hill there to the place where the cliffs are?'

Mary Kate grinned assent. She was a child who set a proper value on words and used as few as possible in conversation. Meldon wondered why the Members of Parliament had gone straight past the human habitations and the works of Higginbotham, which might be supposed to interest them, to the desolate region where only very active sheep grazed. He decided that they must have gone to look at the view, and he thought less of them. The tourist—the mere unmitigated tourist—with no political or social objects before his mind, goes to look at views. No one else—certainly no proper, serious-minded Member of Parliament—would waste his time over a view.'

'Mary Kate,' he began again after a pause. 'You're Michael O'Flaherty Tom's Mary Kate, aren't you?'

'I might then.'

'What's the good of saying you might when you know you are? You can't get over me with that sort of talk. Do you see that?'

He held up between his finger and thumb Major Kent's second sixpence.

Mary Kate grinned.

'Well, take a good look at it. Now, tell me this. Is Thomas O'Flaherty Pat your grandfather?'

'Is it me grandda you mean?'

'It is. Is Thomas O'Flaherty Pat your grandda?'

'He might,' said Mary Kate.

'Well, go you up to him wherever he is and tell him this: that the gentleman who does be measuring out the land wants to see him tomorrow morning at half-past eight o'clock. Do you understand me now?'

'I do surely.'

'Well, what are you to tell him?'

'I'm to tell him that the gentleman from the Board who does be measuring out the land wants to take the house off him.'

'Well,' said Meldon, 'you can put it that way if you like. And mind this, Mary Kate—are you listening to me now?—mind this, if your grandda isn't there at half-past eight o'clock the house will be took off him whether he likes it or not. But if he's there, maybe it won't. Do you understand that?'

'I do.'

'Well, now, there's one thing more. You're a mighty clever little girl, Mary Kate. I suppose now you can speak the Irish just as well as you can the English. Well, then, you be up at your grandda's house at the same time tomorrow, so as you'll be able to tell him what the gentleman says to him and tell the gentleman what he wants to say.'

'Sure, there's no need.'

'I know there's no need just as well as you do. But you're to be there all the same. Will you promise me now that you'll go?'

'I do be in dread of the gentleman,' said Mary Kate doubtfully.

'And well you may after plaguing the life out of him all day for barley sugar. Oh, I heard about your goings on. But don't you be afraid. That'll be all right.'

'Will he be for beating me?'

'He will not. I made it all right with him, and he won't raise a hand to you, so you needn't be afraid. Just you face up to him and tell him what your grandda says about the house. Now, here's the other sixpence for you. Be a good girl and mind what I said, and maybe you'll get another sixpence yet.'

Meldon left the child and strolled down to the pier. He was gratified to see the two strangers in their punt rowing off to the *Aureole*. Their taste for scenery was evidently satisfied. He paddled out to the *Spindrift* very well satisfied with himself. He found Major Kent and Higginbotham sitting over the chessboard in the cabin. The Major had just been checkmated for the fourth time and was in a very bad temper. Higginbotham had taken quite the wrong way of soothing him. There is nothing more irritating than to have the mistakes of the past brought up and explained, all their foolishness exposed. Higginbotham, with that curious memory which only chess-players possess, had insisted on going over each of the four games he had won and showing to the Major where the weakness of his moves lay. Meldon interrupted the fourth demonstration.

'Wake up, you two,' he cried as he entered the cabin, 'and let's get tea. I'm as hungry as if I hadn't touched food today. I'll tell you what it is, Higginbotham; I wouldn't like to be an inhabitant of this island of yours when there's a famine on. I never came across such a place in my life for raising an appetite on a man. You ought to get your Board to run it as a health resort for dyspeptic people who can't or won't eat.'

'Dyspeptic people,' said the Major sullenly, 'are the ones who eat too much.'

'Oh! Well you know the kind of people I mean. I may have got the name wrong. I'm not a boss at scientific names and I never said I was. I leave that to you and Higginbotham. You like talking about pliocene clay and such things. Hullo! Where are you going?'

The Major had risen from his seat and was making for the galley. He disliked the mention of pliocene clay. It seemed to him that it might lead to inquiries from Higginbotham about the geological survey of the island.

'I'm going to light the stove,' he said.

'Oh, I'll do that,' said Meldon. 'I know you hate messing about with coal and paraffin oil. It dirties your hands. You and Higginbotham spread the cloth and get out the cups and things.'

'I'm afraid I can't stay for tea,' said Higginbotham. 'I've got a lot of writing to do.'

'Nonsense,' said Meldon hospitably. 'You can't really want to write. No posts go out from this island.'

'No, they don't. But I'm expecting some members of our Board round before the end of the month, and I like to have a report of my work written up. I didn't realise that it was so late till you came on board.'

'Very well, Higginbotham, we won't interfere with your work. The Major and I both know what official work is. We're sorry to lose your company, but of course we quite understand. Major, if you put Higginbotham ashore in the punt, I'll light the stove. Goodbye, old fellow. Mind you don't forget to be up at old O'Flaherty's tomorrow at 8.30. It's most important. Are you ready, Major?'

Major Kent was already busy at the stove and refused to leave it. It was Meldon who took Higginbotham to the pier. When he returned the stove was lit, the kettle on it, and Major Kent was waiting for him.

'J. J.,' said he, 'I'll stand no more of this. If you want to entertain Higginbotham you must do it yourself. You know I'm no good at chess. What do you mean by dumping a man like that down on me for the afternoon?'

'I thought you'd like a game,' said Meldon.

'You thought nothing of the sort. You knew I was no match for a fellow who has won championship cups and things. He talked to me about the Sicilian defence. What do I know about the Sicilian defences?'

'If he hadn't had Sicilian defences to talk about he'd have talked about geology, and that would have been a great deal more unpleasant for you.'

'I don't see why he need have been kept here to talk at all.'

'My dear Major, aren't you a little unreasonable? I had to keep Higginbotham occupied in some way. I had to keep him off the island. Don't you see that if he landed he'd have been almost certain to knock up against one or other of those Members of Parliament? Then he'd have let the whole thing out—geological survey, school, and all. You wouldn't have liked that. You told me yourself you wouldn't like it.'

'He'll see them tomorrow anyway. It'll be all the same in the end.'

'He may not see them tomorrow. They may be gone out of this. You don't realise, Major, what a restless animal the modern Member of Parliament is. He never stops long in one place. He can't, you know. The British Empire has grown so enormously of late that the Members of Parliament simply have to dart round to get a look at it at all. Besides, even if Higginbotham does see them it won't matter. I have everything fixed up for tomorrow. By the evening we'll have our hands on the treasure and be in a position to laugh at the whole Government. Ah! There's the kettle boiling.'

A few minutes later Meldon entered the cabin with the teapot in his hand.

'I was just going to tell you,' he said, 'when the kettle boiled and interrupted me, that I've made it all right about old Thomas O'Flaherty Pat. He won't track us tomorrow.'

'What did you do?' said the Major a little anxiously. 'Did you disguise yourself again?'

'I did not then,' said Meldon, 'but I don't deny that I more or less disguised Mary Kate's grandda, and for the matter of that, Mary Kate herself and Higginbotham. I resorted to what you military men call a stratagem.'

'What did you do?'

'Well, maybe as you've been a magistrate since you've given up the army, you'll understand me better if I say that I established an alibi.'

'I wish you'd talk sense, not that I care what you did. I'm past caring.'

'An alibi,' said Meldon, 'is what they call it when a man is in another place from where the prosecuting counsel wants him to be. Now I don't want old O'Flaherty down on the pier tomorrow morning when we land. I don't want Higginbotham either. For the matter of that I don't particularly care about seeing Mary Kate there. So I've settled things in such a way that they'll all three of them be somewhere else between half-past eight and half-past nine tomorrow morning. That's the alibi. See?'

'I do not.'

'Well, I can't help your not seeing. The facts are just the same as if you did. We want to get off to that hole tomorrow without being tracked by old T. O. P., or talked at by Higginbotham. That's so, isn't it? Very well, we'll get off, unseen and unknown. That's what comes of managing these things with some little intelligence.'

'What about the Members of Parliament, if they are Members of Parliament?'

'As I think I told you before,' said Meldon, 'They'll probably be gone tomorrow morning. But even if they're not, it won't matter. They went off this afternoon up to the top of the mountain to look at the view. Now fellows who go wandering about after scenery aren't likely to interfere seriously with us. We needn't bother about them.'

9

MELDON's stratagem was entirely successful. Not only did Higginbotham and old O'Flaherty keep their engagement punctually, and Mary Kate go to act as interpreter, but almost all the rest of the inhabitants of the island went to listen to the discussion. The pier and the fields through which it was necessary to pass in order to reach the path down the cliff were entirely deserted. Meldon carried a bathing towel slung round his neck. The Major had a basket with some luncheon in it. After landing they took a look at the *Aureole*. The two strangers were busy on deck.

'What on earth are they doing?' said the Major.

'It looks to me uncommonly like as if they were trying to pull the halyard clear of the block at the throat,' said Meldon. 'If they do they may reeve it again themselves. I'm not going over to help them.'

'But what can they want to do that for?'

'I'm sure I don't know. Maybe they've got a new one on board. The old one's pretty bad. I shouldn't wonder if they wanted to get rid of it. But anyhow it's no business of ours. Come along.'

'I wish very much,' said the Major an hour later, when they were scrambling along the rocks below the cliff, 'that there was some nearer way to this beastly treasure-hole of yours.'

'Well, there isn't; not unless you like to let yourself down off the top of the cliff where the old boy was sitting yesterday, or off the other one on the north side of the bay. I think it dropped more sheer. By the way, that mightn't be a bad idea for getting the treasure up. You could stand on the top and let down a bag to me. I'd fill it with doubloons and then you'd haul up. See? It would be a great deal easier than carrying the stuff all round here and up the path. We'd run it down the hill to the pier in half an hour.'

'It would be easier,' said the Major. 'But it will be time enough to arrange about that when you've got the gold.'

They reached the shelf of rock outside the cave at last.

'It's a pity you can't swim,' said Meldon. 'You look hot enough to enjoy the cold water this minute.'

Meldon himself stripped, stood for a minute on the edge of the rock stretching himself in the warm air. Then he plunged into the water. He lay on his back, rolled over, splashed his feet and hands, dived as a porpoise does. Then, after a farewell to the Major, he struck out along the channel. In a few minutes he felt bottom with his feet and stood upright. He heard the Major shout something, but the echo of the cliffs around him prevented his catching the words. He swam again towards the shore. The Major continued to shout. Meldon stopped swimming, stood waist-deep in the water, and looked round. The Major pointed with his hand to the cliff at the end of the channel. Meldon looked up. A man with a rope round him was rapidly descending. Meldon gazed at him in astonishment. He was not one of the islanders. He was dressed in well-fitting, dark blue clothes, wore rubber-soled canvas shoes and a neat yachting cap. He reached the beach safely and faced Meldon. For a short time both men stood without speaking. The Major's shouts ceased. Then the stranger said—

'Who the devil are you?'

'I am the Rev. Joseph John Meldon, B.A., T.C.D., Curate of Ballymoy. Who are you and what are you doing here?'

'Damn it!' said the stranger.

'I wish,' said Meldon, 'that you wouldn't swear. It's bad form.'

'Damn it!' said the stranger again with considerable emphasis.

'I've mentioned to you that I'm a parson. You must recognise that it's particularly bad form to swear when you're talking to me. You ought to remember my cloth.'

The stranger grinned.

'There's devilish little cloth about you to remember this minute,' he said. 'I never saw a man with less. But any way, I don't care a tinker's curse for your cloth or your religion either. I'll swear if I like.'

'You don't quite catch my point,' said Meldon. 'I don't mind if you swear yourself blue in the face on ordinary occasions. But if you're a gentleman—and you look as if you wanted to be taken for one—you'll recognise that it's bad form to swear when you're talking to me. Being a parson, I can't swear back at you, and so you get an unfair advantage in any conversation there may be between us—the kind of advantage no gentleman would care to take.'

'Well, I'm hanged.'

'Think over what I've said. I'm sure you'll come to see that there's something in it. By the way, I seem to recognise the rope you've got round you. If I'm not greatly mistaken, it's the throat halyard of my boat. I know it by the splice I put in where I cut away a bit that was badly worn. It's a remarkably neat splice. Now, if you don't mind my saying so, you're a fool to go swinging over a cliff at the end of that rope. It's rotten.'

'Like everything else in your damned—I mean to say your infernal old boat. You may be a parson, but I call you a common swindler if you're the man who hired that boat to my friend Langton.'

'Are you a Liberal or a Conservative?' asked Meldon in a cheerful, conversational tone.

'What the devil—I mean, what on earth has that got to do with you?'

'Oh, nothing, of course. Only as you're a Member of Parliament I naturally thought you'd like to talk politics, and it would be easier for me if I knew to start with which side you were on.'

'I'm not a Member of Parliament.'

'Well, I suppose Mr Langton is. It's all the same thing. I

might have guessed he was something of the sort when I saw him in that fur coat. Is he a Liberal or a Conservative?'

'Are you an escaped lunatic?'

'Don't lose your temper,' said Meldon. 'If he isn't a Member of Parliament, say so, calmly and quietly. There's nothing, so far as I know, insulting about the suggestion that you and he are Members of Parliament. Lots of fellows are quite keen on getting into Parliament and spend piles of money on it. I think myself that it's rather a futile line of life. But then I'm not naturally fond of listening to other fellows' speeches. It's all a question of taste. Some people like that kind of thing well enough. I don't blame them. There's nothing to be ashamed of in writing M.P. after your name. There's certainly nothing to get angry about in my supposing that you do. But if you like, we'll drop the subject. What did you say your name is? Mine, I think I told you. It's Meldon—Joseph John Meldon, B.A.'

'And what are you doing here, Mr Joseph John Meldon?'

'Bathing. What are you doing?'

'I'm bird's-nesting.'

'Ah!' said Meldon. 'Now I was very keen on bird's-nesting myself when I was a boy. I remember one time going off to an island in the lake near my old home, swimming, you know, and coming back with four waterhen's eggs in my mouth. One broke on the way and it happened to be a bit—you know what I mean—a bit high. I sometimes think I can taste it still. I couldn't spit it out on account of the other three——'

'How long do you mean to stand there talking?'

'I'm in no hurry,' said Meldon. 'It's early yet, and it isn't every day I get the chance of talking to a Member of Parliament.'

'I've told you once already that I'm not a Member of Parliament.'

'Come now, I can understand modesty, and I can understand a man's adopting a disguise. I've done that myself before now. But it's a bit too thick when it comes to trying to persuade me that you're not a Member of Parliament. Is there any kind of man, except an inquiring English M.P., who'd come off to Inishgowlan in a five-tonner and swing off the face of a cliff on a rotten rope? What would anybody else do it for? Tell me that. Where would be the sense in it? You tell Higginbotham you're not a Member of Parliament if you like, and he'll maybe believe you, though I doubt if even Higginbotham would. Or try it on with Major Kent. He's an innocent sort of man. But there's no good talking that way to me. If you're not a Member of Parliament, what are you?'

'Perhaps you'll believe me and clear out of this if I tell you that my name's Buckley, Sir Giles Buckley, and that I haven't been in this cursed country, or England either, for the last ten years until a week ago.'

A sudden light flashed on Meldon's mind. Old Sir Giles Buckley, the grandfather of the man in front of him, had known about the Spanish treasure. He had heard the story, just as Captain Kent had, from Lady Buckley. No doubt he, too, had written it down in some diary, or had left notes of his expedition in search of the treasure. This man—this disreputable, disinherited son of the last Sir Giles—had of necessity been heir to Ballymoy House and the papers it contained. The situation became clear to Meldon. Here was a rival treasure-seeker, a man evidently possessed of information superior to that of Major Kent's grandfather, for he came straight to the very spot which Meldon had taken much pains to discover.

'I'm delighted to meet you,' said Meldon. 'Your father was always a liberal subscriber to the funds of the church in our parish. I hope you mean to keep up his subscription. The rector has been worried a lot over the loss of what your father used to give. It's most fortunate my meeting you in this way. I'll explain the situation to you in a moment. When the Church of Ireland ceased to be established by law—Gladstone, you know, I think it was in 1869——'

'I'm not going to subscribe one penny to your church,' said Sir Giles. 'I haven't any money, and if I had I wouldn't give a solitary shilling towards paying a fellow like you.'

'Well, anyhow it can do you no harm to understand how we're situated. Under the Act of Disestablishment the existing clergy——'

'Damn it!' said Sir Giles.

Then he pulled vigorously at the rope which was still round his armpits and shouted, 'Langton, Langton, haul up, will you? Have you gone to sleep? Haul up, I tell you. Not too quick. Do you want to knock my brains out?'

He swung slowly up, clinging with both hands to the rope above his head and pushing himself off the face of the cliff with his feet. Meldon, with a broad grin on his face, watched him reach the top and then turned and swam back to the rock where the Major waited.

'I say, Major,' he gasped, 'those fellows aren't Members of Parliament after all, and the treasure is certainly in that hole.'

'I could see you standing up to your middle in water talking to a man. I couldn't hear a word you said, of course. Who is he?'

'He's Sir Giles Buckley, and that's why I say the treasure is certainly in that hole.'

'I don't,' said the Major, 'precisely see how the one thing follows from the other.'

Meldon climbed out of the water and began to rub himself briskly with his towel.

'You wouldn't,' he said, 'but it does follow. Nothing could follow more plainly. It's like a beastly syllogism. Here's a man—two men, in fact—who have no earthly business in Inishgowlan. It's impossible even to invent a motive for their coming here now that we know that they're not Members of Parliament. Very well. They're here all the same, and one of them risks his life on a rotten rope to get down the face of a cliff to a certain hole at the bottom of it. What would he do that for?'

Meldon paused.

'I don't quite see yet,' said the Major, 'how you prove that there is treasure in that hole.'

'Very well, I'll start at the thing from the other direction.

Hitherto I've been proceeding on what's called the inductive method of reasoning. Bacon, you know, was the man who invented that. Now I'll try deduction. Who else besides ourselves knows about that treasure?'

'We don't know. At least I don't. You're trying to prove the treasure to me at present by some method or other.'

'Major, at times you'd make a saint go near swearing. Have I got to go through the whole story of the wreck of that Spanish galleon again? If you don't trust me you might at least believe your own grandfather. He said the treasure was here. Now, who else knew about it? Old Sir Giles Buckley did. Now, assume that he wrote down what he knew, just as your grandfather did. There's nothing more likely. His son never reads the paper any more than your father did. But you read your grandfather's diary after the death of the late Sir Giles. You follow me so far?'

'I follow you all right, but why don't you put on your clothes? I'd have thought you'd have had enough of standing about in your skin for one day.'

'I'm not going to dress yet,' said Meldon. 'I may have to swim down the channel again at any moment. Suppose Sir Giles takes it into his head to drop over the cliff the minute he thinks that my back is turned. I can't afford to let him nip into the hole by himself.'

'Do you mean to stand there stark naked day and night until Sir Giles chooses to leave the island?'

'No, I don't. In another hour the tide will have risen, so that nobody can get into the hole. The mouth of it will be covered and the whole thing full of water inside. Hullo! There's Sir Giles and Langton with him sitting on the cliff opposite us just where old T. O. P. sat yesterday. They're watching us. Very well, let them watch. I'll dress.'

'You may as well for all the good you're likely to get out of that hole.'

'Just you wait,' said Meldon, 'till I get into my shirt and trousers and I'll explain to you.

'Now, where was I? Oh, yes! Sir Giles Buckley dies. His

son, that playboy sitting on the cliff opposite, gets next to nothing out of the property, but he collars some family papers. He reads them. He sees, just as I saw, just as any man with a glimmer of intelligence would see, that he's got a soft thing in this treasure. He doesn't care about being recognised in Ballymoy, where he very likely owes money, so he sends a friend to hire a boat for him. He gets my boat and off he comes.'

'I don't see that you've proved anything,' said the Major, 'except that there's one other ass in the world as giddy as yourself.'

'Unpack the luncheon,' said Meldon. 'Your temper will improve while you eat. There's just one thing left which puzzles me.'

'I shouldn't have supposed that there was anything in the world that could puzzle you.'

'Well, there aren't many things,' said Meldon frankly. 'In fact, I've not yet come across anything which regularly defeated me when I gave my mind to it, but I don't mind owning up that just for the moment I'm bothered over one point in this business. How did Buckley know about the hole in the cliff? How did he locate the exact spot where the treasure lies? He does know, for he walked straight up to it without hesitation. The minute he landed yesterday he went up to the top of that cliff. I thought that he was just a simple Member of Parliament looking for a view, but I was wrong. He was prospecting about for the best way of getting at that hole. Now, how did he know? We only arrived at it by a process of exhaustive reasoning based on a careful examination of the locality. He walks straight up to it as if he'd known all along exactly where to go.'

'Perhaps he reasoned it out before he started.'

'He couldn't. No man on earth could. I couldn't have done it by myself. It wasn't till I got to the spot that I was able to reconstruct the shipwreck and track the working of the Spanish captain's mind. That disposes of your first suggestion. Got another?'

'Perhaps his grandfather knew the spot and made a note of it.'

'Won't wash either. We know that his grandfather couldn't find the treasure any more than yours could. If he'd known about that hole in the cliff he would have found the treasure.'

'Always supposing it's there,' said the Major.

Meldon glared at him.

'If it's there! Major, you're the Apostle Thomas and the Jew Apella and the modern scientific man rolled into one for invincible scepticism. Is it possible to convince you of anything? Tell me that.'

For a time they ate in silence. Now and then Meldon glanced at the cliff opposite to assure himself that Sir Giles and Langton were still there. At last he said—

'It appears to me that Langton must be mixed up in the business somehow. Why did Sir Giles bring him? He isn't any good at sailing the boat. He doesn't look as if he'd be much good for anything. Depend upon it, he must have given the tip about the hole, but how he comes to be in the know I don't precisely see. However, one thing is pretty clear. We've got to keep a very sharp eye on those two gentlemen opposite.'

'Unless you mean to sit here day and night,' said the Major, 'I don't see how you're going to do it.'

'I told you before that you can only get into that hole from about three-quarters low water to a quarter flood. Buckley knows that too, for he's seen the place. He won't come here at high tide nor yet at half tide. What we've got to do is to watch him at the other times. That gives us a chance to eat and sleep.'

'I expect he'll watch you, too. That is to say, if he's really after the treasure.'

'Let him. I'll back myself to get the better of any man living at a game of hide-and-seek. Don't you worry yourself about his watching us, Major. I'll arrange a plan for circumventing him. Look at the way I've diddled Higginbotham and old Thomas O'Flaherty Pat and Mary Kate. What's to stop me dealing with Buckley on similar lines?'

Half an hour later, having finished their luncheon and smoked their pipes, Major Kent and Meldon started to scramble back. The tide had risen sufficiently to prevent any one not an experienced diver from getting into the hole. As they neared the pier they saw Sir Giles Buckley and his friend Langton rowing off to the *Aureole* in their punt.

'That's all right,' said Meldon. 'Now we can take it easy and think things over till tomorrow morning. They won't attempt to get down that cliff in the dark. Hullo! Here's Higginbotham coming out of his tin wigwam to meet us. Do you know, I think Higginbotham is becoming rather a nuisance. I'm beginning to feel that I could get on nicely without Higginbotham. I wonder if we could get rid of him off the island anyhow?'

'Unless you cut his throat and sink the body,' said the Major, 'I don't see how you can.'

'I'd be sorry to do that. I've rather a liking for Higginbotham, though he is a bit of an ass. He used to come out with me sometimes of a Sunday afternoon when I was going to see my little girl in Rathmines. He used to talk to the mother on those occasions and I've always had a feeling of gratitude to him ever since. No; Higginbotham's a nuisance, but I wouldn't wish him any bodily harm. I won't agree to your cutting his throat, Major, so drop the idea. Besides, you never can tell but he might come in useful to us in some way. He's done us no harm so far, thanks to the way I've managed him. Hullo, Higginbotham! How did you get on with the old boy about the house this morning?'

'That's what I wanted to talk to you about,' said Higginbotham. 'There was some sort of misunderstanding.'

'Do you tell me that? Well, now, I'm greatly surprised. I thought I'd left everything coiled down clear for running so that there couldn't have been a hitch. Tell me now, Higginbotham, you didn't try to revenge yourself in any way on Mary Kate, did you?'

'Mary Kate! Oh, is she the little girl who came about the sugar candy?'

'Don't hark back to that sugar candy. I've told you before, Higginbotham, that the Major and I aren't going into that sugar-candy row either on one side or the other. We're dead-sick of the whole subject. You've gone and botched a perfectly simple business with dear old Thomas O'Flaherty Pat. I don't know what you've done exactly, but I strongly suspect that you've made yourself offensive in some way about Mary Kate. Why can't you leave that child alone?'

'I didn't do anything to her,' said Higginbotham. 'I didn't even remember that she was the same child. But what between nobody except the old man being able to speak Irish and him not being able to speak anything else——'

'Now, that's all nonsense,' said Meldon, 'and you know it. Mary Kate speaks both languages fluently. I'm here acting for the National Board of Education, as I told you before, and I've made it my business to find out what Mary Kate knows and what she doesn't. You can't have taken the child the right way. I expect you've been trying to come the Government official over her, and it won't do. No child would stand it, especially a high-spirited little creature like Mary Kate. You ought to cultivate a more ingratiating manner. You mean well, I know; but good intentions aren't everything.'

'The fact is——' said Higginbotham.

'Look here. I had a long talk this morning with Sir Giles Buckley. You know Sir Giles?'

'No, I don't. Who is he?'

'He's something in the Castle. I forget this moment what his particular tack is, but I know he's an important man. Major, do you recollect what Sir Giles is? Does he run the Crimes' Acts, or is he the man who bosses the Royal Commissions?'

'I don't know. I never——'

'Oh, well, never mind. I think he specialises, so to speak, in Royal Commissions; but it doesn't really matter much. If you read the newspapers you'll be familiar with his name. He happens to be going round Ireland at present with Langton, his private secretary——'

'Not Euseby Langton?' said Higginbotham.

'Euseby Langton! I don't know. I didn't ask his Christian name. By the way, who is Euseby Langton? I seem to recognise the name, but somehow I can't quite fix the man.'

'I don't think you knew him; but I did very well. He was in the library in College in our time—some sort of an assistant there. He got sacked. They always said it was drink, but I don't know. He went abroad somewhere afterwards.'

'I remember,' said Meldon, 'but this is a different man—couldn't possibly be the same, you know.'

'Well,' said Higginbotham, for Meldon had relapsed into silence, 'go on.'

'Go on with what?'

'With what you were telling me about Sir Giles Buckley.'

'Oh! Ah! Yes, Sir Giles, of course. Well, I put in a good word for you. I explained that you were doing the best you could with Thomas O'Flaherty Pat. He seemed rather anxious about that business. I said I expected it would pan out right enough in the end if he gave you a free hand. He evidently had some notion of stepping in to settle it himself. Now, what I want to know is this: would you like him to try his hand at it, or would you rather he left you alone to work it in your own way?'

'Of course if Sir Giles—it would be very kind of him——'

'Very well. I'll arrange that. You leave it to me, Higginbotham. And for goodness' sake don't go talking to Sir Giles about it yourself. You've no tact. You know you haven't. You'd just put your foot into it again the way you did with Mary Kate.'

'I won't go near him till you tell me.'

'That's right. Stick to that. I'll see him as soon as I can and I'll let you know. Goodbye for the present, old chap.'

'Thanks, awfully, Meldon. I'm really more obliged to you than I can say. If ever I can do you a good turn of any sort——'

'Don't mention it. I'm only delighted to do what I can to help you. Goodbye.'

After dinner Major Kent and Meldon sat on the deck of the

Spindrift and smoked. On the deck of the *Aureole* sat Sir Giles Buckley and Langton, who also smoked. Neither party made any attempt to go on shore. The Major tried two or three times to start a conversation and was severely snubbed. Meldon declared that he wanted time to think things over quietly. The situation was obviously a difficult one, and frivolous talk on such subjects as a slight fall of the barometer or the possibility of getting some fresh milk was quite out of place. After finishing his pipe, the Major dropped off to sleep in an uncomfortable position. At about half-past five Meldon woke him up.

'I think I've fixed that fellow Langton,' he said.

The Major yawned.

'Have you?' he said. 'What have you done to him?'

'I haven't done anything to him yet. What I mean is that I've discovered where he comes in, how he happened to be in a position to give Sir Giles the tip about the hole under the cliff. You heard what Higginbotham said about Euseby Langton. Well, I recollect that this fellow signed the agreement I drew up about the *Aureole* "E. Langton." He's evidently Higginbotham's man.'

'He might not be,' said the Major. ' "E. Langton" might stand for Edward Langton or Edgar Langton or Ethelbert Langton.'

'It might stand for Ebenezer Ledbeater, but I'm pretty sure it doesn't. It stands for Euseby Langton. Euseby Langton got the sack for drink, and this fellow looks as if he drank a lot, which also goes to show that he's the same man.'

'Well, suppose he is?'

'The next point is where did Euseby Langton get sacked from?'

'I forget. I wasn't listening to Higginbotham.'

'Well, luckily enough I was. Euseby Langton got sacked from Trinity College Library. He had some sort of job there poking about among catalogues and things. Now you may not be aware, Major, of the fact that Trinity College Library is the biggest in the world. There are books in it that no man has ever read. Nobody could. I couldn't myself, even if I gave my whole time to nothing else. What's to hinder our friend Langton from picking up the tip about the place where the treasure is from some book in the library?'

'There's no such book.'

'I wouldn't be too sure of that. There are some extraordinary books in that library—books that aren't in the college course anywhere—that even the men who go in for honours know nothing about. Besides, it mightn't be a book exactly. It might be a manuscript—not a large illuminated missal of a thing stuck in a glass case for every fool to stare at, but some quiet, unobtrusive, rather tattered manuscript which had lain for years, perhaps centuries, under a pile of other manuscripts. That's the sort of place the information would be.'

'I don't see how it could.'

'It might, in fact, be the log of the Spanish captain himself. You know there's an organ in the big examination hall that was taken out of a Spanish Armada ship. Well, if they fetched a thing like an organ all the way to the college, you may be pretty sure that they fetched lots of manuscripts too. Once Euseby Langton got a taste for hunting up old manuscripts, he'd be just as likely as not to hit upon the log of our captain.'

'But you said he drank. Is it likely he had a taste for manuscripts?'

'He's almost sure to have had. Most probably it was the manuscripts that drove him to drink. They would, you know, unless he was exceptionally strong-minded, and Langton clearly wasn't that. Now suppose——'

'You can suppose any rigmarole you like.'

'I explained to you before, Major, the nature of a scientific supposition or hypothesis. It always strikes the outsider at first as a rigmarole. I needn't go into that again. What we have to deal with is fact—hard fact—and to get some sort of reasonable explanation of things as they are. It's quite evident that Sir Giles and Langton know that the treasure is in the hole under that cliff. It's also evident that Langton gave Sir Giles the tip. It follows that Langton must have found the thing out somewhere. I don't say for certain that he found it in a manuscript in the college library. I only say that, considering all the circumstances of the case, he's more likely to have found it there than anywhere else. That may not strike you as a very good hypothesis; but unless you have a better one to propose, it seems to me quite good enough to go on with.'

'All right, go on with it. But I don't see where you expect to arrive.'

'I'll arrive, if you want to know, at a nice comfortable income and a good, well-furnished house, a place I can take my little girl to with some sort of satisfaction. That's where I'll arrive and I'm putting the treasure at the lowest possible figure.'

10

MELDON was very little troubled by the problems and perplexities which pressed on him. He turned into his bunk at nine o'clock and slept the unbroken sleep of a just man until six the next morning. Then he got up and plunged overboard for his morning dip. He swam in the direction of the *Aureole* and was rewarded by seeing Langton come on deck in his pyjamas. A few minutes later Sir Giles emerged, and the two stood in consultation watching the *Spindrift*. Meldon, having had as much of the water as he cared for, climbed on board and waved a greeting to the *Aureole* with his towel. He noticed while he dressed that Sir Giles and Langton did not go below together. Either one or the other of them remained on deck to watch the *Spindrift*. Meldon roused the Major and then got breakfast ready. The meal, in spite of the Major's opposition, was eaten on deck.

'It's quite evident to me,' said Meldon, 'that those fellows mean to watch us. They're pretty certain that we're after the treasure, and they don't intend to let us get round to the hole in the cliff without them.'

Major Kent snorted contemptuously. He, too, had slept well and had wakened in one of those moods of sound common sense which are strongest in men of Anglo-Saxon temperament during the early part of the day. The idea of treasure-seeking seemed to him more than ever absurd as he sat in the morning sunshine eating fried bacon and drinking tea. That two strangers in an ordinary and somewhat battered yacht like the *Aureole* should be spying upon his actions, as if he and they were conspirators, was a grotesquely impossible thought. Such things might have happened in the sixteenth century, or might happen even now in places like Russia. They couldn't be real during the twentieth century anywhere in the dominions of His Britannic Majesty.

'I must make arrangements for dealing with them,' said Meldon.

'J. J.,' said the Major, with another snort of contempt, 'I've had enough of this play-acting. You and I aren't children that we should spend our time pretending we are brigands and hunting other fellows about in smugglers' caves. I'll have no more of it.'

'Do you mean to tell me that you don't believe those two fellows are watching us, afraid of their lives that we should succeed in dodging them and getting the treasure?'

'Of course I don't believe anything of the sort. It's absurd on the face of it. I don't deny that it was odd their turning up yesterday at the very place you fancied there was treasure hidden; but as for their being after it or watching us, I simply don't and won't and can't believe a word of it.'

'Very well. I'll have to prove it to you.'

'You'd prove anything,' said the Major—'any blessed thing,

once you start talking, but you won't convince me. I've heard too many of your proofs.'

'I'll prove it this time by the evidence of your own eyes and ears. You say that Sir Giles and Langton aren't watching us and don't mean to track us if we go after the treasure. Very well, I'll demonstrate to you that they are and do.'

He stood up and hauled the punt alongside.

'Get in,' he said to the Major.

'Why should I get in? I don't want to go ashore?'

'You'll get in because I tell you and because once and for all you're going to be shaken out of that vile attitude of sceptical superiority which you've chosen to assume.'

Major Kent shrugged his shoulders and submitted. Meldon stepped into the punt after him and began paddling towards the pier.

There was a stir on board the *Aureole*. Langton was on watch when Meldon shoved off from the *Spindrift*. He went below at once. Then he and Sir Giles came on deck together and pulled their punt alongside. Meldon, who could watch the *Aureole* as he rowed, judged from the look on his face that Sir Giles Buckley was in a bad temper.

'I'd be prepared to bet now,' he said, 'that Sir Giles is swearing like anything this minute. I expect he hadn't finished his breakfast and hates being routed out at this hour to follow us. Don't you look round, Major. If you do it's ten to one you upset this patent punt, and I shouldn't care to rely on Sir Giles to pick you up in his present mood.'

Having reached the pier, Meldon, followed unwillingly by Major Kent, set out briskly towards the south end of the island.

'Where are we going now?' asked the Major.

'We're going to convince you. If you don't like it, you can lay the blame on your own sceptical nature. Look round now and tell me if the other two aren't following us.'

They were. The Major unwillingly admitted the fact.

'They're certainly coming this way,' he said. 'But I don't see why you should take it for granted that they're tracking us.'

'Come on,' said Meldon.

He reached the house of the woman to whom he had talked on the occasion of his second interview with Mary Kate. He tapped at the door and entered, dragging the Major after him.

'Good-morning to you, Mrs O'Flaherty,' he said. 'I'm glad to see the baby looking well.'

'He's finely, thanks be to God.'

'Do you happen to want to have him vaccinated or anything of that sort?'

'I do not.'

'I dare say you're right. I asked the question because there's a gentleman coming along this way in a few minutes who's a great doctor. He's on his holiday, of course; but I'm sure he'd vaccinate a fine boy like yours if you asked him to.'

'Would he give me a bottle for the old woman, do you think?'

'He would, of course. What's the matter with her?'

'She's ravelling in her talk this long time, and sorra the bit she'll stir out of her bed, and me with all the work to do and never a one to give me a hand.'

'That's the very sort of case this doctor likes best. Come along with me now and we'll speak to him. But don't be calling him "doctor" to his face. It's a kind of lord he is. Call him "Sir Giles" when you speak to him.'

Meldon, Mrs O'Flaherty with her baby in her arms, and Major Kent, who lingered a little behind, set out to meet Sir Giles and Langton.

'Good-morning, Sir Giles,' said Meldon. 'Good-morning, Mr Langton. You got home safe yesterday off that cliff? That's right. Take my advice and don't risk it again. There isn't a bird's egg in the world worth a broken neck. Do you happen to have a bottle about you?'

Sir Giles scowled. Meldon's good-humoured greeting evidently irritated him.

'No,' he said. 'I haven't.'

'Oh, well,' said Meldon, 'it can't be helped. I dare say you have one on the yacht.'

'I don't know what you're talking about,' said Sir Giles. 'Do you, Langton?'

'Damned if I do,' said Langton. 'What are you talking about, eh?'

'Bottles,' said Meldon. 'I was asking if you had a bottle on the yacht.'

'What the devil is it to you whether I have or not?' said Sir Giles.

'Oh, nothing to me—nothing whatever—only Mrs O'Flaherty wants a bottle for her old mother-in-law. Isn't that so, Mrs O'Flaherty?'

'It is, your honour. It is, Sir Giles. The old woman's ravelling in her talk this long time, and what's more, she won't stir out of her bed; and if your honour would give her a bottle——'

'Come now,' said Meldon, 'you won't refuse her, Sir Giles. It's a small request. What's a bottle to you one way or another? Slip back to the yacht and get her one. It won't take you an hour. The Major and I will wait about till you come back.'

He winked at the Major as he spoke—a large obvious wink, which neither Sir Giles nor Langton could fail to notice.

'Now look here, Mr John James Meldon——' said Sir Giles.

'Joseph John,' said Meldon, 'not that it matters; only just in case anything should turn up afterwards, it's as well to be accurate.'

'I really don't know,' said Sir Giles, 'whether you're more knave or fool, but if you think you're going to send me back to the yacht on a hunt after a bottle or some such ridiculous thing while you go round the base of the cliffs again, you're greatly mistaken.'

'Mrs O'Flaherty,' said Meldon, 'Sir Giles's temper is a little short this morning, but he's a good man at heart. Try him for the bottle again tomorrow and you'll very likely get one. Good-morning, Sir Giles. Good-morning, Mr Langton. This is better than grubbing about among fusty old manuscripts in the College library, isn't it? Come along, Major. We'll be getting back.'

'I suppose,' said Major Kent, when they reached the pier, 'that there wouldn't be any use in my asking for an explanation of that performance?'

'I told you before I started,' said Meldon, 'that I was going to offer you ocular and oral demonstration that those fellows mean to track us, and won't let us stir in the direction of the cliffs without them. Now you've got it. I hope you're convinced.'

'Couldn't you have done it without that bottle foolery?'

'Well, I might. To tell you the truth, Major, the bottle incident was not part of my original plan. It's what I call a brilliant improvisation. It came on me like a flash when I saw that plump baby of Mrs O'Flaherty's, and thought how the poor little beggar had never been vaccinated. It developed in my mind when she began talking about her mother-in-law. After that the thing simply worked itself out, and worked well. I don't take any credit for it, not the least. But I'm rather pleased with the results. In the first place I've convinced Sir Giles that I'm a perfect fool.'

'He's not far out if he believes that.'

'Whether he is or not, Major, remains to be seen. In the second place I've convinced you that he and Langton mean to keep a close watch on us, which was the thing I set out to do originally. I have convinced you, haven't I?'

'I think you're all mad together,' said the Major. 'I don't understand what's going on between you.'

'You mean that you won't understand. You could, of course, if you liked.'

'What do you intend to do now?'

'For the present, nothing. When the time comes for eluding the vigilance of Sir Giles, I'll elude it. There will be difficulties, of course. Higginbotham will be a difficulty—so, very likely, will Mary Kate. In the meanwhile we'll sit down here and wait till the tide rises and makes it impossible to get at the treasure. They are watching us from the hill beyond there.

I don't believe they mean to try for it themselves today. Now I come to think of it, they can't; for they didn't bring the rope with them. Come along, Major, we may safely go back on board.'

'This,' said Meldon, as he paddled the collapsible punt towards the *Spindrift*, 'is out-and-away the best holiday I've ever had. I tell you, Major, it's fine.'

'I'm glad you're enjoying yourself. Sure you wouldn't like to slip off home and take out the rest of your time with your little girl?'

'I wouldn't leave the treasure,' said Meldon, 'at this stage of the proceedings, not if Gladys Muriel went down on her bended knees to beg me. I wouldn't do it even if Sir Giles and Langton weren't here. Now that they have come, and added a spice of real adventure to the hunt, I wouldn't go away to marry the eldest daughter of the Emperor of Germany. I'm enjoying myself.'

There was no doubt that Meldon spoke the literal truth. Excitement and pleasure beamed from his very eyes. He sent the Major to get the dinner ready while he lay on deck, and with his eye just over the low gunwale of the yacht, watched Sir Giles and Langton row back to the *Aureole* in their punt. He ate his dinner hurriedly, breaking in upon the meal at short intervals to mount the companion-ladder and take a look at the *Aureole*.

'Patience and calm,' he said after one of these excursions, 'are the great things after all. There's a French proverb about getting a thing in the end if you only wait quietly.'

'I suppose you think you're practising those virtues now,' said the Major.

'I know I am. A man with less self-control would have darted off to the cave this morning and probably had a free-fight with Sir Giles, which would have ended in Higginbotham taking possession of the treasure in the name of the Government. Whereas I sit here quietly and wait for the next move on the part of the enemy.'

'Oh, that's the game now, is it?'

'That's the game. Let Sir Giles show his hand and I'll deal with him.'

For some time it appeared that Sir Giles also intended to play a waiting game. He and Euseby Langton sat on the deck of the *Aureole* and watched the *Spindrift*. They gazed at Meldon and the Major through binoculars when they had seen all they could with the unassisted eye. Meldon, in return, got out a pair of glasses and stared at them. The afternoon became very hot. The water of the bay lay in an unbroken sheet around the boats, and glowed a sullen reflection of the light. The Major fetched some cushions from the cabin, made himself really comfortable, and went to sleep.

At about four o'clock there was a stir on board the *Aureole*. Langton dragged the punt alongside. He and Sir Giles got into her and pulled for the shore. Meldon, watching them intently through his glasses, observed that they took no rope with them. He made up his mind that they did not intend to descend the cliff. The tide was still too high to permit of any one entering the hole. Yet it seemed evident to Meldon that this expedition to the shore must have some object. He became very anxious to discover what they were at. It was easy enough to row on shore after them and then follow them, as they had followed him in the morning. But he realised that on an island without trees or hedges it would be totally impossible to follow them without himself being seen; and their plan, whatever it was, would certainly not be carried out before his eyes. Scanning the land with his glasses, he detected Mary Kate sitting in the shade of Higginbotham's house to watch the strangers land. His mind was made up in a moment. He shook the Major.

'Give me another sixpence,' he said; 'I'm going ashore.'

'My money's in the pocket of my other trousers,' said the Major; 'and they're hanging beside my bunk. Take what you want and for Heaven's sake leave me to have my sleep in peace. It's the only comfort I get since I came to this island.'

Meldon made all the speed he could in the canvas punt, a craft singularly ill-suited to a man in a hurry. He reached the pier shortly after Sir Giles and Langton had landed. Mary Kate, who had hesitated for some time between the desire to follow the strangers and the hope of another sixpence from the approaching Meldon, was on the pier to meet him. She grinned amiably when he greeted her.

'Mary Kate,' he said, 'I've got another sixpence for you. You'll be the richest girl in the island in a few days if this goes on.'

'I will so.' She spoke in a tone of conviction.

'Well now, go you up after those two gentlemen and just watch what they do. You needn't go too close to them. And, listen to me now: if it should happen that they speak to you, just you take a leaf out of your grandda's book and answer them in Irish, "Ní Beurla"—what do you call it? You know how to do it, don't you?'

Mary Kate nodded. The instructions were not absolutely lucid, but she grasped their meaning.

'Not another word out of your head now, mind that. And look as stupid as you can. I'll run down and pay a visit to your aunt. Isn't she your aunt?'

'She is not.'

'Well, you know who I mean, anyhow. Mrs O'Flaherty beyond there, the one that owns the baby with the nice fat legs. You drop down there as soon as ever those two gentlemen go back to their yacht, and tell me what they've been doing. I needn't explain to you, Mary Kate, that I wouldn't be setting you on a job of this kind if those two fellows weren't a pair of bad ones. The fact is they're land-grabbers—the worst kind of land-grabbers. That will probably convey to you better than anything else the sort of fellows they really are.'

He noticed that Mary Kate's attention had wandered, but he continued speaking for his own satisfaction.

'If that isn't exactly the literal truth, as people like the Major would say, it's the nearest thing to the truth that you're at all likely to understand. It will convey to you a perfectly true idea of the character of the men. You understand what I mean, Mary Kate, when I say they're land-grabbers, don't you?'

The child wasn't listening to him. Her eyes were on the now distant figures of Sir Giles and Langton. Even if she had listened, it is doubtful whether the word 'land-grabber' would have conveyed anything to her. Politicians rarely, if ever, visit Inishgowlan, and the people, even the grown men, are uninstructed in the simple principles of modern nationalism. It had never been worth the while, even of a publican, to grab the land on Inishgowlan. In any case, whether she had understood him or not, Meldon's motives for having the strangers watched would not have interested Mary Kate. It was sufficient for her that she was to be paid sixpence for doing what natural curiosity would have prompted her to do without a bribe.

Mrs O'Flaherty seemed surprised to see Meldon. She was churning, plunging up and down an old-fashioned dash in the most primitive kind of churn. She was dressed in a sleeveless garment, tucked in to an old red petticoat which seemed likely, as her body swayed, to work its fastenings loose and fall off. Drops of milk, splashed from the churn, bespattered her. She was exceedingly hot, partly from her exertion, partly with annoyance at the lamentable howls of her baby, who had of necessity been left to the care of the old woman in the room off the kitchen. She was at first far from being well pleased at seeing a visitor. She was not, indeed, embarrassed by the scantiness of her costume, but she foresaw that in mere politeness she might be obliged to stop churning, and to stop at a certain stage of the process is fatal to the production of butter. Meldon's first words reassured her.

'Give me the dash,' he said, 'and go you in and get the baby.'

'I will not,' she said. 'I'd be spoiling your good clothes on you if I let you do the like of this work.'

'Did you never hear that there's no luck when the stranger that comes in doesn't put a hand to the churn?'

'Faith, and that's true. But who'd think of the likes of you knowing it?'

'I know more than that,' said Meldon. 'I know things that

would surprise you now, wise as you are. Give me the dash, I say.'

He took it from her and began to work vigorously. Mrs O'Flaherty watched him.

'Maybe now it isn't the first time you've done that,' she said.

'It is not, nor the second. But go you and take your baby. The shouts of him is enough to stop the butter coming.'

She returned in a few minutes with the child, quickly pacified, in her arms.

'Where's himself?' said Meldon. 'Why shouldn't he be giving you a hand at this work?'

'Sure he does do a turn for me odd times, when he wouldn't be earthing up the potatoes, or saving the hay, or burning the kelp or the like of that.'

Meldon began to feel hot.

'The butter's a mighty long time coming,' he said.

'You may say that. Whether it's the warmth of the day or maybe—but sure you're tired. It's terrible hard work for them that's not used to it. Give it up to me now.'

'Very well; I'll have a try at the baby. Come here to me, Anthony Tom. Did you say Anthony Tom was the name you had on him?'

'It is not, then, but Michael Pat.'

Meldon took Michael Pat in his arms. He was very successful as a nurse, but he found the work almost as hot as the churning. Michael Pat had reached the age at which happiness is found in perpetual motion, and it was necessary to keep on jumping him up and down.

'I'll tell you what it is,' said Meldon at last. 'I'd rather be saving hay or burning kelp, or doing any other mortal thing, than trying to mind a baby and make butter at the same time. Men have a much better time of it than women as things are arranged at present.'

'They might,' said Mrs O'Flaherty, 'but what would they be doing if it wasn't for the women?'

'That's true,' said Meldon; 'but it isn't saying that men don't have the best of it.'

'And for the matter of that, how would the women get along wanting the men?'

'There's something in that, too.'

'Sure, God is good, and the troubles He does be sending is no worse for me than another. If so be that Michael Pat doesn't be cutting or burning himself when I have him reared to be out of my arms, I've no cause to be complaining. And himself is a good head to me.'

Meldon danced Michael Pat vigorously. The sweat ran down his face, but he stuck to his work, realising more and more clearly the strenuousness of a woman's life. At last he spoke again, jerkily for want of breath.

'Mrs O'Flaherty, ma'am, tell me this. Is there e'er a branch of the Woman's Suffrage Association in this island?'

'I never heard tell of any such a thing.'

'Well, take my advice. Found one at once. It may not do you much good, but it will relieve your feelings. You're suffering under an intolerable injustice.'

'Is it the Government you mean?' said Mrs O'Flaherty, whose husband occasionally read a copy of the *Ballymoy Tribune*.

'It is not; it's the men. What you want is what's called sexuo-economic independence of women. Just wipe Michael Pat's mouth with something, will you. I haven't a handkerchief on me, and he's dribbling worse than I could have believed possible.'

The half-door of the cabin was pushed open, and Mary Kate entered. At the sight of Meldon with Michael Pat in his arms she stood still and grinned broadly.

'Thank God!' said Meldon fervently. 'Come here, Mary Kate. Sit down on the creepy stool there by the hearth and take the baby.'

Mary Kate hung back, still grinning.

'Do what the gentleman bids you,' said Mrs O'Flaherty.

Mary Kate obeyed reluctantly. She foresaw that it might be very difficult for her to escape from Michael Pat if she once accepted the charge of him. She had the makings of a feminist in her. She valued her independence.

'Tell me now,' said Meldon, 'did you do what I bid you?'

'I did,' said Mary Kate.

'And have the gentlemen gone back to the yacht?'

'They're after going this minute.'

'And where were they?'

'Beyond.'

'Listen to me now, Mary Kate. I'm not going to spend the rest of the day dragging information out of you as if each word you say is a tooth that it hurts you to part with. Tell me now straight, and no more nonsense—where did they go?'

'It's yourself that's the stubborn little lady,' said Mrs O'Flaherty. 'Why wouldn't you be speaking to the gentleman when he wants to be listening to you?'

'They were up beyond at my grandda's.'

'At Thomas O'Flaherty Pat's! Were they talking to him?'

'They were not, then, for himself wasn't in it.'

'What were they doing?'

'Looking at the Poll-na-phuca.'

'At the what?'

'That's the hole that there does be in the field back west of the house,' said Mrs O'Flaherty. 'Poll-na-phuca is the name there does be on it on account of them that's in it.'

'Is that all they did?'

'Sorra a thing else.'

'Well,' said Meldon, 'that beats all. I must be getting away now, Mrs O'Flaherty. I've had a delightful afternoon. Goodbye. Goodbye, Mary Kate. Be kind to Michael Pat. Remember that you were once that size yourself, and somebody had to sit on a stool and hold you.'

He walked down to the seashore, selected a large flat stone, and sat down on it. He was very much puzzled by the account which Mary Kate had given him of the movements of Sir Giles and Euseby Langton. He could not understand why they had gone up to Thomas O'Flaherty Pat's cabin or why they had looked at the hole in the field. He recalled the appearance of the cabin. It was a very dilapidated place, standing by itself two fields higher up than the cottage in which Mary Kate's father lived. He went over all he knew about the field with the hole in it. It was, so Higginbotham said, a very small and barren field. There was no fence round the hole; Higginbotham had lamented that. A heifer had fallen into it and got killed. There was nothing, so far as he could see, which could possibly interest Sir Giles about the cabin, the field, or the hole. Why should a man, out on a search for treasure, care to view the scene of a heifer's death? A heifer is not a very important animal, even on Inishgowlan. He recollected that Poll-na-phuca meant the fairy's hole. He had understood from Higginbotham that the place was regarded by the islanders with some awe as the home of malevolent spirits. But this threw no light on his problem. He could not suppose that Sir Giles was an amateur of folk-lore, so enthusiastic as to suspend his treasure search for the purpose of investigating a local superstition, however interesting.

Meldon's pipe went out, half-smoked. He wrinkled his forehead and half-shut his eyes in bitter perplexity. It hurt him that he could not understand what Sir Giles had been doing. At last he rose from his stone with a deep sigh and walked ten or fifteen yards along the shore. He found another flat stone and sat down on it. He knocked the plug of tobacco out, refilled his pipe and lit it. He deliberately gave up the problem which he could not solve, and set himself to work on another. He decided that he must himself reach the hole where the treasure lay at the earliest possible moment the next day, and that Sir Giles must be prevented from following him. He smoked steadily this time, and his face gradually cleared of the wrinkles the other problem had impressed upon it. At last he smiled slightly. Then he grinned. He knocked the ashes out of his pipe and put it in his pocket. He picked up a few pebbles and flung them cheerfully into the sea. Then he rose and walked back to Mrs O'Flaherty's cottage.

The churning was over. Mrs O'Flaherty was working the

butter with her hands at the table. Mary Kate still sat with the baby on her knee.

'Good-evening to you, Mrs O'Flaherty,' said Meldon.

'Is it yourself again? Faith, I thought you were gone for today anyway.'

'I looked in again to see if Michael Pat was all right after the shaking I gave him. Would you sooner be churning the butter or churning the baby, Mrs O'Flaherty? Or would you rather be taking them in turns the way we did this afternoon? I see you've got him asleep there, Mary Kate. Just put him into the cradle now and he'll be all right.'

'Mind, but he'll wake on you,' said Mrs O'Flaherty, 'and me in the middle of squeezing the butter.'

'He will not. Do you think I don't know when a baby's asleep? You wouldn't wake him now if you put him into the churn head first. Do what I bid you, Mary Kate. That's a good girl. Now the next thing you have to do is to run up to the iron house where the gentleman lives that does be measuring out the land and tell him I want to see him this evening. He's to get some one to put him off to the yacht; do you understand? I'm not coming ashore again. Will you do that for me, like a good girl?'

'I might.'

'Well then, do. And look here. If he isn't there, just you sit down outside the door and wait till he comes. Now off with you. I'll follow in a minute or two. It wouldn't do for you and me to be seen walking about together every hour of the day, Mary Kate. They might say we were courting; and that wouldn't suit you any more than myself. Goodbye to you, Mrs O'Flaherty. I'm really off this time, but very likely I'll look in tomorrow to see Michael Pat and the butter. Will you be off out of this, Mary Kate? You'll spoil the look of your mouth for life if you stand there grinning much longer.'

Meldon walked to the pier, passed it, and went down to the sandy beach which lay beyond. There were three curraghs drawn up and laid, as the custom is with such boats, bottom upward on the sand. One of them Meldon recognised as that in which Higginbotham had come off to the *Spindrift*. It was the property of Jamesy O'Flaherty. Meldon passed it and looked at the next. The canvas bottom revealed a large rent. It could not possibly go to sea. The third was sound. Meldon knelt down and looked under it. The oars were there as he expected. He went back to the pier, embarked in the collapsible punt, and rowed out to the *Spindrift*.

He found that Major Kent had finished his nap and was reading, for want of other literature, the sheet of a week-old newspaper. It was spotted with grease and a good deal crumpled, having, in fact, been used to wrap up the bacon which they ate at breakfast. The occupation showed that the Major was very much bored. He gave frank expression to his feelings.

'How much longer do you intend to spend mousing round this wretched little island, J. J.? I'm about sick of it. This isn't my idea of a cruise at all. I mean to up anchor and slip across to Inishmore tomorrow for a change.'

'Don't you do anything of the sort. You'll be sorry all your life afterwards if you do. I don't mind telling you that we're just on the very verge of bagging the treasure.'

'I don't believe it.'

'I'll give you my word, Major, that if you stay here tomorrow, I'll be ready to go anywhere you like the next day. The next twenty-four hours, or thirty-six hours at the outside, will see the thing through.'

'That's all very well. But if your treasure-hunting consists in sitting here all day watching those other two fellows on the *Aureole*, I tell you plainly it's not good enough.'

'If it's a little excitement you want, you shall have it tomorrow. I was thinking things out a bit after I finished nursing Michael Pat, and——'

'Finished what?'

'Nursing Michael Pat, the baby Sir Giles wouldn't vaccinate this morning. But you're a slow-witted man, Major. It's one of your great faults. Everything has to be explained to you. I suppose I must begin at the beginning.'

'I wish you would.'

'Well, I will. But first of all, I may as well mention that I've planned a *coup d'état* for tomorrow. I'm not sure that I've got the expression quite right. Perhaps I ought to say a *coup de théâtre*; but you know what I mean, anyhow.'

'I don't; but I might make a guess if you'd begin at the beginning instead of in the middle or at the end.'

'The epic poet,' said Meldon, 'always begins in the middle. It's a well-known literary law that all first-rate narrative begins in the middle. If you don't know the middle of a thing, how on earth can you appreciate the beginning? My coup—we'll call it simply a coup, so as to get over the difficulty of not knowing exactly which sort of coup it is—comes off tomorrow, but it begins this evening. I don't expect you to play up to me. That would probably be beyond you, but I hope you'll try and not actually give the show away when Higginbotham comes.'

'Oh, Higginbotham's in it, is he?'

'Of course Higginbotham's in it. So is Mary Kate, so is Sir Giles, so is Langton, so are you and I. It wouldn't be a coup of any sort if we weren't all in it.'

'If it involves my adopting another disguise—— But what's the good of my talking?'

'None. Just you listen. I went on shore this afternoon to find out what Sir Giles and the other man were after. I took sixpence with me for Mary Kate. I set the dear little girl on to watch Sir Giles while I went and nursed Michael Pat—a fine, plump baby, Michael Pat, but boisterous.'

'Is he part of the coup?'

'No. I should like to have him in it if I could, but I can't manage it. Well, after a time Mary Kate returned and told me that Sir Giles and the man who owns the fur coat went up to Thomas O'Flaherty Pat's field and looked at the hole there is in it.'

'Is the hole part of the coup?'

'It is not. The fact is I don't quite see how the hole comes in. That's what has me so set on bringing off my coup without delay. If I understood why they looked at that hole I might see my way to checkmate their move whatever it is. But I don't. They may have a game on, or they may not. I'm not going to give them a chance.'

'Perhaps,' said the Major, 'you'll get to the coup soon.'

'I wanted to tell you about the coup first thing; but you kept nagging at me to go back to the beginning. Now I've gone back to the beginning and you're discontented because you haven't got the end straight off. You're a very hard man to please.'

'All I mean,' said the Major, 'is that it's near tea time.'

'That reminds me that Higginbotham may be here at any moment. Listen now. There seem to me to be only two available boats on this island, Jamesy O'Flaherty's curragh and another.'

'There's a third. I saw three on the beach this morning.'

'One of those has a hole in her bottom you could put your foot through; so there are only two to be considered. Now if Jamesy O'Flaherty was to go off tomorrow to Inishmore in his curragh and if I could put the other one *hors de combat*, so to speak——'

'Knock a hole in her, I suppose.'

'Now would I do a thing like that to a curragh that belongs to a poor man, for all I know to the contrary to Mary Kate's father? I wouldn't if you paid me. All I mean to do is to temporarily conceal her oars so that she can't be rowed. Now if Jamesy's curragh is off at sea and the other one is not available, and if the *Aureole's* punt were to go adrift, I don't quite see how those two jokers could get ashore, do you?'

'So that's the coup, is it?'

'Yes. You see it requires some management. There are three distinct points. First, Jamesy O'Flaherty's curragh must be sent off. Next, the other curragh must be dealt with. Finally we must hope that the *Aureole's* punt will go adrift during the night.'

'It won't,' said the Major. 'Why should it?'

'Oh, yes, it will. I mean to see to it myself that it goes adrift.'

'Do you mean to set Higginbotham afloat in it?'

'No, I don't. I told you before that I had a regard for Higginbotham. I don't want to send him off without oars in an unseaworthy punt. I wouldn't do it to any man, much less to a fellow who used to come up with me every second Sunday to Rathmines when I——'

'Don't begin again about your little girl.'

'I wasn't going to mention my little girl. But as you've introduced the subject of little girls I must say that I think your tone about women is most discourteous. You display what I may call a graceless want of chivalry. I'm not a feminist myself or anything extreme of any kind, but I think a man ought to show some respect to women, and not be always sneering at them as you are. After all, Major, if you hadn't had a mother where would you be now? You ought to try and remember little things like that.'

'Would there be anything unchivalrous,' said the Major, 'in asking where Higginbotham does come in if he's not to go to sea in Sir Giles's punt?'

'It's my punt, not Sir Giles's. But we needn't argue about that. The thing's quite simple. Higginbotham is to go to Inishmore in Jamesy O'Flaherty's curragh.'

'Oh, is he?'

'Yes. He's to start early, about six a.m.'

'Why?'

'Because I don't see how I'm to get Jamesy O'Flaherty off to Inishmore for the day in his curragh unless I make Higginbotham hire him for the purpose. Besides, I want Higginbotham out of the way, too. If he's on the island he'll do some sort of mischief, with the best intentions, of course, and spoil the whole coup. There's no saying what a kind-hearted man like Higginbotham would do when he found out that Sir Giles and Langton were shut up on the *Aureole* and couldn't get ashore. He might hunt us up and make us go off for them. No; I don't want even to inconvenience Higginbotham more than I can help; but I can't have him on this island tomorrow.'

'The whole thing seems to me enormously complicated,' said the Major. 'I don't see how you can expect it to work without a hitch. All I insist on is that you don't bring me into it.'

'It's perfectly simple,' said Meldon. 'I don't see where a hitch can come in if the thing's properly worked.'

11

MAJOR KENT and Meldon had finished their eggs and were eating bread-and-jam when Higginbotham, rowed by Jamesy O'Flaherty, reached the *Spindrift*. At the sound of a bump against the yacht's side Meldon went on deck.

'Come along, Higginbotham,' he said. 'Come below and have a cup of tea. Jamesy O'Flaherty, do you make your curragh fast and get on board. I'll bring you up a glass of whisky in a minute.'

He shepherded Higginbotham into the cabin. The Major rose to his feet nervously. He foresaw that the process of persuading Higginbotham to set out for Inishmore in a curragh at six the next morning would be trying.

'I think,' he said, 'I'll go on deck and have a chat with Jamesy O'Flaherty.'

'Do,' said Meldon, 'and take a glass of whisky with you. I want to have a quiet talk with Higginbotham.'

The Major departed, well satisfied that he would escape taking part in the quiet talk which was to follow.

'Help yourself to some tea,' said Meldon to Higginbotham, 'and make yourself comfortable with a slice of bread-and-jam. I think I mentioned to you yesterday that Sir Giles Buckley is rather a big bug in his own way.'

'You said he was something in the Castle.'

'He is. I hinted, I think that either Crimes Acts or Royal Commissions were his particular line. I was wrong there. I confused him for the moment with another man whose name is somewhat similar. The fact is that Sir Giles is the man whom they keep unattached, as it were, to take up any particular job that happens to be prominent at the moment. It may be a famine, or it may be crochet, or sick nurses, or Christmas-trees for workhouse children. Whatever it is, Sir Giles is the man who runs it. At present it happens to be tuberculosis.'

'I never heard of there being any such man in the Castle.'

'I dare say not. You official people get into very narrow grooves. You all of you seem to think that your own footy little Board is the only one in the country. Whereas there are lots and lots of others besides the one you happen to be connected with. Not that I mean to suggest that Sir Giles is a Board. He isn't. He's simply, as I said, unattached.'

'Still, I think I must have heard of him if he's what you say.'

'You might not. I tell you, Higginbotham, there aren't half a dozen men in Ireland who could tell you even the principal kinds of regular officials; and when it comes to unattached freelances like Sir Giles, hardly anybody knows exactly what they are. I'm liable to make mistakes about them myself, as you saw when I spoke about Sir Giles yesterday.'

'Still——'

'I may not be using technically correct language when I call Sir Giles an unattached official. I dare say there's some other name for what he is which you would recognise if you heard it. But the gist of the matter is the same, however you express it. He's in charge of the anti-tuberculosis movement, fighting the Great White Plague. That's what he's here for. This morning he made an examination of young Mrs O'Flaherty's baby, little Michael Pat. You might have seen him going off in that direction at about half-past eight.'

'I did.'

'You saw him talking to her on the side of the road and her with the baby in her arms?'

'Yes. I happened at the time to be going——'

'Well, there you are. If Sir Giles isn't investigating tuberculosis on behalf of the Government, why should he bother his head about making a prolonged and minute examination of Mrs O'Flaherty's baby? Tell me that.'

'I don't know. I suppose it's all right.'

'Well, then, don't contradict me flat when I'm giving you information which may come in useful to you. The fact is that Sir Giles wants you to help him tomorrow.'

'But—but I don't know anything about tuberculosis.'

'Nobody supposes you do. What he wants you to do is to go over early tomorrow to Inishmore in Jamesy O'Flaherty's curragh and make a list of all the cases of consumption you can find. You know the people, or at any rate you ought to, and of course Sir Giles doesn't. His plan is to follow you later on in the *Aureole*. You're to start about six a.m. Allowing an hour and a half for the row over, you'll be there by seven-thirty. After you've had a bit of breakfast—Sir Giles was most particular that you should breakfast properly—he thinks you might catch the thing yourself if you went at it on an empty stomach. After breakfast you're to stroll round the island and keep your eye lifting for consumptives. You needn't drag them out and lay them on the beach or anything of that sort. Just take a note of any case you come across so that when Sir Giles arrives there'll be no unnecessary waste of time.'

'I never heard of such a job in my life.'

'Very likely not. But you ought to recollect, Higginbotham, that you'd never heard of Sir Giles till I told you about him. And you'd never heard of the anti-tuberculosis crusade.'

'I had heard of that.'

'Oh, had you? Well, this morning you saw with your own eyes the way Sir Giles was examining little Michael Pat.'

'I didn't say I saw him examining the child. I said I saw——'

'Don't go back on what you've just admitted. You said you were watching Sir Giles this morning. I don't call it a very gentlemanly action. But there's no use making the matter worse now by denying that you did it.'

Higginbotham stroked his moustache nervously. He took off his spectacles and rubbed the glasses with his handkerchief. He cleared his throat.

'I can't do a thing like that,' he said. 'I don't know how.'

'It'll be all right,' said Meldon. 'Call on the parish priest when you land; he'll help you.'

Higginbotham still displayed signs of uneasiness.

'Why does Sir Giles send me this message through you?' he asked. 'Why doesn't he speak to me himself.'

'He tried to. He and I were searching the island for you all afternoon. He went up to old Thomas O'Flaherty's place to look for you. I told him that you were likely to be there, but you weren't.'

'I heard he was up there. I thought he might have been speaking to the old man about——'

'Well, he wasn't. He was simply looking for you. Now, Higginbotham, the question is simply this: will you go or will you not? I'd go myself in a minute, only I thought you'd like to get the chance. I've nothing to gain by being civil to Sir Giles, but you have. Why, man, your whole future depends upon the kind of impression you make upon these big officials. You know the way they talk to each other in their clubs after luncheon. I tell you there's very little they don't know about every inspector and engineer in the country. If you've any sense you'll make yourself as pleasant and obliging to Sir Giles as you possibly can. I hope you don't mind my speaking plainly. It's for your own good.'

'I think,' said Higginbotham, 'that I'll row over now and see Sir Giles myself.'

'You'd much better not.'

'Why?'

'Oh well, I don't like repeating these things. But of course it's pretty well public property. The fact is——'

Meldon took a cup from the table, put it to his lips, slowly raised his elbow and threw back his head.

'Only in the evenings,' he continued, 'after he's left the

office. He never allows it to interfere with his work in the slightest.'

Higginbotham gasped. Meldon nodded solemnly.

'Naturally,' he went on, 'the poor fellow doesn't care about having unexpected visitors dropping in on him during the evening.'

'Good God!' said Higginbotham.

'Yes, it's frightfully sad. In every other respect he's a splendid fellow, one of the very best. We keep it as quiet as we can, but, you can see it for yourself. You've only got to look at Langton's face to see it. You told me yourself that he'd got sacked out of the College Library for drink.'

'But Sir Giles!'

'Oh, tarred with the same brush. Birds of a feather, you know. You see now why it wouldn't do for you to be going over there this evening. You're an official yourself, and I need scarcely say that a subordinate official is the very last kind of man who should mix himself up in a business of this kind.'

'I see that, of course.'

'I needn't say, Higginbotham, that it's no pleasure to me to repeat stories of this kind. I wouldn't have said a word if you hadn't forced me. I'm extremely sorry for Sir Giles and for poor Langton. What a promising career that man had before him! With his taste for manuscripts and the whole College Library at his disposal, he might have made a European reputation. Drink's an awful curse.'

'But I thought you said he wasn't the same man.'

'I may have said that at the time. I naturally wanted to shield Sir Giles as long as I could. But he is the exact same man. Poor old Euseby Langton! But we'll drop the subject now. I don't care to spend the whole evening gloating over other men's infirmities. The point I want to get at is this: will you go to Inishmore tomorrow morning?'

'I suppose I'd better.'

'Quite right. Take my word for it you'll be glad afterwards you did. And now, as you've got to make an early start I daresay you'd like to be getting home. Don't let Jamesy O'Flaherty oversleep himself in the morning.'

'Major,' said Meldon, when Higginbotham had departed, 'I've settled that all right. Higginbotham and the curragh go to Inishmore tomorrow. They start at six a.m.'

'How did you arrange it?'

'Don't ask me. I had a tough job.'

Meldon lit his pipe and puffed great clouds of smoke. His nerves required steadying after the conversation with Higginbotham. For a time he remained silent.

The Major was filled with curiosity—the morbid curiosity which makes some men eager to gaze on sights which fill them with horror. He pressed Meldon to tell him how the expedition to Inishmore had been arranged.

'I'm glad we'll get that treasure tomorrow,' said Meldon. 'I don't believe it will be possible to keep Higginbotham going much longer without his suspecting that there is something up. He's becoming extraordinarily sceptical about the things I tell him. I give you my word, Major, that at times tonight it took me all I knew to persuade him that I was telling the truth.'

'I shouldn't wonder.'

'I've made up my mind,' said Meldon, after another pause, 'that, if we get anything like the haul I expect tomorrow out of the Spanish captain's hoard, we'll give Higginbotham a good bagful of doubloons for himself. We owe it to him to do him a good turn of some sort. I don't feel that we've treated him quite fairly. It's rough on a man to set him searching for tubercle bacilli all day long on an island by himself. It's not in Higginbotham's regular line of work and I'm afraid he won't like it at all. I'm sorry I had to do it.'

'What have you done?'

'I've just told you. I've sent him off to Inishmore to make a kind of census of all the consumptive people on the island. I told him he'd better get the parish priest to help him. By the way, what sort of a fellow is the parish priest of Inishmore?'

'He's a man called Mulcrone.'

'Has he a sense of humour? I mean, will he see the joke afterwards, or is he the kind who'll make a row?'

'He can see ordinary jokes. At least he has something of a reputation for making them, but whether he'll see your kind of joke, of course I can't say.'

'Oh, well, it won't much matter what he does once we have the treasure, and there's very little between us and it now. I think I'll turn in, Major. I'm a bit fagged. Michael Pat took more out of me this afternoon than I suspected at the time. I advise you to turn in too. We've a long day before us to-morrow. Good-night.'

Half an hour later Meldon from his bunk addressed Major Kent, who had been on deck to wash his teeth.

'Major, Higginbotham's not nearly such a fool as you appear to think. If I were you I'd slide off that geological survey story of yours quietly and unobtrusively. Don't try and keep the thing up. I doubt very much whether you'll be believed if you do. Any disguise you assume in future when dealing with Higginbotham had better be very carefully tested beforehand. Good-night.'

12

NEXT morning Meldon awoke earlier than usual. He turned out of his bunk at half-past five, and, as yachtsmen often do, began the day by tapping the barometer. It had fallen during the night and was still falling. He went on deck and looked round him. There was no sign visible as yet of a change in the weather. Everything pointed to the certainty of at least one more hot day. He returned to the cabin and shook Major Kent.

'It's not time for you to get up yet,' he said. 'But I thought I might as well warn you that you'll have to be dressed and ready to start by half-past six.'

'I'm not going on a fool's errand at any such hour in the morning,' growled the Major.

'I thought you'd very likely say that when you woke. That's the reason I shook you up a bit before it was absolutely necessary. Some people are at their best when they first wake. All really great men are. I am, myself. Other people wake slowly and are uncommonly short in their temper for an hour or so after they get up. That's the sort you are. If you had a wife I'd pity her at breakfast-time.'

Meldon went on deck again and surveyed first the *Aureole*, then Higginbotham's hut. At the end of a quarter of an hour he returned to the Major.

'It's all right,' he said. 'Higginbotham is stirring and I see Jamesy O'Flaherty fiddling about at the curragh. They'll be off in a few minutes. You'd better be getting up if you want half an hour to dress yourself. We'll breakfast on shore.'

'I won't.'

Meldon made no answer to this flat refusal. He went on deck again and stared through the glasses at the beach beside the pier. He saw Higginbotham embark in the curragh, watched Jamesy O'Flaherty take the oars, shove off and begin to row steadily. He returned to Major Kent.

'He's gone,' he reported. 'I hardly dared to hope he would, but he has. In a few minutes he'll be out of the bay. Then I'll swim across to the *Aureole* at once.'

'What for?'

'To deal with the punt, of course. There's a nice little westerly breeze, and when I cast loose the painter she'll drift quietly out to sea.'

'J. J., I've stood a lot of your foolery, but I'm not going to allow you to commit theft before my eyes and I'm not going ashore without my breakfast.'

'I'll take your two points separately,' said Meldon. 'There doesn't seem to be any connection between them. First, there's no theft in taking my own punt and sending her out to sea. Second, you must come on shore at once or else the other fellows will wake. They can't get off the *Aureole* when they do, of course. But I'd rather not have them howling after us. It wouldn't look well if we refused to go back for them. People might say afterwards that we'd taken their punt from them. Whereas if we're well out of the way before they wake we can't be blamed for their being stuck all day on the *Aureole*.'

'It's ten to one they see you setting the punt adrift, and then there'll be a nice row.'

'They won't. What would have them up at this hour of the day? They know jolly well that the tide won't be low enough to get into that hole at the bottom of the cliff till about ten o'clock. They won't expect us to stir till after eight, anyhow. But I can't stop here arguing with you. You get a few bits of bread and some butter and sardines and things together, and I'll be off.'

Meldon dropped over the side of the *Spindrift* and struck out for the *Aureole*. He watched her keenly as he swam, and saw no signs of life on board her. The morning breeze ruffled the surface of the water slightly. The tiny ripples beat against his chin and cheek. The sun shone red through a faint haze. Meldon swam joyously. He was filled with the spirit of adventure and with delightful anticipations of success. The *Aureole* lay with her bow pointing to the shore. The punt was astern of her. Now and then she pulled at her painter just sufficiently strongly to life it from the water and haul it taut. Then, while the drops still fell from it, the rope grew slack again and the punt ran up a little towards the yacht. The gurgling wash of the ripples against her side was pleasant to hear. Meldon gripped her by the stern, steadied himself, and lay almost flat on the water with his legs near the surface to avoid the suction of the punt. Then with a sharp jerk of his arms he raised himself till his chest touched the gunwale. He climbed cautiously on board, loosed the painter from the ring in the bow and lay still for a minute or two, watching the distance between him and the *Aureole* widen slowly. The breeze was light, and the punt did not drift very fast. Still, she moved towards the mouth of the bay. Sir Giles and Langton were apparently sound asleep. Meldon slid quietly into the water again and started on his return journey to the *Spindrift*. Now and then he turned over on his back and swam for a few yards with his eyes fixed on the *Aureole*. There was no sign of awakening on board of her.

He climbed into the *Spindrift* by the bight of rope he had left hanging over the side for his accommodation.

'Major,' he said in a delighted whisper, 'the coup has come off. Where's my shirt? Isn't it extraordinary the way things move about during the night. I could have sworn I left it on the end of my bunk. Ah! I have it. Now the sooner we're off the better. Slip the breakfast into the punt and get in yourself. Go on, man. If you want to argue, argue when we're on shore. We haven't a minute to lose. I wouldn't trust that beast Langton not to sneak up in his pyjamas to have a look at us. He did yesterday.'

Major Kent, grumbling and protesting, was hustled into the punt. Meldon followed him and paddled briskly to the shore. There was no one, not even Mary Kate, on the pier when they reached it.

'Now,' said Meldon, 'get that punt ashore and fold her up. We're going to take her with us.'

'Why should we drag the punt? We'll only be cutting her to pieces on the rocks.'

'Why? Because in the first place, as you'd see if you troubled yourself to think for a single instant, if we leave her here some fool will go off to the *Aureole* in her when those fellows begin to shout for help. In the next place, because you can't swim, and we'll want her to carry you up the channel to the bottom of the cliff. I must say that these collapsible punts, beastly as they are to row in, have certain good points. We couldn't have carried the ordinary wooden boat all round the island. Just you fold her up while I go over to the curragh there on the shore.'

Major Kent lifted the punt out of the water and folded her flat. Then he looked up and saw Meldon, with four oars on his shoulders, going up the hill towards Higginbotham's house.

'What are you doing?' he called.

'I found four oars,' said Meldon, 'and I'm going to put them in through one of the windows of Higginbotham's house. Nobody will think of looking for them there. I wish to goodness you wouldn't shout at me like that. You'll waken every man on the island before you've done, to say nothing of Sir Giles and Langton.'

The Major pursued Meldon up the hill and seized him by the arm.

'J. J.,' he said earnestly. 'I call this theft.'

He had the true English respect for law in spite of the fact that both him and his father had spent their lives in Ireland. The very thought of an unhallowed interference with property shocked him inexpressibly.

'You can call it arson if you like,' said Meldon, who had nothing but Irish blood in his veins, 'or malicious injury, or agrarian outrage, or intimidation. I don't care if you call it cattle-driving or even boycotting. I'm going to stow the oars away all the same. I can't have the owners of the curragh rowing off to the *Aureole* and putting Sir Giles on shore as soon as our backs are turned.'

Meldon breasted the hill and reached the iron hut. He tried each of the four windows in turn. They were all bolted. With the end of one of the oars he deliberately smashed a pane of glass.

'For Heaven's sake, don't,' said the Major.

'I must; Higginbotham will probably grumble, but that can't be helped. He'd no right to go away and leave his house barred and bolted as if he was afraid of burglars.'

'He very well might be afraid of burglars when you're about.'

'Now look here,' said Meldon as he shoved the oars through the broken pane, 'I don't mind your being abusive, not the least bit. You've been calling me a liar and a burglar and other bad names since ever I brought you to this island. I haven't resented it a bit and I don't. But I tell you what I do dislike, and that's your abominable unreasonableness. I can't bear men who are carried away by mere words and don't stop to think about the meaning of what they say. What is burglary? Isn't it taking a man's own things out of his house when he's not looking? You agree to that definition, I suppose. Very well. What am I doing? I'm putting other people's things into a man's house when he's not looking. Now that's just the exact, bang opposite to what burgling is. Therefore, I'm not a burglar. In fact, I'm the very antithesis of a burglar. You may not know what an antithesis is, but——'

'I do know, so you need not trouble to explain.'

'Very well, I'll pursue my line of reasoning. Burglary is wrong. You hinted that yourself a minute ago. But the antithesis of wrong is right. What I'm doing is the antithesis of burglary. Therefore——'

'There's no need to go on talking that rot,' said the Major. 'It doesn't impress me in the least.'

'I feared it wouldn't. Never mind, Major, even if you don't pocket a single doubloon—and I'll be greatly surprised if you're not weighted down with them before morning, but even if you don't pocket one, you're getting a liberal education. The things I've told you about geology, entomology, theology, ethics, and philosophy in general, since we came to this island would set up an ordinary professor handsomely.'

Meldon slung the folded punt across his shoulders, took a last look at the *Aureole* and started to tramp up to the head of the path which led down the cliff to the western beach of the island. Major Kent, with the paddles, the rowlocks, and the basket which contained the breakfast, followed him. The inhabitants of Inishgowlan are not early risers. A few women peered out through the doors of the cabins. Nobody attempted to speak to them or follow them. Neither Thomas O'Flaherty

Pat nor Mary Kate appeared at all. Meldon and the Major walked rapidly. At the top of the cliff they paused.

'We're pretty safe now,' said Meldon, 'and we'll take a few minutes' rest, but we won't breakfast till we're down among the rocks.'

He swung the punt off his shoulders as he spoke, sat down and wiped his brow.

'If I'm not mistaken,' said the Major, 'there's some one on the deck of the *Aureole* now.'

Meldon stood up and looked eagerly.

'There is,' he said. 'You're quite right. See now, they're both on deck. Well, they can stay there.'

'What'll they do now?'

'Shout, I should think. I can't myself see what else there is for them to do. Sir Giles might swim, but it's not likely the other fellow can. That sort of man never does anything really useful. Anyway, if they do swim, they can't carry all their tackle with them for getting down the cliff. All the same, I think we'll move on a bit.'

'I'm inclined to go back to them,' said the Major. 'I don't like—— After all, they've not done anything to us.'

'It's not what they've done so much as what they want to do which makes me determine to keep them there. Recollect, Major, they're after the treasure.'

'Well, haven't they as good a right to it as we have? I like to play fair.'

'They have not as good a right as we have. I deny that entirely. Think of the use those fellows would make of the treasure if they got it. You told me yourself that Sir Giles was a bad hat—so bad that his own father left the family property away from him, as much of it as he could. Langton's no better. You heard what Higginbotham said about his drinking, and he must have a hideously corrupted mind after poking about for years among those manuscripts in the College Library. You don't know how bad most manuscripts are. That's the reason they remain manuscripts. No decent printer would set them up in type. I tell you, if those two fellows get a hold of the treasure, they'll spend it in ways that will make the Spanish captain shiver in his grave, and I don't expect he was exactly a squeamish man. It's nothing but a public duty to prevent their getting a hold of the money, even if we never touch a penny of it ourselves.'

'I don't see what all that, even if it's true, has to do with their right to take the treasure if they can, always supposing there is any treasure to take.'

'I wish you wouldn't qualify everything you say with a whole string of "ifs". It robs your conversation of piquancy. But come on now. We must get out of this. They might see us with their glasses. When we've had our breakfast, I'll explain to you why Sir Giles has no right to the treasure.'

They made their way down the steep path and reached the rocks at the foot of the cliff. Meldon laid the punt down carefully. The basket was unpacked and a sufficient supply of bread, butter, sardines, potted meat, and jam were spread out on a flat stone. For a while, Meldon ate without speaking. An early swim, a long walk, and an hour or two of anxious excitement, whet a man's appetite for breakfast. Major Kent began to hope that he would escape an explanation of his own moral right to the treasure. He was disappointed. Meldon, his appetite sated, lit a pipe and leaned back comfortably against a rock.

'We may as well take it easy for a bit,' he said. 'The tide won't be out far enough to let us get into that hole for another two hours, and it won't take us more than one to get there.'

He smoked contentedly for a few minutes and then began to speak again—

'You read *The Times*, Major, so I suppose you take some interest in politics.'

'I know that the Nationalists are blackguards, if that's what you mean.'

'I'm not talking now of these petty little local squabbles. When I say politics, I refer to the great stream of European thought, to the wide movements discernible among all civilised peoples.'

He waved his hand towards the ocean to indicate the immensity of his subject.

'I don't know anything about that,' said the Major.

'I thought you wouldn't, but you ought to. Are you aware that our modern civilisation is on the very verge of a bust-up? No? Well, it is. The Governments of the various countries are, generally speaking, unaware of the catastrophe which threatens them; or, if they guess anything, are foolish enough to think that they can stifle an explosion by sitting on the safety-valve. You catch my meaning, I suppose?'

'You appear to mean,' said the Major, 'that all Kings, Princes, Presidents, Prime Ministers, and Parliaments are fools.'

'Precisely. They all are.'

'It's a pity you don't tell them so.'

'I will. I've always intended to tell the first one I met. Look at Russia. Choke full of anarchists and nihilists. Look at Portugal. They're murdering kings and rioting in churches. Look at Finland, admitting women to their Parliament; not that I object to women in the way you do, Major. I think they're all right in their proper place. I only quote Finland as an instance of the general tendency I'm speaking of. Look at New York, with its Socialist riots. Look at Austria-Hungary, or Italy, or any other country you choose to name. Look at the Labour Members in the English House of Commons. Now what does all that mean?'

'I don't know in the least, and I don't care. Things were always pretty much the same. There's nothing new in the condition of the world that I can see.'

'You may not see it, but there is. We're on the brink of a revolution—the biggest thing of the kind that there has ever been. And the cause of it is the concentration of wealth in the hands of a few people who are using it for purely selfish purposes. Any student of sociology will tell you the same thing. It's a well-known fact. Now what is our duty under the circumstances? What is the duty of every well-disposed person who values the stability of civilisation? Obviously it is to prevent the selfish, depraved, and fundamentally immoral people from acquiring wealth; to see that only the well-intentioned and public-spirited get rich. That is the general principle. Now apply it to the particular case we are discussing. On this island there is untold wealth in solid gold.'

'I suppose,' said the Major, 'that I shall come to believe that in the end. I hear it so often that I shan't be able to help myself.'

'There are just two parties who stand a chance of possessing themselves of it. There's no one else in the running for this particular scoop.'

'What about Higginbotham and Thomas O'Flaherty?'

'You might just as well say, what about Mary Kate and Michael Pat? They're not in it. Higginbotham is a Government official, to mention only one point, and is so much occupied in ameliorating the condition of the people that he simply wouldn't have time to spend the money, even if he got it. No. There's us and there's Sir Giles and Langton. That's all. Now, *ex hypothesi*—you know what I mean by *ex hypothesi*, don't you?'

'I do, but don't let that stop you if you have any fancy for explaining it. I shan't mind listening.'

'Your suggestion, Major, as one of the members of our District Council said the other day, when some one accused them all of being drunk, is quite uncalled for. It's only for your sake, to quiet your conscience about the treasure, that I'm going into the matter at all. My own mind is quite clear. I haven't any doubts about Sir Giles.'

'If that's all, you needn't go into it any more.'

'All right. I won't. Have another sardine? There are two left in the tin. Now that I've finished my pipe I feel that I could do with one of them. In fact I could manage them both if you don't want the other.'

'I don't.'

'Sure? Oh, well, rather than let them go to waste, I'll eat them.'

He took them one after the other by their tails, and, throwing his head back, dropped them into his mouth. With his penknife he scraped out of the pot some fragments of jam which lingered near the bottom. There was no more bread. Having finished this scanty second breakfast he stood up and stretched himself. Then he announced that it was time to start. Major Kent rose unwillingly and took up the paddles. Meldon swung the punt on to his back again.

'No sign of old T. O. P. this morning,' he said. 'We've successfully given him the slip. I expect he's cowering in his gloomy cabin, meditating on fresh ways of defeating Higginbotham. Sir Giles and Langton have probably stopped shouting for help by this time. They're too hoarse, I expect, to shout any more. They are now reduced to gnashing their teeth silently and muttering frightful oaths. Higginbotham is searching for bacilli on Inishmore. Poor Higginbotham! I'm afraid it'll be a dull and trying day for him. But we'll make it up to him afterwards. Mary Kate is, I hope, doing her duty by her little cousin Michael Pat and making things a bit easier for young Mrs O'Flaherty. When we get back to Ballymoy, Major, we'll send a good stiff bottle off to the old woman. Remind me of that, will you, in case it slips my memory. On the whole, things look rosy for you and me—a great deal rosier than I ever recollect them looking before. Come along now, we've no more time to waste.'

13

It is not easy to carry a punt—even the kind of punt that folds up—over rugged and slippery rocks. Meldon stumbled frequently and fell three times. He cut his elbow and reopened the rent in the knee of his trousers which he had laboriously sewed up after his first expedition round the coast of the island. His cheerfulness was untouched by misfortune. His energy carried him far ahead of Major Kent, who had the lighter load. Even when he found himself on his hands and knees among seaweed and pools he preserved the punt from injury. He arrived at last at the point on which he had decided that the Spanish galleon must have struck, scrambled round it and reached the ledge of rock above the channel. He was breathless, dishevelled, and so hot that he wished very much to swim rather than row to the hole in the cliff. He put the temptation aside. Major Kent, labouring heavily with the paddles over one shoulder, appeared at the corner. Meldon unfolded and stretched the canvas punt. He made fast the rope, which he had used as a sling, to the ring in her bow, and launched her very carefully. He insisted on embarking at once when the Major arrived.

'No sign of any one swinging down over the cliff today,' he said, looking over his shoulder as he paddled up the channel. 'Sir Giles is otherwise and perhaps less innocently occupied. He is certainly swearing frightfully. He is very likely at this moment cutting Langton's throat.'

'It isn't Langton's throat he'll cut. Langton didn't set his punt adrift.'

'I dare say he'd rather cut mine if he could, but in the sort of temper he's in at present it'll be almost necessary for him to murder somebody at once.'

'But what has he against Langton?'

'Oh, you can't always account for deeds of that sort. They are what the French call crimes of passion. By the way, did you ever read Lombroso on Crime? You ought to. He's a tremendous fellow for the physical characteristics of the criminal. I'd like him to have a look at Sir Giles. I expect—— Hullo! here we are!'

The punt grounded at the very mouth of the hole. There were still a few inches of water in the entrance, and the little beach on which Sir Giles had stood two days before was not yet uncovered. Meldon stepped out of the punt, knelt down, and peered into the hole.

'It's all right,' he said. 'We can get in easily. It doesn't matter if we get a little wet.'

He took the painter of the punt in his hand and crawled into the hole. In a couple of minutes his voice, sounding hollowly, reached Major Kent.

'Come along. It's only the entrance that's really narrow. It's quite a large cave when you're inside, and not nearly so dark as you'd expect. You don't have to crawl more than a few yards in the water. The ground rises rapidly and it's quite dry where I am now.'

Major Kent disliked very much the idea of crawling even a few yards through water; but he knew that it was no use holding back. Meldon was quite capable of emerging and dragging him by main force into the hole. Very unwillingly he stooped down and crept forward.

'It's not a bad place, is it?' said Meldon, 'and a pretty good size. You can sit straight up here and hardly bump your head at all.'

He made fast the painter of the punt to a large stone as he spoke. 'She'll be all safe. The tide will leave her high and dry in another half-hour. I wonder how far this cave goes? I expect the Spanish captain dumped his treasure right at the far end. Come along.'

It was difficult to get along at first. Walking over large round stones which roll about when trodden on is never easy. It becomes extremely troublesome when it is only possible to proceed either on all fours or bent double—when the roof is so low that an unguarded movement results in a blow on the head. But things got pleasanter after a little while. The ground sloped rapidly upwards. Meldon and the Major were soon above high-water mark. Then the stones on which they walked were no longer so smoothly rounded and were much less liable to roll.

'What beats me about this cave,' said Meldon, 'is that it isn't darker. It doesn't seem to get any darker either as we go on.'

The roof rose higher. It became possible to walk upright. Major Kent stretched himself at last to his full height and looked round him. The rocks on each side had widened out, leaving a space between them. They and the roof were quite visible in a dim light which came from the depths of the cave.

'It's interesting to think,' said Meldon, 'that the last human feet which trod these stones were those of the Spanish captain and his crew. It must have been tough work dragging the cases of bullion along through that narrow part. We can't have much farther to go now. I see what looks like the end in front of us. But I can't understand where the light comes from.'

He went on a few yards and then gave a sudden shout—a kind of cheer—half-smothered by excitement. He ran forward, stumbling desperately among the loose stones, but picking himself up and bounding on with outstretched arms. Major Kent, stirred at last out of his grumbling indifference, ran after him. Meldon stopped abruptly. Before him, laid on a slab of rock at the side of the cave, were two iron chests. Their lids stood wide open. They were perfectly empty.

'Good God!' said Major Kent, 'there was something here after all. I must say, J. J., I didn't believe in your treasure till this minute, and now it's gone.'

'It's gone,' said Meldon, 'but it can't be gone far. Every argument for believing that it's still on the island holds good. Don't you lose heart. What we've got to do now is to turn to and find out where it's gone and who's got it.'

He took another glance at the empty chests and then looked on from where they lay.

'This isn't the end of the cave,' he said. 'It takes a sharp bend to the right. See how the light, coming round the corner, strikes that wall. Let's go on and see where the cave does end and where the light comes from.'

'I don't see,' he said as he stumbled on, 'how Sir Giles can have got it. I've watched him like a cat does a mouse. The only time he got away from me was yesterday afternoon when he went up to Thomas O'Flaherty Pat's house, and I had Mary Kate watching him then. Great Scott! What's that?'

The crash of some heavy body falling on the boulders set the whole cave echoing. Meldon stood still in astonishment.

'If you ask me,' said the Major, 'I should say that the roof's falling in. We'd better clear out of this while we can.'

'I don't care,' said Meldon, 'if the roof does fall in. I don't care if the whole island crumbles into bits and comes rattling down on top of my head. I'm going to see this business through.'

He went forward very cautiously, peering in front of him, until he reached the place where the cave bent to the right. He stood still for a minute. Then he turned and went back to where the Major waited.

'It's Sir Giles,' he said. 'He's come down through the roof, and he's standing there looking up while something is being lowered to him. I have it, Major. The hole in Thomas O'Flaherty Pat's field! Mary Kate told me they were looking at it yesterday. What an ass I was not to think of it before! Of course, it opens straight down into this cave. It couldn't do anything else. Why didn't I think of that sooner? Come on, now, Major. As Sir Giles is here, we may as well have a talk with him.'

Taking Major Kent by the arm he stepped forward, turned the corner, and came in sight of Sir Giles Buckley, who was lighting a lantern. Meldon recognised it at once as the riding-light of the *Aureole*.

'Good-morning, Sir Giles,' he said. 'You won't need that lantern. The cave is quite light.'

Sir Giles started and turned quickly.

'Oh, it's the damned parson,' he said. 'I more than half expected you'd be here.'

'I don't mind owning,' said Meldon, 'that I did not expect to see you. You swam ashore from the yacht, I suppose.'

'No, you didn't expect me. I dare say you thought you had me boxed up for the day when you played that fool's trick, setting my punt adrift.'

'It's my punt, not yours. But as we're on the subject of the punt, how did you get ashore?'

'As soon as I found she was gone,' said Sir Giles, 'I got up the mainsail and went after her. Any one who wasn't a perfect ass would have known beforehand that I'd do that. You must think that everybody in the world is as big an idiot as you are yourself. Did you suppose that I'd sit still and whistle hymn-tunes until you came back and put me ashore?'

'I didn't suppose anything of the sort. I thought you'd swear every oath you knew five or six times over and then cut Langton's throat.'

'You drivelling imbecile!'

'Go on,' said Meldon, 'call me any other name that occurs to you. When you've finished perhaps you'll walk down the cave a bit and I'll show you whether I'm a fool or not.'

He turned and walked away, followed by Major Kent. Sir Giles eyed them doubtfully for a minute and then went after them. When he reached the slab of rock on which the chests lay, Meldon turned and made sure that Sir Giles was at his heels. With a dramatic gesture he pointed to the chests.

'Empty, Sir Giles,' he said. 'Look in and make sure. Quite empty.'

'Have you got the stuff?' said Sir Giles, 'Damn it! You can't have it. I don't believe you've touched it.'

'Believe whatever you like, but there's one thing you may bet on with perfect safety. Whether we've got it or not, you haven't, and what's more you never will. Now, who's the fool, the ass, the idiot, and the drivelling imbecile?'

Sir Giles glared at Meldon. It was evident that he was in an extremely bad temper. His face became first white and then crimson. He opened his mouth to speak, but no sound issued from it except a sort of hoarse gurgle produced apparently far down in his throat.

'Don't let your temper get the better of you,' said Meldon. 'It's foolish, besides being bad form. And remember what I said to you the day we first met about swearing. Excuse my reminding you of that, but I can't help thinking that you mean to curse as soon as ever you can. You have all the appearance of a man who is struggling to find expression for strong feelings of some kind.'

Sir Giles stuttered out an oath. Having succeeded in giving utterance to one intelligible syllable, he obtained all at once complete command of his powers of speech. He poured forth a series of voluble imprecations and expressed hopes for Meldon's future which would have startled the author of the most emphatic of the Psalms. He was interrupted by a loud crash from the depths of the cave. He started violently:

'What the devil's that?'

'It's uncommonly like the noise you made yourself when you came down through the roof. My own opinion is that it's Langton. He'd be likely enough to drop in to see that you didn't sneak off with any more than your own proper share of the treasure. Come along and we'll see.'

He went up again to the place where he had met Sir Giles. Langton, who had descended very much more rapidly than he wished, sat on a stone nursing a bruised knee.

'Good-morning, Mr Langton,' said Meldon. 'I'm delighted to see you. I hope you haven't hurt yourself. As far as I could judge by the noise, you must have come down rather hard. However, I'm glad you're here. You must take Sir Giles in hand and look after him a bit. He very nearly had a fit just now. You ought to see to it that he takes some kind of cooling medicine three times a day—bromides, or castor-oil, or something of that sort. Any chemist would make the mixture up for you if you told him the kind of thing you wanted. Or if there's no good man in your neighbourhood try one of those soothing syrup stuffs you'll see advertised in Christmas numbers. I dare say they're all right. I hesitate as a rule about recommending patent medicines, but you can see for yourself that your friend wants something.'

'What the devil brings you here?' said Sir Giles. 'I told you to wait at the top for me. Who's going to haul us up now, I'd like to know?'

Langton, still nursing his knee, sat in sulky silence. Meldon looked up at the hole above his head. Peering over the edge of it was the benevolent and aristocratic face of Thomas O'Flaherty Pat. His long white beard dropped down. His white hair completed a kind of moonlight aureole round his head. His face expressed a mild and entirely courteous interest in the doings of the men below him.

'It's all right,' said Meldon to Sir Giles. 'There's a dear old fellow up there, a great friend of mine, who'll do what he can to pull you up. I'm sure. He's not very strong, and he may not be able to haul you quite the whole way, but he'll do his best. And you're taking risks in any case. I see you're using the throat halyard of my boat again in spite of the warning I gave you the day before yesterday. If I were you I'd make Langton lie down flat underneath you as you go up. He'd break your fall a good deal in case——'

'Come out of this,' said Sir Giles, taking the rope from Langton and fitting it round his own armpits. 'I'll go mad if have to stand here any longer listening to that ape gibbering. Hi! You above there! Haul up!'

'I forgot to mention,' said Meldon, 'that the old gentleman doesn't understand a word of English. My friend Higginbotham, who has important business to transact with him, is learning Irish on purpose to be able to carry on the necessary conversations.'

Sir Giles plucked furiously at the rope and shouted again.

'There's no use trying to make him understand by shouting,' said Meldon, 'he's not the least deaf. The best thing you can do is to wait here quietly till the Major and I get away in our punt and back to the far side of the island. It'll only take us about two hours. You and Langton can talk things over together while you're waiting. I'll send up a little girl called Mary Kate who understands both languages. You can tell her what you want and she will explain it to her grandfather. But I do ask you to remember, Sir Giles, that she's a little girl. I don't want to rub it in about your language, but there are some things that a girl of ten years old—you know what I mean.'

Sir Giles stooped and took up a large stone in both hands.

'If you utter another word,' he said, 'I'll bash in your skull with this.'

'If you'd keep calm,' said Meldon, 'you'd run much less chance of bursting a blood-vessel. You ought to be able to realise that I'm giving you sound advice and speaking for your own good.'

Sir Giles raised his two hands above his head with the stone between them. He held it there, poised for several seconds, taking aim at Meldon. The rope round his armpits tightened suddenly. He was lifted from his feet. He dangled in mid-air, hands and feet hanging down. When he was about eight feet above the ground he ceased to ascend. He writhed and wriggled, with the result that he began to spin rapidly round and round at the end of the rope.

'If I were you,' said Meldon, 'I'd drop that stone. It adds considerably to your weight. I told you before that old Thomas O'Flaherty Pat is anything but a strong man. I'm sure he's doing his best, but it looks to me as if he was pretty nearly played out. It's trying him too high to make him hoist both of you and the stone at once. I'll send it up to you afterwards if you really want it. But I can't see what use it will be to you. There are plenty of stones up above. The island is simply covered with stones, every bit as good as that one.'

The ascent commenced again and continued jerkily with many pauses, until at last Sir Giles disappeared through the hole.

'I think,' said Meldon to the Major, 'that you and I may as well be dodging off home now. Goodbye, Mr Langton. We can't be of any further use to you. Sir Giles will pull you up all right. If I were you I wouldn't be in too great a hurry to go. His temper won't be by any means improved by the argument he'll have with Thomas O'Flaherty Pat. You can't imagine how trying it is to argue with a man who can't understand a word you say and can't speak so as you can understand him. That old fellow has just one sentence, something about 'Ní beurla'. He says it over and over again in a way that would get on the nerves of a cow. It takes a cool man to stand it. Higginbotham gets quite mad, and even I have to keep a tight grip on my temper. The effect on Sir Giles will be frightful. And he has that stone with him. He would insist on clinging to it. Good-bye, Mr Langton.'

Meldon and Major Kent went down the cave together. The tide had completely ebbed, and it was possible to crawl through the entrance without getting wet. The punt, which lay high and dry, was carried down to the water and launched. Meldon, as usual, took the paddles.

'One thing,' he said thoughtfully, 'seems perfectly clear. Sir Giles hasn't got the treasure. If he had he wouldn't have got into such a beastly temper.'

'That coup of yours about the punt didn't precisely come off,' said the Major with a grin. 'He rather had you over that, I thought.'

Meldon ignored the taunt.

'The question now is,' he said, 'who has the treasure? The position seems to me to require some thinking out. It is becoming complex. I'm glad we have a long, quiet afternoon before us.'

They reached the shelf of rock, disembarked, and folded up the punt.

'I wish,' said Meldon, 'that you hadn't insisted on my finishing off those two sardines this morning. I'm very hungry now.'

'You'll get nothing more to eat till you get back to the *Spindrift,* unless you happen to come across that crab which which you lost the first day we were here.'

'I wouldn't eat a raw crab any way. I'm not a cannibal. Come on and let us get back as quick as we can.'

The disappointment of the morning and the sharp appetite which followed hard work in the open air affected even Meldon's temper. He spoke no more for some yards ahead of Major Kent. Gradually the extreme interest of the treasure-hunt took possession of his mind again and returned his cheerful self-confidence.

'You'll admit now,' he said, 'that I reasoned perfectly correctly about that treasure. The Spanish captain hid it precisely where I said he did.'

'There was only one point you went wrong about,' said the Major. 'You said the treasure was in that cave and it wasn't.'

'It was, originally. I couldn't be expected to foresee that some one would remove it and hide it again in another place. That's what has happened. Now that I know it's gone, I'll turn to and reason out where it's gone to. If it hasn't got any rightful owner we'll get it yet.'

'What do you mean by a rightful owner?'

'A live man,' said Meldon. 'If it was removed and hidden by some fellow that's dead and gone, then he's no more the owner of it now than the Spanish captain is. If there is a rightful owner, of course we're done. I'm not going to commit robbery even for the sake of getting that treasure.'

'I'm glad to hear that, anyway.'

'Now, there are just two people at present alive who can possibly have that treasure. One is Higginbotham. The other is Thomas O'Flaherty Pat. I'll take Higginbotham first.'

'What's the good of that? If Higginbotham has it he will keep it.'

'Still it would be interesting to know. In favour of Higginbotham it may be urged that he has evidently made a very careful investigation of this island. You see how glibly he came out with that information about the pliocene clay. Now would he have known that if he hadn't, so to speak, got at the inside of the island? That sort of clay doesn't lie about on the surface for everybody to see.'

'Why shouldn't it?'

'Oh, just because those fundamental things never do lie on the surface. A fellow wouldn't find out what your backbone consisted of by just looking at your skin, would he? He'd have to put you on an operating table and cut a hole in you to find that out. It's just the same with islands. Higginbotham knew that this island consisted of pliocene clay. Very well, it follows that he must have gone beyond the surface of the island.'

'Prompted, I suppose, by an unholy curiosity.'

'Prompted by a stern sense of duty. He is employed by the Government at an enormous salary, no doubt, to find out all he can about this island. Naturally he either digs a hole or goes down some hole already in existence. Now, so far as we know, Thomas O'Flaherty's hole is the only one there is. Therefore it seems likely that Higginbotham went down it. If he did he found the treasure and has it now.'

'It's all the same to us who has it. As I said before, if Higginbotham has it, he'll keep it.'

'I didn't say Higginbotham had it. So far I've only considered what is to be said in favour of what I may call the Higginbotham hypothesis.'

'Don't start on hypotheses again J. J. I'm sick of the sound of the word.'

'I can't help it if you are. The proposal of an hypothesis is the only known method of finding out truth. I tell you, Major, I've gone pretty deep into these philosophic and scientific questions, and I know what I'm talking about. You ask any first-rate man and he'll tell you the same thing. Now, against Higginbotham there's just one broad fact to be argued, but I candidly confess it seems to me to be decisive. Higginbotham isn't the kind of man who would come upon hidden treasure even by accident. He has too much of the official mind. It's almost impossible to think of a Congested Districts Board official gloating over Spanish gold. That puts Higginbotham out of court. There remains Thomas O'Flaherty Pat. You'll recollect that I've always had my suspicions of that old man. The way he followed us the first day we went round the cliffs was peculiar, to say the least of it. His persistent refusal to speak a word of English points to the fact that he has something or other to conceal. I shall have to go into his case very carefully indeed. But here we are at the foot of the path. I can't climb up a cliff with a punt on my back and talk at the same time. I'll have to put off discussing old O'Flaherty till we get to the top.'

After a quarter of an hour's hard work Meldon reached the

head of the path, drew a long breath, and took a look at the bay below him. Then he laid down the punt hurriedly and turned to the Major, who was still struggling upwards.

'There's another yacht in the bay,' he said—'a big steam yacht.'

Major Kent hurried over the last few steps of the climb.

'You're right,' he said. 'There is. If I'd known that this was to be a kind of Cowes week at Inishgowlan I wouldn't have come near the place. I suppose the next thing will be some fellow coming round and asking us to act on the committee of a regatta.'

'That's a biggish boat,' said Meldon. 'The man who owns her must be pretty wealthy. Now what has he come here for?'

'Treasure-hunting, of course,' said the Major. 'Nobody comes here for anything else.'

'Don't jump at conclusions in that way. There's nothing so unphilosophic as forming conclusions on insufficient evidence, and in this case you simply haven't any evidence at all.'

'It wasn't a conclusion,' said the Major. 'It was an hypothesis. Of course if you've any better hypothesis to offer——'

'I have. I believe, in fact I'm practically certain, that the men on that yacht are Members of Parliament.'

'You said that about Sir Giles and you turned out to be wrong.'

'That's just what makes me so sure I'm right now. I'll explain it to you in one minute. You've sometimes played pitch-and-toss, I suppose—I mean as a boy.'

'I have.'

'Very well. Now suppose the other fellow tossed the penny. You called heads and it turned out that you were wrong. You'd be practically certain it was tails, wouldn't you? There you are, then. I was wrong about Sir Giles being a Member of Parliament, therefore I'm nearly sure to be right when I say that this man is.'

'I don't see that. Not that it's any use arguing with you.'

'If you don't see a simple thing like that, it isn't any use.'

'All the same I will,' said the Major. 'Just for once I'll show you what rot you talk. You said it must be either heads or tails.'

'I didn't. I said it was nearly sure to be either heads or tails. The penny might light in a mud head and stand on its edge.'

'It's no use reasoning with you.'

'It isn't,' said Meldon, 'if you won't reason right.'

'Look here. You say if it isn't heads it's nearly sure to be tails. But suppose he tossed another coin. That's what's happened in this case.'

'It's just the same with any coin. There are only two sides to the best of them.'

'What I mean is this. Here's a fresh yacht altogether. Quite a different yacht from the *Aureole* with quite different people in her. It isn't a case of heads or tails at all.'

'I don't in the least see what you mean, and I don't believe you see yourself. But you may take my word for it, Major, that there is at least one Member of Parliament in that yacht. There may be more, but I'll bet my hat there's one. Don't bother your head any more about that. These things only make you irritable. We'll get along back to the *Spindrift* and have a bite to eat. Then I'll take a long, quiet afternoon thinking things out. If I get them sized up to my satisfaction I may go on shore before tea and have a look at Michael Pat. In the evening I'll find out how Higginbotham got on with the tuberculosis bacilli on Inishmore.'

14

MELDON stretched himself along the seat of the *Spindrift's* cabin. He had dined very heartily off tinned corned beef and potatoes, followed by several cups of strong tea. He had lit his pipe and felt happy. The unpleasant duty of washing up the plates and cups was postponed until after the evening meal, when one job could be made of all the crockery dirtied during the day.

'There's one good thing about a morning's work such as we have had,' he said. 'Even if you haven't pulled off the exact thing you went out to do, you enjoy your dinner and your smoke afterwards tremendously. I expect there are fellows at this moment sitting in London restaurants and clubs and places smoking half-crown cigars after gorging themselves with iced soufflés and pâtés of various kinds, who aren't getting half the satisfaction that I am out of this pipe of common twist.'

Major Kent grunted. He was disinclined for philosophic argument.

'There's something in one of Horace's odes about it's not being Sicilian feasts but hard work and a good conscience which bring real satisfaction. I can't recollect the exact words, but if I had a Horace I could find them.'

'I wouldn't give Horace too much credit for the remark, even if he made it. An obvious truth of that sort must, I should think, have been discovered by Adam.'

'Adam couldn't have discovered it,' said Meldon. 'As long as he had a quiet conscience he did no work, and when he had to work his conscience was at him day and night.'

Major Kent allowed this to pass without contradiction.

'Besides,' said Meldon, 'I doubt very much whether Adam understood the use of tobacco. If he did I don't see how the secret could have died out. It was Sir Walter Raleigh, as well as I recollect, who brought—— Hullo! There's somebody hailing us.'

'*Spindrift* ahoy!'

The shout floated through the open skylight of the cabin while Meldon spoke.

'I wonder if that's Higginbotham back from Inishmore,' said Major Kent. 'I hope he hasn't brought a consumptive patient with him. If he has you may deal with him yourself, J. J. It's no affair of mine and I won't help.'

'I hope it's not Higginbotham; I don't feel in the mood for dealing with Higginbotham just now. It's as likely as not that he'd be unreasonable about the bacillus hunt.'

The hail was repeated: 'Ahoy there! *Spindrift* ahoy!'

'It can't be Higginbotham,' said Meldon. 'He always comes on board without hailing. It must be that new Member of Parliament off the steam yacht.'

'Let's lie low then and pretend we're not here.'

'Nonsense. Members of Parliament are often extremely amusing. We'll have him in and listen to him talking about the Irish problem. Get out the whisky, Major. These fellows all drink whisky when they come to this country, whether they actually like it or not. I'll fetch him on board.'

He went on deck and discovered to his surprise Sir Giles Buckley and Langton in the *Aureole's* punt alongside.

'Hullo!' he said. 'What brings you here? If it's a new throat halyard you want you may as well go straight back again. We haven't a rope to spare, and I warned you to be careful about the one you had.'

'The throat halyard is all right,' said Sir Giles. 'We haven't come about that. We want to have a little chat with you and your friend.'

He smiled as he spoke. Langton also smiled. It was evident that they had agreed together to be civil and agreeable.

'Very well,' said Meldon. 'Come on board if you like.'

His tone was not very cordial. Sir Giles evidently felt the necessity of making some sort of an apology before he accepted the invitation.

'I should like to explain,' he said, 'that I'm sorry for losing my temper with you in the cave this morning. I don't make any excuse for myself, of course, but——'

'It's all right,' said Meldon more graciously. 'In fact, I ought to apologise first. I played you rather a shabby trick with the punt this morning.'

'Oh, that was nothing. We didn't mind, did we, Langton?'

'Not a bit,' said Langton. 'We laughed.'

'Come below,' said Meldon, 'and have a drink.'

Sir Giles and Langton seated themselves at one side of the table in the *Spindrift's* cabin. Major Kent and Meldon faced them. A bottle of whisky and two syphons of soda-water stood on the table. Tumblers were filled and the ceremony of pledging each other duly performed. Then Sir Giles spoke:

'Langton and I were naturally disappointed this morning when we found that those chests in the cave were empty. I think I may take it for granted that you two gentlemen were disappointed too, though I'm bound to say you didn't show it.'

'You may take it that way for the sake of argument, if you like,' said Meldon cautiously. 'But I don't admit that we have any reason to be disappointed. It all depends on who emptied the chests.'

'Come now,' said Sir Giles. 'We quite understand that you don't want to give yourselves away. But we don't believe you have the treasure. In fact we're certain you haven't. I think it will pay you better in the long run to be straight with us. We're all of us out of it at present. What I've come to propose is this. Let us join forces and find the stuff wherever it is. I don't deny that Langton and I would rather keep it all to ourselves. So, no doubt, would you and your friend. But we'd rather go shares with you than lose it altogether. And that's what will happen if we spend our time chasing each other round and round this wretched little island as we've been doing for the last three days.'

'What do you propose to do?' said Meldon.

'First of all I would suggest that we table all the information we have about the treasure. We'll tell all we know and you'll tell all you know. To show you that we mean to play fair I don't mind speaking first.'

'Very well,' said Meldon. 'We agree to that. Go ahead with your story and I'll tell ours afterwards.'

'After my father's death,' said Sir Giles, 'I got the family place, house, furniture, and so forth, and precious little else. I gave orders to have the furniture sold and the lawyer sent me out a bundle of old papers. I wouldn't have bothered myself about the papers at all, only that just at the time they came I had nothing in the world to do. I don't mind owning that I was pretty well stony-broke just then and was stuck in a lodging in a dirty little French town. I read the papers. Among them was an old diary kept by my grandfather. It appears that he paid a visit to this island in 1798, and——'

'You needn't go into that,' said Meldon. 'We have papers ourselves which give us all the information your grandfather had. Major Kent's grandfather kept a log, as he called it, of that expedition. I expect that both the old gentlemen wrote down pretty much the same thing—all they knew about the matter.'

'I didn't think anything of it,' went on Sir Giles, 'until I happened to meet another stony-broke Englishman.'

'I'm an Irishman,' said Langton.

'It's all the same thing,' said Sir Giles.

'I beg your pardon,' said Langton. 'It's not the same thing at all.'

'Gentlemen,' said Meldon, 'if this conference is to go on it must be conducted on strictly non-political lines.'

'What!' said Sir Giles.

'My friend, Major Kent,' said Meldon, 'is a strong Unionist, and I can't allow him to be compromised by any political arguments of a Nationalist kind.'

Sir Giles gaped at him.

'I wasn't talking politics,' he said. 'I wasn't thinking about politics. As a matter of fact, I don't care a hang for any politics.'

'Langton was talking politics,' said Meldon, 'and you were arguing with him. He said he was an Irishman and you said he wasn't. Any one with any experience of this country knows where that sort of talk leads to. The Major can't be expected to stand it. He's a Unionist, one of the loyal and oppressed minority, and it isn't right to outrage his feelings by introducing politics into what ought to be a simple business discussion.'

Sir Giles checked what was evidently a strong impulse to curse.

'Go on with your story,' said Meldon. 'I'm sorry for having to interrupt, but do try and keep politics out of it. You were just telling us that you met Langton.'

'I met Langton,' said Sir Giles, 'who was also at the time stony-broke. We got yarning together, having nothing better to do. Naturally we talked a good deal about money, the thing both our minds were dwelling on, because we hadn't got any. I told Langton the story of my grandfather's diary and the Spanish treasure on Inishgowlan. It turned out that Langton had read somewhere——'

'In Trinity College Library,' said Langton, 'before I resigned my post there.'

'Resigned?' said Meldon with a grin.

'If politics are barred,' said Sir Giles, 'so are offensive remarks. I have agreed to respect Major Kent's feelings about the Union Jack, though I'm blest if I understand how they come in. You must not insult my friend Langton.'

'I apologise,' said Meldon. 'We'll be non-sectarian as well as non-political.'

'You tell this part, Langton,' said Sir Giles.

'There's not much to tell. While I was in the College Library I came across an old manuscript written in Spanish. It was a good deal mutilated—in fact there was neither beginning nor end to it. It appeared to be the log of one of the Armada captains. It began with an account of being shipwrecked on a small island off the west coast of Ireland. The island wasn't named, nor was the situation described, but he told how he and his crew left the island in two curraghs. Their own boats were, I suppose, destroyed. Before they went——'

'They hid the treasure,' said Meldon.

'Precisely. They couldn't take it in the curraghs. They meant to go back for it.'

'Did he mention the hole in Thomas O'Flaherty's field?'

'Yes.'

'I see. I could not understand how you got at that. This is most interesting. Go on.'

'There isn't much more to tell,' said Sir Giles. 'We put our stories together——'

'Oh, but I want to hear what happened to the Spaniard,' said Meldon.

'It doesn't matter about him. The log broke off abruptly, didn't it, Langton? What we did was, put our stories together. We made up our minds that the thing was good enough to try for. The sale of the furniture in Ballymoy House brought in some money. I sent Langton over to hire a small yacht. He knew nothing about boats, and you stuck him badly with your old *Aureole*.'

'I don't like that,' said Meldon. 'We agreed to be non-sectarian and you go introducing religion.'

'I only said you stuck him over the boat. There's nothing religious about that remark.'

'There is,' said Meldon. 'To stick a man is a form of swindling, and swindling is a distinct breach of one of the Ten Commandments. There isn't a sect of Christians in the world which doesn't profess to have more or less respect for the Ten Commandments, therefore your remark about sticking Langton over the boat is in the highest degree sectarian and a distinct infringement of the terms of our agreement.'

'I've knocked about a good deal in my day,' said Sir Giles, 'and I've met lots of queer people. In fact, I thought I'd met every kind of man there is in the world. But I'm hanged—"hanged" isn't swearing, it's only a form of emphasis—I'm hanged if I ever met quite as queer a fellow as you.'

'What do you propose to do now?' said the Major.

It was his first contribution to the discussion, and the other three men looked at him in surprise.

'Before going into that,' said Sir Giles, 'we'd like to hear what you know about the treasure. You've had our story. Let us hear yours.'

'We've no story,' said Meldon. 'We had the information in

Major Kent's grandfather's log, pretty much the same as what you got from your grandfather. That's all.'

Sir Giles and Langton looked at each other. Suspicion was in both their faces.

'We had nothing else to go on,' said Meldon.

'Then how did you find the cave?'

'By inductive reasoning,' said Meldon. 'By careful observation, and a proper use of what is called the scientific imagination.'

'If you won't be open and above-board with us,' said Sir Giles, 'there's no use our talking to you. It's neither fair nor honourable of you to keep a card up your sleeve in this way when we've laid all ours on the table.'

'I've got no card up my sleeve,' said Meldon. 'As a matter of fact, I don't play cards, so I wouldn't be likely to have one about me—up my sleeve or anywhere else. I haven't played cards since I left college, and even there I didn't cheat.'

'Do you expect us to believe that out of all possible places on this island where that treasure might have been hidden you lit on that cave straight off by accident?'

'I don't expect you to believe anything of the sort. What I said was, that I arrived at the cave by a process of reasoning. You may not be able to reason yourself, but there's no use denying that other people can.'

'Strikes me as a bit thick, that. What do you say, Langton?'

'It's a damned lie,' said Langton.

'Now, if I said a thing like that to either of you,' said Meldon, 'you'd lose your tempers and try to break my head with a stone. But I happen to have some self-control.'

'I believe,' said the Major to Meldon, with a broad grin, 'that this is the first time you've spoken the truth since we came to this island, and it's the only time you haven't been believed.'

'We may as well go,' said Sir Giles. 'There's nothing to be gained by standing here arguing with men who have no sense of honour or decency.'

Langton gulped down the remains of his whisky and water

and stood up. A sharp bump against the yacht's side shook him into his seat again.

'What the devil's that?' said Sir Giles.

'It must be Higginbotham,' said Major Kent. 'He always does that. He's come on board twice before, and each time he has rammed the yacht as if he were a torpedo specially paid to knock holes in the sides of ships.'

'I'll fetch him down,' said Meldon. 'Don't go yet, Sir Giles. You'll like Higginbotham when you meet him, I'm sure. He'll want to talk to you about tuberculosis. He's frightfully keen on every kind of consumption, and he's got it into his head that you're interested in the subject.'

He rose to go on deck. Before he succeeded in getting clear of the table Higginbotham descended rapidly, legs first, into the cabin. He was flushed, eager, and evidently in a condition of great nervous excitement.

'I've just got back,' he said. 'I came off at once—I haven't a minute to spare—to tell you that the *Granuaile* is in.'

'What is the *Granuaile*?' said Sir Giles.

'Oh, I beg your pardon. I didn't see that you were here, Sir Giles. I was going over to your yacht to tell you. I thought you'd like to know. It will be time enough to give my report later on, won't it? I can't stay now.'

'What's the *Granuaile*?' said Sir Giles. 'Let's get that first.'

'She's the C.D.B. yacht, and the——'

'For God's sake, man, don't talk alphabetical riddles. What's the A.B.C.?'

'C.D.B.,' said Meldon mildly, 'stands for Congested Districts Board. Mr Higginbotham is part of the C.D.B. He's the Board's representative on Inishgowlan.'

'The Chief Secretary is here,' said Higginbotham. 'I can't possibly stay. I'm expecting him up at my place every minute. I must be there to meet him. Goodbye. I suppose you'll come ashore soon and pay your respects. Goodbye for the present.'

He backed rapidly up the companion ladder and disappeared. A minute later there was a sound of scraping and another bump against the yacht's side.

'Am I to understand,' said Major Kent, 'that the Chief Secretary is on the island?'

'Apparently he is,' said Meldon. 'I wasn't expecting him, but now that he has turned up we must all try to make his stay as pleasant for him as possible.'

'Who is the Chief Secretary?' said Sir Giles. 'What is he Chief Secretary of? Is it that A.B.C. thing which the last lunatic talked about?'

'You've lived abroad,' said Meldon, 'or else you'd know that the Chief Secretary is the principal boss of the Government of this country. In fact, he *is* the Government. He's far and away a bigger man than the Lord-Lieutenant, although he doesn't wear such good clothes or look so ornamental. He varies, of course, from time to time according to circumstances, that is to say, according to whether the English people think they'd like a Conservative or a Liberal for Prime Minister. At present he's a man called Willoughby—the Right Honourable Eustace Willoughby, M.P. By the way, Major, I told you there was sure to be a Member of Parliament on that steam yacht. I turned out to be right, you see, in spite of your sneers. I don't happen to have met this Chief Secretary, but they tell me he's not a bad sort of man in private life. I shall look forward to having some quiet chats with him while he's here.'

'You won't get them,' said the Major, in a determined tone. 'I'm off at once.'

'Whatever he is, he has nothing to do with us,' said Sir Giles. 'We've got our own business to see to. Come now, Mr Meldon, before we go, you may as well tell us the truth about how you found that cave.'

'There's no use my repeating what I've said before. I've told you all we know about the matter. If you don't choose to believe me, don't believe me. I can't help it.'

Sir Giles scowled at him.

'Very well, Mr Parson, if you are a parson, which I doubt. We've offered to run this business in partnership with you and to go shares. It was a fair offer and you've refused it. You won't have me for your friend. You'll find me a nasty enemy to deal with. I tell you straight I mean to handle that treasure before I leave the island. Come along, Langton.'

Meldon went on deck with them, saw them into their punt, and waved a cheerful farewell as they rowed away. Sir Giles, who was rowing and faced the *Spindrift*, scowled in reply, and, to Meldon's intense delight, began to swear.

15

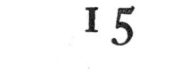

MAJOR KENT came on deck. He was agitated and showed signs of being in a hurry. Without speaking a word to Meldon he went to the end of the boom and began to unlace the cover of the mainsail. Meldon watched him take it off, roll it up, and stow it in the sail locker.

'What are you at now?' said Meldon.

'I'm going to get up sail and go home at once. I'll listen to no more talk from you, J. J. I've had too much of it already. My mind is made up. I'll not stay in this place another hour.'

'Why?'

'Why?' said the Major, who was casting loose the ties which bound the mainsail to the boom. 'Do you ask me why? Didn't you hear Higginbotham saying that the Chief Secretary is on the island. I'm not going to stay here to be made look like a fool over all the lies you've told. What could I say to the man if I met him?'

'Do you mean about the geological survey?'

'Yes I do. Of course I do. And about Sir Giles being a medical missionary or whatever the fool lie you told about him was. And about the National Board of Education building a school. Higginbotham is sure to tell him everything you've said.'

'You may make your mind quite easy so far as the school is concerned. That is no business of the Chief Secretary's. The Education Board is the one thing in the country that he has no control over. That came out in Parliament some time ago, as you ought to remember.'

'Well, what about the geological survey? You said I'd been sent here by the Chief Secretary and the Lord-Lieutenant. And what about Sir Giles and the tuberculosis?'

'Take one thing at a time, Major, like a good man, and don't confuse yourself. You're afraid he'll be angry because I said he sent you here to make a geological survey of the island. I assure you he won't even be surprised. You don't know these Cabinet Ministers, and of course it's hard for you to realise the life they lead. Now just listen to me. That man, Eustace Willoughby, spends his time mainly in receiving deputations. Hundreds and hundreds of deputations wait on him every week. There isn't a public body in the country, not so much as an Association of Licensed Publicans, which doesn't send two or three deputations to each Chief Secretary. I expect he's receiving one this moment, headed by Thomas O'Flaherty Pat. To every deputation he says something—something nice and sympathetic. He must, you know. That's how he earns his salary. Now I put it to you as a sensible man, can he possibly recollect all the things he's said to all the deputations? He can't, of course. You put a bold face on it. Speak to him civilly but without any show of timidity. Tell him that you went to him as part of a deputation from the Irish Incorporated Geological Surveyors' Institute, and that he sent you to this island. He won't know in the least what you're talking about, but he'll be afraid to give himself away by saying he doesn't remember. He'll believe what you say. He must.'

'I don't mean to give him the chance. I'm going home.'

'Well, if you funk it,' said Meldon, 'though I can't myself see what there is to be afraid of, I'll go on shore and talk to him. I'll settle the matter all right. You can trust me not to let you in for anything unpleasant.'

'I wouldn't trust you an inch. I've trusted you a great deal too much already, and look at the fix I'm in. I'm going straight home.'

'Think of the treasure.'

'I wouldn't give you the chance of talking to the Chief Secretary for £500 down. You'd make things worse than they are at present, if that's possible.'

'Do think of the treasure,' said Meldon persuasively.

'There's no treasure, or if there is, somebody else has got it. I tell you I wouldn't stay here to be ballyragged and bullied by a Chief Secretary for all the treasure in the world.'

'I'm not putting the matter before you in that selfish way at all. Do try to be a little altruistic, Major. I am speaking about the treasure from the point of view of public duty. Either Higginbotham or Thomas O'Flaherty Pat, probably the latter, has the treasure. But that scoundrel Sir Giles means to steal it. I could see it in his eye that he meant to, and so could you. Sir Giles, as you know, is a man who sticks at nothing. He wanted to murder me today with a stone. We're the only people on the island who are in a position to interfere with his abominable plans. If we go away he'll do poor old Thomas O'Flaherty out of his hard-earned gold. He'll rob Mary Kate of her inheritance, of the money that would make life brighter for her. I tell you, Major, I've got to be very fond of that little girl and I won't let the thing be done. Or, if it's Higginbotham that has the money, Sir Giles will go at night and cut Higginbotham's throat. You wouldn't like to think of poor Higginbotham lying all gory in a lonely grave in Inishgowlan, far from his family burying-place and the associations of his innocent youth. It'll be your fault, remember, if he does, because you won't stay here to protect him. I should think that Higginbotham's ghost, a most objectionable-looking spectre, will haunt you to the end of your life. And you'll richly deserve it.'

Major Kent made no answer. He loosed the halyard from the belaying pin at the foot of the mast.

'You're still determined,' said Meldon, 'after all I've said, to get up sail.'

'Yes; I'm going home.'

'You may get up sail but you'll not go home.'

'Why not?'

'Because there's no wind, as you could have seen for yourself long ago if you hadn't been off your head with nervousness. It may amuse you to hoist the sails and get up anchor, and then drift about, up and down the bay, till night-time. The only result will be that you'll go foul of the *Aureole* or the *Granuaile*. If that's what you want to do, I'll help you, of course; but I must say it seems to me a rotten way of spending the afternoon.'

Major Kent sat down on the deck and glared at Meldon.

'Why couldn't you have told me that before,' he said, 'instead of standing there and talking like a born fool?'

'I preferred,' said Meldon, 'to appeal to your higher nature first. I'd like to have seen you doing your plain duty voluntarily. There's very little credit in staying here simply because there's no wind to take you away.'

Major Kent smiled feebly.

'I give up,' he said. 'Say what you like to the Chief Secretary; make any muddle you can. You'll most likely land me in prison before you've done. You'll certainly have every newspaper in the three kingdoms making fun of us. I can't help it. I can do no more. I don't even mean to try.'

'You needn't; I'll manage all right. All you have to do is to keep cool and avoid fuss and excitement. Come on shore and let us interview the Chief Secretary at once. I expect we'll find him quite a reasonable man. After all, a fellow can't climb right up to the top of the tree, become a Chief Secretary, a Cabinet Minister, and all that sort of thing, without being more or less reasonable. As long as a man is reasonable it's always quite easy to get on with him. The people who kick up rows and make themselves unpleasant are the smaller kind, the men with prejudices and ridiculous conventional views. Willoughby must have knocked about a good deal in his day.

I know he's been ragged a lot by Suffragettes, and that shakes a man up. I expect we'll find him quite amusing.'

A boat pulled by two men with a coxswain in the stern left the pier and headed for the *Granuaile*. Major Kent saw her and pointed her out.

'Perhaps he's leaving at once,' he said; 'the yacht has steam up still.'

Meldon got the glasses and took a long look at the boat, following her in her course to the *Granuaile*.

'He's not in that boat,' he said. 'He wouldn't be pulling an oar himself. That wouldn't be suitable for a man in his position, and the fellow who's steering is evidently one of the yacht's officers. He has gold buttons on his coat. Besides, they'd be sure to fly a white ensign, or whistle "God Save the King", or make some kind of show if they had a Chief Secretary on board; whereas that's just a plain, ordinary boat.'

He laid down the glasses and looked at the pier.

'I see a stranger standing there with Higginbotham,' he said; 'a plump, little man in light grey clothes with a Panama hat. Give me the glasses again. He has a small, brown moustache and a thick, short nose. I can see him distinctly. It's certainly the Right Honourable Eustace Willoughby. I'd know him anywhere by his likeness to a cartoon there was of him in *Punch* a couple of weeks ago. I wonder, now, why the boat's going off and leaving him there?'

He shifted his position and looked at the *Granuaile* again.

'By Jove! The yacht's getting up anchor and hoisting the boat on the davits. She's off somewhere in the dickens of a hurry. But why have they left the Chief Secretary behind? What will he do? He can't surely mean to stop the night in Higginbotham's wigwam. There's only one bed, and I happen to know that it's full of broken glass. It was just underneath the pane I smashed this morning when I hove the oars in through the window. All the bits of glass went into the bed; I saw them. This is becoming serious. The *Granuaile* is certainly off. He must mean to sleep in Higginbotham's bed. He'll probably lose his temper if he does. No man likes being cut about the body with broken glass just as he's going off to sleep. I wouldn't like it myself, and I expect it would be perfect torture to a plump man like Willoughby. What had I better do?'

'I don't know,' said the Major. 'I dare say you're sorry now that there's no wind. I think if I were you I'd go ashore and try to slip round some back way and sweep out Higginbotham's bed before night.'

'I won't do that. I hate sneaking, underhand ways of doing things. Let us be gentlemen, Major, whatever else we are. We'll go ashore with our heads up. We've nothing to be ashamed of.'

'You may go by yourself. I won't. I'll stay on the yacht till there's breeze enough to take her out of this.'

'Very well, I'll go alone. After all, the man is a stranger here, and whether there's glass in his bed or not we ought to try and cheer him up. Higginbotham isn't very interesting. I'm sure he's boring Willoughby already. I expect the poor man is feeling a bit lonely too, seeing the *Granuaile* go off. By the way, I wonder where she's going to? She headed for the south point of the island, and that looks rather as if she meant to fetch Inishmore. I hope to goodness Higginbotham hasn't been talking about Sir Giles and the tuberculosis. I'd like to have a chance of making a good impression before I have to begin explaining that business. I wish Sir Giles hadn't gone off in a ridiculous huff. If we'd been friends I might have got him to stand over the tuberculosis and it would have been all right. The Chief Secretary couldn't well contradict a baronet, whatever he might think in his own mind. It isn't my fault Sir Giles took offence the way he did. I was telling him the literal truth. I couldn't start inventing a lot of lies just to please him.'

'I don't see why you couldn't. You've invented plenty the last few days.'

'I'm going on shore now,' said Meldon. 'I see Willoughby and Higginbotham strolling up together towards the hut. I don't suppose he's likely to go to bed at this hour of the afternoon, but in case of accidents I'll go at once.'

'The only thing you seem to mind about is that broken glass. It doesn't seem to me nearly so serious as the other things.'

'It isn't. Considered by itself, it isn't really serious at all. The thing is that Higginbotham won't know how it got there. He won't have any explanation to offer. The Chief Secretary, gashed and bleeding, will blame the wrong man. He'll think that Higginbotham has been playing off some new kind of apple-pie bed on him and he'll be upset about it. That will ruin Higginbotham's prospects in life. That's why I'm anxious about the bed. I must get off at once.'

'Go on,' said the Major, with a sigh. 'The Lord alone knows what you'll do when you get ashore. Things can't be much worse, anyway.'

'Don't be gloomy,' said Meldon, as he got into the punt. 'Just trust me a little. I'm not at the end of my resources yet, by any means. After all, what's a Chief Secretary? I suppose he's only flesh and blood like the rest of us. And besides, he's a migratory kind of bird. He's here today, and back in his native England tomorrow.'

Higginbotham, his face white with anxiety and distress, ran down the hill from his hut and greeted Meldon as he came alongside the pier.

'Meldon,' he said, 'I'm awfully sorry, but you'd better go back to the yacht at once. Don't come on shore. Like a good man, go back. I can't tell you how sorry I am about it all. He's frightfully angry.'

'Who's angry?' said Meldon, stepping ashore with the painter in his hand. 'Do try to be intelligible, Higginbotham, and don't speak till you've got your breath. I hate having things gasped out at me. Who's angry?'

'The Chief Secretary.'

'Has he gone to bed yet?'

'No, he hasn't. Why should he go to bed? He's up at my place sitting on a chair. I left him just for a moment when I saw you coming ashore. I ran down to warn you, in case you thought of coming up.'

'If he hasn't gone to bed,' said Meldon, 'I don't see that he's anything particular to be angry about.'

'It's about Major Kent and the geological survey of the island. He said he'd never heard of such a thing in his life. He said a most unwarrantable use had been made of his name. I can't tell you all he said. He called it intolerable insolence. I give you my word, Meldon, I wouldn't have mentioned the matter if I'd had the slightest idea that you were only pulling my leg. I really believed you. Why didn't you tell me?'

'If I'd told you I shouldn't have pulled your leg. What on earth would be the use of playing off a spoof on a man and at the same time telling him you were doing it? I wish you'd be reasonable, Higginbotham.'

'Fortunately I didn't mention the National School or Sir Giles Buckley. When I saw how things really were, I dried up at once. I'm more sorry than I can possibly tell you. Somehow I never thought——'

'That'll do,' said Meldon. 'Don't go on apologising. I don't blame you in the least. You acted in a perfectly natural way.'

Meldon stooped and made fast the painter of the punt.

'You're not coming ashore, are you?' said Higginbotham. 'Don't do it. Please don't. Go back to the yacht.'

'I'm going up to have a chat with the Chief Secretary,' said Meldon.

'But he won't speak to you, I know he won't. I tell you he's simply savage.'

'It's for your sake I'm going. I want to prevent your getting into trouble. I don't want to have your prospects blighted on account of any misunderstanding with the Chief Secretary.'

'But I'm not in any trouble. I assure you he doesn't blame me. He said so himself. It's only you he's angry with.'

'If he's not angry with you now, he very soon will be. As soon as ever he gets into bed he'll be wanting to tear you limb from limb, unless I go up and straighten things out.'

'But why? What has he to be angry with me about?'

'You'll find that out as soon as he gets into bed.'

Meldon began to walk towards the hut. Higginbotham's fears came back on him and rendered him almost inarticulate. He seized Meldon by the arm and tried to hold him forcibly. With actual tears in his eyes he entreated his friend to stop. He ejaculated unintelligible sentences about 'awful rows', 'legal proceedings', and 'public disgrace'. He even mentioned high treason.

'Don't be an ass,' said Meldon. 'I'm going up to talk sense to that Chief Secretary. If everybody else he comes across is as much afraid of him as you are, it's quite time that somebody that isn't took him in hand. Pull yourself together, Higginbotham, and come up with me. I want you to introduce me. It's awkward walking in on a man you've never met without an introduction.'

Higginbotham shook his head. After a last appeal he sat down helplessly on the grass. Meldon walked on towards the hut.

16

THE Chief Secretary lay back in Higginbotham's hammock-chair. There was a frown on his face. His sense of personal dignity was outraged by the story he had just heard. He had not been very long Chief Secretary of Ireland and, though not without a sense of humour, he took himself and his office very seriously. He came to Ireland intending to do justice and show mercy. He looked forward to a career of real usefulness. He was prepared to be opposed, maligned, misunderstood, declared capable of every kind of iniquity. He did not expect to be treated as a fool. He did not expect that an official in the pay of one of the Government Boards would assume as a matter of course that he was a fool and believe any story about him, however intrinsically absurd. He failed to imagine any motive for the telling of such a story. There must, he assumed, have been a motive, but what it was he could not even guess.

Meldon entered the hut without knocking at the door.

'Mr Willoughby, I believe,' he said cheerily. 'You must allow me to introduce myself since Higginbotham isn't here to do it for me. My name is Meldon—the Rev. J. J. Meldon, B.A., of T.C.D.'

The Chief Secretary intended to rise with dignity and walk out of the hut. He failed because no one can rise otherwise than awkwardly out of the depths of a hammock-chair.

'Don't stir,' said Meldon, watching his struggles. 'Please don't stir. I shouldn't dream of taking your chair. I'll sit on a corner of the table. I'll be quite comfortable, I assure you. How do you like Inishgowlan, now you are here? It's a nice little island, isn't it?'

Mr Willoughby succeeded in getting out of the chair. He walked across the hut, turned his back on Meldon, and stared out of the window.

'I came up here to have a chat with you,' said Meldon. 'Perhaps you wouldn't mind turning round. I always find it more convenient to talk to a man who isn't looking the other way. I don't make a point of it, of course. If you've got into the habit of keeping your back turned to people, I don't want you to alter it on my account.'

Mr Willoughby turned round. He seemed to be on the point of making an angry remark. Meldon faced him with a bland smile. The look of irritation faded in Mr Willoughby's face. He appeared puzzled.

'It's about Higginbotham's bed,' said Meldon, 'that I want to speak. It's an excellent bed, I believe, though I never slept in it myself. But——'

'If there's anything the matter with the bed,' said Mr

Willoughby severely, 'Mr Higginbotham should himself represent the facts to the proper authorities.'

'You quite misunderstand me. And in any case Higginbotham can't move in the matter because he doesn't, at present, know that there's anything wrong about the bed. By the time he finds out it will be too late to do anything. I simply want to give you a word of advice. Don't sleep in Higginbotham's bed tonight.'

'I haven't the slightest intention of sleeping in it.'

'That's all right. I'm glad you haven't. The fact is'—Meldon's voice sank almost to a whisper—'there happens to be a quantity of broken glass in that bed. I need scarcely tell a man with your experience of life that broken glass in a bed isn't a thing which suits everybody. It's all right, of course, if you're used to it, but I don't suppose you are.'

Mr Willoughby turned, this time towards the door. There was something in the ingenuous friendliness of Meldon's face which tempted him to smile. He caught sight of Higginbotham standing white and miserable on the threshold. He made a snatch at the dignity which had nearly escaped him and frowned severely.

'I think, Mr Higginbotham,' he said, 'that I should like to take a stroll round the island.'

'Come along,' said Meldon. 'I'll show you the sights. You don't mind climbing walls I hope. You'll find the place most interesting. Do you care about babies? There's a nice little beggar called Michael Pat. Any one with a taste for babies would take to him at once. And there's a little girl called Mary Kate, a great friend of Higginbotham's. She's the granddaughter of old Thomas O'Flaherty Pat. By the way, how are you going to manage about Thomas O'Flaherty's bit of land? There's been a lot of trouble over that.'

Mr Willoughby sat down again in the hammock-chair and stared at Meldon.

'Of course it's your affair, not mine,' said Meldon. 'Still, if I can be of any help to you, you've only got to say so. I know old O'Flaherty pretty well, and I may say without boasting that I have as much influence with him as any man on the island.'

'If I want your assistance I shall ask for it,' said Mr Willoughby coldly.

'That's right,' said Meldon. 'I'll do anything I can. The great difficulty, of course, is the language. You don't talk Irish yourself, I suppose. Higginbotham tells me he's learning. It's a very difficult language, highly inflected. I'm not very good at it myself. I can't carry on a regular business conversation in it. By the way, what is your opinion of the Gaelic League?'

A silence followed. Mr Willoughby gave no opinion of the Gaelic League. Meldon sat down again on the corner of the table and began to swing his legs. Higginbotham still stood in the doorway. Mr Willoughby, with a bewildered look on his face, lay back in the hammock-chair.

'I see,' said Meldon, 'that you've sent your yacht away. That was what made me think you were going to sleep in Higginbotham's bed. I suppose she'll be back before night.'

'Really——' began Mr Willoughby.

Meldon replied at once to the tone in which the word was spoken.

'I don't want to be asking questions. If there's any secret about the matter you're quite right to keep it to yourself. I quite understand that you Cabinet Ministers can't always say out everything that's in your mind. I only mentioned the steamer because the conversation seemed to be languishing. You wouldn't talk about Thomas O'Flaherty Pat's field, and you wouldn't talk about the Gaelic League, though I thought that would be sure to interest you. Now you won't talk about the steamer. However, it's quite easy to get on some other subject. Do you think the weather will hold up? The glass has been dropping the last two days.'

Mr Willoughby struggled out of the hammock-chair again. He drew himself up to his full height and squared his shoulders. His face assumed an expression of rigid determination. He addressed Higginbotham.

'Will you be so good as to go up to the old man you spoke of——'

'Thomas O'Flaherty Pat,' said Meldon. 'That's the man he means—you know, Higginbotham.'

'And tell him——' went on Mr Willoughby.

'If you're to tell him anything,' said Meldon, 'don't forget to take some one with you who understands Irish.'

'And tell him,' repeated Mr Willoughby, 'that I shall expect him here in about an hour to meet Father Mulcrone.'

'I see,' said Meldon. 'So that's where's the yacht's gone. You've sent for the priest to talk sense to the old boy. Well, I dare say you're right, though I think we could have managed with the help of Mary Kate. She knows both languages well, and she'd do anything for me, though she has rather a down on Higginbotham. It's a pity you didn't consult me before sending the steamer off all the way to Inishmore. However, it can't be helped now.'

Higginbotham departed on his errand and shut the door of the hut after him. The Chief Secretary turned to Meldon.

'You've chosen,' he said, 'to force your company on me this afternoon in a most unwarrantable manner.'

'I'll go at once if you like,' said Meldon. 'I only came up here for your own good, to warn you about the state of Higginbotham's bed. You ought to be more grateful to me than you are. It isn't every man who'd have taken the trouble to come all this way to save a total stranger from getting his legs cut with broken glass. However, if you hunt me away, of course I'll go. Only I think you'll be sorry afterwards if I do. I may say without vanity that I'm far and away the most amusing person on this island at present.'

'As you are here,' said Mr Willoughby, 'I take the opportunity of asking you what you mean by telling that outrageous story to Mr Higginbotham. I'm not accustomed to having my name used in that way and, to speak plainly, I regard it as insolence.'

'You are probably referring to the geological survey of this island.'

'Yes. To your assertion that I employed a man called Kent to survey this island. That is precisely what I do refer to.'

'Then you ought to have said so plainly at first, and not have left me to guess at what you were talking about. Many men couldn't have guessed, and then we should have been rambling about at cross purposes for the next hour or so without getting any further. Always try and say plainly what you mean, Mr Willoughby. I know it's difficult, but I think you'll find it pays in the end. Now that I know what's in your mind, I'll be very glad to thrash it out with you. You know Higginbotham, of course.'

'Yes.'

'Intimately?'

'I met him this afternoon for the first time.'

'Then you can't be said really to know Higginbotham. That's a pity, because without a close and intimate knowledge of Higginbotham you're not in a position to understand that geological survey story. Take my advice and drop the whole subject until you know Higginbotham better. After spending a few days on the island in constant intercourse with Higginbotham you'll be able to understand the whole thing. Then you'll appreciate it. In the meanwhile I'm sure you won't mind my adding, since we are on the subject—and it was you who introduced it—that you ought not to go leaping to conclusions without a proper knowledge of the facts. I said the same thing this morning to Major Kent when he insisted that you had come here to search for buried treasure.'

Mr Willoughby pulled himself together with an effort. He felt a sense of bewilderment and hopeless confusion. The sensation was familiar. He had experienced it before in the House of Commons when Irish Members of both parties asked questions on the same subject. He knew that his only chance was to ignore side-issues, however fascinating, and get back at once to the original point.

'I'm willing,' he said, 'to listen to any explanation you have to offer; but I do not see how Mr Higginbotham's character alters, or can alter, the fact that you told him what I can only describe as an outrageous lie.'

'The worst thing about you Englishmen is that you have such blunt minds. You don't appreciate the lights and shades, the finer nuances, what I may perhaps describe as the chiaroscuro of things. It's just the same with my friend Major Kent. By the way, I ought to apologise for him. He ought to have come ashore and called upon you this afternoon. It isn't the want of loyalty which prevented him. He's a strong Unionist, and on principle he respects his Majesty's Ministers whatever party they belong to. The fact is he was a bit nervous about this geological survey business. He didn't know exactly how you'd take it. I told him that you were a reasonable man and that you'd see the thing in a proper light, but he wouldn't come.'

'Will you kindly tell me what is the proper light in which to view this extraordinary performance of yours?'

'Certainly. It will be a little difficult, of course, when you don't know Higginbotham, but I'll try.'

'Leave Mr Higginbotham out,' said the Chief Secretary irritably. 'Tell me simply this, were you justified in making a statement which you knew to be a baseless invention? How do you explain the fact that you told a deliberate—that you didn't speak the truth?'

'I've always heard of you as an educated and cultured man. I may assume therefore that you know all about pragmatism.'

'I don't.'

'Well, you ought to. It's a most interesting system of philosophy quite worth your while to study. I'm sure you'd like it if you understood it. In fact, I expect you're a pragmatist already without knowing it. Most of us practical men are.'

'I'm waiting for an explanation of the story you told Mr Higginbotham.'

'Quite right. I'm coming to that in a minute. Don't be impatient. If you'd been familiar with the pragmatist philosophy it would have saved time. As you're not—though as Chief Secretary for Ireland I think you ought to be—I'll have to explain. Pragmatism may be described as the secularising of the Ritschlian system of theological thought. You understand the Ritschlian theory of value judgments, of course?'

'No, I don't.' Mr Willoughby began to feel very helpless. It seemed easier to let the tide of this strange lecture sweep over him than to make any effort to assert himself.

'Do you mind if I smoke?' he said. 'I think I could listen to your explanation better if I smoked.'

He took from his pocket a silver cigar-case.

'Smoke away,' said Meldon. 'I don't mind in the least. In fact I'll take a cigar from you and smoke too. I can't afford cigars myself, but I enjoy them when they're good. I suppose a Chief Secretary is pretty well bound to keep decent cigars on account of his position.'

Mr Willoughby handed over the case. Meldon selected a cigar and lit it. Then he went on—

'The central position of the pragmatist philosophy and the Ritschlian theology is that truth and usefulness are identical.'

'Eh?'

'What that means is this. A thing is true if it turns out in actual practice to be useful and false if it turns out in actual practice to be useless. I dare say that sounds startling to you at first, but if you think it over quietly for a while you'll get to see that there's a good deal in it.'

Meldon puffed at his cigar without speaking. He wished to give Mr Willoughby an opportunity for meditation. Then he went on—

'The usual illustration—the one you'll find in all the textbooks—is the old puzzle of the monkey on the tree. A man sees a monkey clinging to the far side of the trunk of the tree. I never could make out how he did see it, but that doesn't matter for the purposes of the illustration. He, the man, determines to go round the tree and get a better look of the monkey. But the monkey creeps round the tree so as always to keep the trunk between him and the man. The question is whether, when he's gone round the tree, the man has or has not gone round the monkey. The older philosophies simply gave that problem up. They couldn't solve it, but the pragmatist——'

'Either you or I,' said Mr Willoughby feebly, 'must be going mad.'

'Your cigar has gone out,' said Meldon. 'Don't light it again. There's nothing tastes worse than a relighted cigar. Take a fresh one. There are still two in the case, and I shall be able to manage along with one more.'

'Would you mind leaving out the monkey on the tree and getting back to the geological survey story?'

'Not a bit. If it bores you to hear an explanation of the pragmatist theory of truth I won't go on with it. It was only for your sake I went into it. You can just take it from me that the test of truth is usefulness. That's the general theory. Now apply it to this particular case. The story I told Higginbotham turned out to be extremely useful—quite as useful as I had any reason to expect. In fact, I don't see that we could have very well gone on without it. I can't explain to you just how it was useful. If I did, I should be giving away Major Kent, Sir Giles Buckley, Euseby Langton, and perhaps old Thomas O'Flaherty Pat; but you may take it that the utility of the story has been demonstrated.'

Mr Willoughby made an effort to rally. He reminded himself that he was a Cabinet Minister and a great man, that he had withstood the fieriest eloquence of Members for Munster constituencies and survived the most searching catechisms of the men from Antrim and Down. He called to mind the fact that he had resolutely said 'No' to at least twenty-five per cent. of the people who came to him in Dublin Castle seeking to have jobs perpetrated. He tried to realise the impossibility of a mere country curate talking him down. He hardened his heart with the recollection that he was in the right and the curate utterly in the wrong. He sat up as well as he could in the hammock-chair and said sternly—

'Am I to understand that you regard any lie as justifiable if it serves its purpose?'

'Certainly not,' said Meldon; 'you are missing the whole

point. I was afraid you would when you prevented me from explaining the theory of truth to you. I never justify lies under any circumstances whatever. The thing I'm trying to help you to grasp is this: a statement isn't a lie if it proves itself in actual practice to be useful—it's true. There now, you've let that second cigar go out. You'd better light that one again. I hate to see a man wasting cigar after cigar, especially when they're good ones.'

Mr Willoughby fumbled with the matches and made more than one attempt to relight the cigar.

'The reason,' Meldon went on, 'why I think you're almost certain to be a pragmatist is that you're a politician. You're constantly having to make speeches, of course; and in every speech you must more or less say something about Ireland. When you are Chief Secretary the other fellow, the man in opposition who wants to be Chief Secretary but isn't, gets up and says you are telling a pack of lies. That's not the way he expresses himself, but it's exactly what he means. When his turn comes to be Chief Secretary and you are in opposition, you very naturally say that he's telling lies. Now that's a very crude way of talking. You are, both of you, as patriotic and loyal men, doing your best to say what is really useful. If the things you say turn out in the end to be useful, why, then, if you happen to be pragmatists, they aren't lies.'

Mr Willoughby stuck doggedly to his point. Just so his countrymen, though beaten by all the rules of war, have from time to time clung to positions which they ought to have evacuated.

'A lie,' he said, 'is a lie. I don't see that you've made your case at all.'

'I know I haven't, but that's because you would insist on stopping me. If you'll allow me to go back to the man who went round the tree with the monkey on it——'

'Don't do that. I can't bear it.'

'Very well. I won't. I suppose we may consider the whole matter closed now and go on to talk of something else.'

'No. It's not closed,' said Mr Willoughby with a fine show

of spirited indignation. 'I still want to know why you told Mr Higginbotham that I sent Major Kent to make a geological survey of this island. It's all very well to talk as you've been doing, but a man is bound to tell the truth and not to deceive innocent people.'

'Look here, Mr Willoughby,' said Meldon, 'I've sat and listened to you calling me a liar half a dozen times, and I haven't turned a hair. I'm a man of remarkable self-control and I appreciate your point of view. You are irritated because you think that you are not being treated with proper respect. You assert what you are pleased to call your dignity by trying to prove that I'm a liar. I've stood it from you so far, but I'm not bound to stand it any longer and I won't. It doesn't suit you one bit to take up that high and mighty moral tone, and I may tell you that it doesn't impress me. I'm not the British public, and that bluff honesty pose isn't one I admire. All those platitudes about lies being lies simply run off my skin. I know that your own game of politics couldn't be played for a single hour without what you choose to describe as deceiving innocent people. Mind you, I'm not blaming you in the least. I quite give in that you can't always be blabbing out the exact literal truth about everything. Things couldn't go on if you did. All I say is, that being in the line of life you are, you ought not to set yourself up as a model of every kind of integrity and come out here to an island which, so far as I know, nobody ever invited you to visit, and talk ideal morality to me in the way you've been doing. Hullo! Here's Higginbotham back again. I wonder if he's brought Thomas O'Flaherty Pat with him. You'll be interested in seeing that old man, even if you can't speak to him.'

Higginbotham started as he entered the hut. He did not expect to find Meldon there. He was surprised to see Mr Willoughby crumpled-up, crushed, and cowed in the depths of the hammock-chair, while Meldon, cheerful and triumphant, sat on the edge of the table swinging his legs and smoking a cigar.

'You'd better get that oil stove of yours lit, Higginbotham,' said Meldon. 'The Chief Secretary is dying for a cup of tea. You'd like some tea, wouldn't you, Mr Willoughby?'

'I would. I feel as if I wanted tea. You won't say that I'm posing for the benefit of the British public if I drink tea, will you?'

It was Meldon who lit the stove and busied himself with the cups and saucers. Higginbotham was too much astonished to assist.

'There's no water in your kettle,' said Meldon. 'I'd better run across to the well and get some. Or I'll go to Michael Pat's mother and get some hot. That will save time. When I'm there I'll collar a loaf of soda-bread and some butter if I can. I happen to know that she has fresh butter because I helped to make it.'

Mr Willoughby rallied a little when the door closed behind Meldon.

'Your friend,' he said to Higginbotham, 'seems to me to be a most remarkable man.'

'He is. In college we always believed that if only he'd given his mind to it and taken some interest in his work, he could have done anything.'

'I haven't the slightest doubt of it. He has given me a talking to this afternoon such as I haven't had since I left school —not since I left the nursery. Did you ever read a book on pragmatism?'

'No.'

'You don't happen to know the name of the best book on the subject?'

'No, but I'm sure that Meldon——'

'Don't,' said Mr Willoughby. 'I'd rather not start him on the subject again. Have you any cigars? I want one badly. I got no good of the two I half-smoked while he was here.'

'I'm afraid not. But your own cigar-box has one in it. It's on the table.'

'I can't smoke that one. To put it plainly, I daren't. Your friend Meldon said he might want it. I'd be afraid to face him if it was gone.'

'But it's your own cigar! Why should Meldon——'

'It's not my cigar. Nothing in the world is mine any more, not even my mind or my morality or my self-respect is my own. Mr Meldon has taken them from me and torn them in pieces before my eyes. He has left me a nervous wreck of the man I once was. Did you say he was a parson?'

'Yes. He's curate of Ballymoy.'

'Thank God I don't live in that parish! I should be hypnotised into going to church every time he preached, and then—— Hush! Can he be coming back already? I believe he is. No other man would whistle so loud as that. If he begins to ill-treat me again, Mr Higginbotham, I hope you'll try and drag him off. I can't stand much more.'

17

MELDON flung open the door of the hut and entered. He at once took possession of the remaining cigar and lit it.

'I met Mary Kate,' he said, 'and I sent her on with the kettle. By the way, Mr Willoughby, have you such a thing as half a crown about you?'

The Chief Secretary plunged his hand into his pocket and brought out a number of coins, gold and silver.

'Take it all,' he said; 'I don't feel as if I should ever want money any more.'

'Thanks,' said Meldon. 'I'll take half a crown. It's for Mary Kate. As a rule I only give her sixpence at a time, but she'll naturally expect more when she's fetching water for a Chief Secretary's tea. Higginbotham generally gives her sugar-candy.'

Meldon's grin and the look of embarrassment on Higginbotham's face hinted to Mr Willoughby of a joke behind.

'I wish,' he said, 'you'd tell me about Mary Kate and the sugar-candy.'

'Oh, that story's hardly worth telling,' said Meldon. 'It was only that she nearly had the face ate off Higginbotham one afternoon.'

'She ate his face! But surely——'

'He wasn't trying to kiss her, if that's what you're thinking of. Higginbotham's not that kind of man at all. Besides, she's quite a little girl, though remarkably intelligent. No. There was some slight misunderstanding about some sugar-candy between her and Higginbotham. Both of them came to me and complained. I did what I could to set the matter right. You've not been troubled about it lately, have you, Higginbotham?'

'No; it's all right now.'

'Is that all I'm to be told?' said Mr Willoughby.

'There's really nothing more to tell, and besides I want, while I think of it, to warn Higginbotham about the condition of his bed. I happened to spill some broken glass and a few oars on to your bed this morning, Higginbotham. It doesn't really matter about the oars. You'd be sure to notice them as you got in, but you might not see the glass. What I advise you to do is to take the blankets and things outside the door and shake them well before you go to bed.'

'I don't suppose it would be any use my asking,' said Mr Willoughby; 'but I should greatly like to know how you came to strew Mr Higginbotham's bed with oars and broken glass.'

'I don't think it would interest you much,' said Meldon.

'I assure you it would. I can't even imagine circumstances under which it would be any temptation to me to put oars—of all things in the world—and broken bottles into another man's bed.'

'It wasn't broken bottles. It was a broken window-pane. The circumstances were these: this morning I wanted to conceal some oars——'

'From?'

'From their owners, and——'

'Oh, from their owners. I see. Stupid of me not to have guessed. Please go on.'

'From their owners, who would, or at all events might, have made a very bad use of the oars if they had been able to get at them. Very well. I naturally thought at once of Higginbotham's bed.'

'I don't see why you say "naturally". It doesn't seem to me at all a natural place to think of. I'm sure I should never have thought of it.'

'It doesn't much matter in this case what you would have thought. Higginbotham's bed was the place I thought of at once; and I am still of opinion, in spite of anything you say, that it was a good place. I couldn't open the window, so I smashed it. That's the whole story. I don't suppose it's as good a one as you expected. But you would have it.'

'It's better than I expected,' said Mr Willoughby, 'and I'm much obliged to you for telling me.'

There was a gentle tap at the door. Meldon jumped down from his seat on the table and took his cigar out of his mouth.

'That's Mary Kate, I expect, with the hot water.'

It was Mary Kate. She entered the room with a sheepish grin on her face. In one hand she carried a kettle of hot water, in the other hand a loaf of soda-bread. The kettle was a good deal the heavier burden of the two, and she had evidently carried it first in one hand and then in the other. Its handle had some flour on it. The bread was mottled with black off the kettle.

'That's a good girl,' said Meldon. 'Here's half a crown for you. How much money is that you have now altogether?'

'It's four shillings,' said Mary Kate.

'There,' said Meldon. 'I told you she was an intelligent child. Now listen to me, Mary Kate. The reason you're getting half a crown this time is that the gentleman over there in the chair is the Chief Secretary. Do you know what a Chief Secretary is?'

'I do not.'

'Well, I haven't time to explain it to you now; but if you come up here tomorrow to Mr Higginbotham he'll tell you all about the Chief Secretary. How's Michael Pat?'

Mary Kate grinned.

'If you're going to grin like that when I ask you questions,' said Meldon, 'you'd better go home.'

He pushed her gently from the room and shut the door.

'Now Higginbotham, put that kettle on your stove and bring it to the boil again. And you'd better take a note of your engagement with that child. It won't do for you to be out when she comes. Now for tea.'

'Mr Meldon,' said the Chief Secretary, 'I'd take it as a personal favour if you'd stay here and see me through the interview between Father Mulcrone and the old man who won't give up his land.'

'Certainly. You're not expecting any sort of a fight, are you? If you are, I'd better go and borrow a stick somewhere.'

'Oh, no. Nothing of that sort. It's only that the priest got rather the better of me yesterday. He made me promise what will cost the Government a thousand pounds and he'll probably want to get as much more out of me this afternoon.'

'That'll be all right,' said Meldon. 'You leave it to me. Give me a free hand, that's all I ask. I'll manage him for you.'

'Thank you,' said the Chief Secretary; 'he's a persistent man, but if anybody can get the better of him I'm sure you can.'

'I suppose,' said Meldon, 'it was either a pier or seed potatoes he wanted the money for. Probably seed potatoes. The place must be rotten with piers already.'

'He wanted both,' said Mr Willoughby. 'It was the potatoes I promised.'

'Well, I'll get out of that if I can. But don't count on it. I may not be able to manage.'

Mr Willoughby looked rather doubtfully at the loaf of bread with the smears of kettle-black which Mary Kate's fingers left on it. He was not reassured by the way in which Meldon cut it up. The plan was simple. Grasping the loaf firmly, he sliced off long strips. These he laid one by one flat along the palm of his hand and held them in position by pressing his thumb into the corners. Then he drew a buttery knife across them. Higginbotham laid out his two cups and his slop bowl. They were quite clean. Meldon's hands were not. When tea was over Meldon suggested that they should smoke.

'I'm sorry,' said Mr Willoughby, 'that I've no more cigars with me. The rest of my supply is on board the *Granuaile*.'

'Higginbotham,' said Meldon, 'stick your head outside the door and see if the steamer is coming into the bay yet. You must try a fill of my baccy, Mr Willoughby. I'm sure Higginbotham will have a spare pipe.'

He pulled a lump of black twist tobacco out of his trousers pocket and handed it to the Chief Secretary. Then he rose and began to search for a pipe. Mr Willoughby eyed the tobacco, turning it over and over in his hand. Higginbotham returned with the news that the *Granuaile* had just appeared round the south point of the bay.

'I fear,' said Mr Willoughby, 'that this tobacco is too strong for me. I think that as the *Granuaile* is so near I'll wait until I can get some more of my own cigars.'

'All right,' said Meldon. 'I'll have a pipe. I'll step down to the pier as soon as I have it lighted and be ready to meet Father Mulcrone. I'll send the boat back for the cigars. In the meanwhile, Higginbotham, you'd better go and collar Thomas O'Flaherty Pat.'

'He promised to come here,' said Higginbotham, 'as soon as ever the *Granuaile* dropped anchor.'

'Don't you rely too much on his promises,' said Meldon. 'That old boy has taken you in once or twice already. You can't believe a word these people say,' he explained to Mr Willoughby. 'Even Mary Kate would lie to you if she stood to gain anything by it. They simply don't know what truth is.'

'Are they pragmatists?' asked Mr Willoughby.

'No; they're not,' said Meldon severely. 'If you had listened to me when I was explaining to you what pragmatism is, you'd know that these people aren't pragmatists. I can't go into the whole question again now, but I'll just say this much: the pragmatists, according to their own idea, know what truth is. And what's more, they're the only people in the world who do. Now what I said about Thomas O'Flaherty Pat and Mary Kate is that they don't know; therefore they can't be pragmatists. That ought to be fairly obvious. I'm off now to meet Father Mulcrone. Goodbye.'

'Mr Higginbotham,' said the Chief Secretary, 'did you follow that reasoning about the pragmatists and Mary Kate?'

'No—not quite. But I didn't take up ethics in College. Meldon did.'

'Did you watch him cut the bread-and-butter for tea?'

'I did. I was sorry he insisted on cutting it. His hands were—— But he's a really good sort at bottom, though he has his peculiarities. I've known him for years.'

'It must have been a great privilege. Did you see the bit of tobacco he offered me?'

'No; was there anything wrong with it?'

'He took it out of his trousers pocket,' said Mr Willoughby, 'and it was quite warm. Mr Meldon is certainly a very remarkable man. I wonder how he'll get on with Father Mulcrone. I wonder will he succeed in capturing all my cigars.'

The *Granuaile's* boat, with Father Mulcrone seated in the stern, approached the pier. Meldon hailed her. The priest, a plump man, with a weather-beaten face and small, keen grey eyes, waved his hand in response.

'Delighted to see you,' said Meldon, as the boat touched the pier and the priest stepped ashore. 'I have heard a good deal about you. My name is Meldon—J. J. Meldon. I'm acting with the Chief Secretary here and he asked me to meet you.'

'How do you do? How do you do?' said the priest.

'Quite well. I needn't ask how you are. Flowers in May are nothing to you in the matter of bloom of appearance.'

Father Mulcrone seemed a little surprised at this warm compliment.

'What does the Chief Secretary want with me now?'

'We'll come to that in a minute. First of all I want to know is there nothing else that would do you except a pier?'

'A pier!'

'Well, seed potatoes, then. I forget for the moment which it was.'

'The season's very backward, very backward indeed,' said the priest, 'and the poor people will be badly off next spring. Unless we get some help from the Government there'll be starvation in our midst.'

'Have you a Board of Guardians on the island?'

'We have not. And I wouldn't say but we're as well without one.'

'I dare say you're right,' said Meldon. 'But about those seed potatoes. The thing for you to do is to get the nearest Board of Guardians to pass a good strong resolution.'

'That might be done.'

'Tell them to put something in about the representatives of the people and the inalienable rights of the tillers of the soil.'

'They'll do that whether I ask them or not.'

'Get that resolution forwarded to the Local Government Board in Dublin. Then wait three weeks.'

'What for?'

'Oh, it's the usual thing. If these things aren't done properly the Chief Secretary can't act, simply can't. Then send a deputation to wait on the President of the Board. You understand me?'

'I do, of course.'

'It'll be as well if you could spare the time to go up with the deputation yourself. Lay the matter before them in temperate language—strong but temperate. Then you'll see what'll happen about the seed potatoes.'

Father Mulcrone winked at Meldon.

'Do you take me for a born fool,' he said, 'that you're talking that way to me?'

'As you've asked me the question straight, I may as well say that I don't take you for anything of the sort. I knew the kind of man you were the minute I set eyes on you. But I promised the Chief Secretary that I'd try and do you out of those seed potatoes if I could.'

'So you thought you'd get him off if you persuaded me to have a lot of resolutions passed and go on a deputation.'

'I did think that, and what's more I think it still. But you wouldn't fall in with the plan.'

'I would not.'

'Very well, then. We'll pass on, as they say, to the next business. There's an old fellow on this island called Thomas O'Flaherty Pat.'

'I know him well,' said the priest.

'Well, you'll hardly believe it, but that old fellow is holding out against the entire Congested District Board. He won't give up his wretched little house and the bit of land round it, hardly big enough to sod a lark, and it with a hole in the middle that would swallow a heifer.'

'I'll talk to him,' said the priest.

'I thought you would. That's the reason I sent for you. Come along. We have him set out waiting for you. At least I told Higginbotham to go and get him.'

Taking Father Mulcrone's arm he walked up towards the hut.

'I almost forgot to tell you,' he said, 'that the great difficulty about old O'Flaherty is that he can't talk English.'

'He'll talk it quick enough when I get at him.'

'I just thought he would.'

'For the matter of that I'm not sure that I wouldn't as soon sort him in Irish.'

'Just as you like, of course,' said Meldon. 'It's all the same to us, so long as you bring him to his senses.'

'What right has a man like him to be thwarting the excellent intentions of the Board?'

'None,' said Meldon; 'and poor Higginbotham, who's brimful of the most excellent intentions you can possibly imagine, is nearly heart-broken about it. You'd be sorry for Higginbotham if you saw him; he's growing thin.'

'I have seen him,' said the priest, 'if he's the inspector the

Board sent out. He was over at Inishmore this morning, just after the yacht left, looking out to see which of the people had consumption.'

They reached the hut and found Mr Willoughby seated in the hammock-chair. Higginbotham was absent in pursuit of the reluctant Thomas O'Flaherty Pat. Mr Willoughby rose at once and offered the chair to the priest.

'No, thank you; no, thank you,' said Father Mulcrone. 'If I sat down in the like of that chair I'd never get out. I'm a heavy man.'

'Father Mulcrone and I will sit on the bed,' said Meldon. 'Oh, it's all right, Mr Willoughby. I'll move the oars and give the quilt a shake. I don't want to set Father Mulcrone down on a pile of broken glass. I've more respect for him than to do that.'

He took the quilt outside the hut and flapped it vigorously up and down.

'I see Higginbotham and the old man coming down the hill together,' he said. 'There's quite a little crowd after them, but we needn't let anybody in unless we like. By the way, Mr Willoughby, Father Mulcrone and I had a chat on the way up from the pier about those seed potatoes. He can't do without them. It's a case of potatoes or coffins for the people on those islands next spring.'

'I feared so,' said Mr Willoughby with a sigh; 'but I'm sure you did your best.'

Higginbotham with Thomas O'Flaherty Pat, a dignified captive, entered the hut. The old man took off his hat and bowed courteously to the men in front of him. He held himself erect. His fine eyes wandered gravely round the hut. His face expressed neither curiosity nor obsequiousness. Mr Willoughby was a gentleman, accustomed to the society of titled hostesses and the manners of exclusive London clubs. Higginbotham could behave gracefully at surburban tennis parties. Meldon and Father Mulcrone were strong and self-assertive men. Thomas O'Flaherty Pat looked and behaved in this company like a genuine aristocrat. He waited for what was to be said to him with an air of courteous aloofness. He appeared fully conscious of a certain superiority in himself, a superiority so self-evident as to require neither assertion nor emphasis.

'You are Mr Thomas O'Flaherty, I think,' said Mr Willoughby.

'Ní beurla agam,' said the old man, bowing again.

Then Father Mulcrone began. He spoke in Irish, rapidly and at some length. Thomas O'Flaherty Pat replied in a few calm words. The priest spoke again, raising his voice indignantly. Again he received only the briefest of answers. A torrent of words followed from the priest. Father Mulcrone had made no idle boast when he said that he could deal with the old man in Irish. He never paused for an instant, never hesitated for a word. Thomas O'Flaherty was moved to quite a long reply. The priest interrupted him frequently, but the old man showed no sign of excitement and spoke all the time with gentle courtesy. When he stopped Father Mulcrone rose from the bed and spoke with unabated volubility. He gesticulated violently, waving his arms and bringing the palms of his hands together with loud smacks. For half an hour the dispute continued, heated argument on the one side, dignified reply on the other. At last Thomas O'Flaherty Pat shrugged his shoulders with a gesture of despair.

'I have him persuaded at last,' said Father Mulcrone, wiping his brow with the back of his hand, 'but I had a tough job of it. A more obstinate man I never met in all my born days.'

'I thought you'd get him in the end,' said Meldon. 'I couldn't understand a word you were saying, of course, but the way you said it made me feel that the poor old fellow hadn't half a chance.'

'If you have the papers ready tomorrow morning,' said Father Mulcrone to Higginbotham, 'I'll see that he signs them.'

'We're all greatly obliged to you,' said Meldon. 'Without your help I really don't know what we should have done.'

'As Mr Meldon says,' added the Chief Secretary, 'we're greatly obliged to you. And now, gentlemen, I hope you'll come and dine with me on the *Granuaile*. I can offer you a small cabin for the night, Father Mulcrone. It's too late to go back to Inishmore.'

'Thanks,' said Meldon. 'We'll go, of course. What do you say, Father Mulcrone? I'm only sorry the Major won't be with us.'

'The Major!' said Mr Willoughby. 'Oh, yes; Major Kent, of course, the geological expert. Go and fetch him, Mr Meldon. I shall be delighted to see him.'

'He wouldn't come if I did,' said Meldon. 'Apart altogether from the survey business he wouldn't come. Nothing would induce him to dine out without a dress-coat, and he hasn't got one on the yacht. That's the kind of man he is. In any case I don't want to go back to the yacht to ask him. There's a breeze getting up now and if the Major got me on board he'd want to up anchor and run home.'

Meldon took possession of the Chief Secretary and led the way to the pier. He looked up at the sky and sniffed the air suspiciously.

'There's a change coming,' he said. 'It will be blowing hard before morning.'

'Which of the two yachts is yours?' asked Mr Willoughby.

'Do you mean which of the two actually belongs to me, or do you mean which do I happen to be cruising in at present?'

'That, said Mr Willoughby, 'sounds like another riddle. Does it by any chance illustrate the pragmatist philosophy?'

'It might, if properly worked out. But I'm too hungry to attempt that now. About those yachts—the one to the south is Major Kent's *Spindrift*. I'm with him for this cruise. The other is my *Aureole*. I've hired her to Sir Giles Buckley. I see him and his friend Euseby Langton coming ashore now in their punt. By Jove! That reminds me. Higginbotham!'

He stood still suddenly. The Chief Secretary also halted. His face expressed patient expectation and a determination not to be surprised. Higginbotham and Father Mulcrone overtook them.

'Higginbotham,' said Meldon, 'did you lock the door of your hut?'

'No I didn't. I locked it this morning when I went——'

'And you found your bed full of oars and broken glass,' said Mr Willoughby. 'I think you're right to leave the door open this time.'

'When I tell you,' said Meldon, 'that Sir Giles is coming ashore in his punt and that he went down the hole in Thomas O'Flaherty's field this morning, perhaps you will go back and lock your door.'

'I will, if you like, but I don't know what you mean.'

'If you don't understand what I'm telling you,' said Meldon, 'you needn't bother about the door; but in that case Thomas O'Flaherty Pat ought certainly to be warned.'

'I thought when I first heard of you,' said Mr Willoughby, 'that you were an impudent liar. Next I decided that you were a lunatic. Then I made sure you were a man of unusual force of character and mental agility. Now I'm getting puzzled about you again.'

'Don't bother about me,' said Meldon. 'I'm sorry for Thomas O'Flaherty Pat, that's all. It makes me a bit nervous to see Sir Giles coming ashore in the dusk of the evening.'

'Who is Sir Giles?' asked Mr Willoughby.

'He's rather a hot lot. In fact, he's a bit of a lad. He'd'—Meldon paused and looked meaningly at the priest, then he whistled—'as soon as drink a pint of porter. You know what I mean, Father Mulcrone.'

'I do,' said the priest; 'I do well.'

'I don't,' said Mr Willoughby. 'I wish you'd explain. Do you know, Mr Higginbotham?'

'I do a little,' said Higginbotham. 'That's to say, I more or less guess.'

'I suppose,' said Mr Willoughby plaintively, 'that it's better for me not to know. I am a mere child compared to you two reverend gentlemen. I ought to be grateful to you for respecting my innocence and for not speaking more plainly than you do.'

A boat from the *Granuaile* lay alongside the pier. The party embarked just as Sir Giles Buckley's punt reached the shore.

'Good-evening, Sir Giles,' said Meldon. 'Surely you're not going down that hole again tonight.'

Sir Giles scowled in reply.

'That gentleman doesn't seem to be on very good terms with you,' said Mr Willoughby.

'He's not just at present,' said Meldon. 'I had a conversation with him this afternoon. He chose to assume that I wasn't speaking the truth, and he hasn't got over it since.'

'I have a certain sympathy with him,' said Mr Willoughby. 'I dare say he knows little or nothing about pragmatism. I went very near getting angry myself when I thought—just for the moment—that you had been deceiving Mr Higginbotham.'

'You got over it all right,' said Meldon. 'Nobody minds a man flaring out now and then as you did. You don't keep on sulking like that beast Sir Giles. You are a more or less reasonable man.'

18

ON board the *Granuaile* Mr Willoughby showed himself a courteous host. He took Father Mulcrone to a cabin and offered to provide him with anything he wanted. But the priest, having foreseen that he would sleep elsewhere than in his own bed, had with him a small bag which contained all that he required. Higginbotham and Meldon were put into another cabin. The party assembled in the saloon and dinner was served.

'You do yourself pretty well on this boat,' said Meldon as he tasted the soup. 'The Major and I have been living principally on sardines and tinned brawn. Higginbotham gets a lobster now and then. I suppose you have more lobsters than you care about in the course of the summer, Father Mulcrone?'

'I get plenty,' said the priest. 'Lobsters, potatoes, and tea. They're the easiest things to get on Inishmore.'

After this the conversation languished. Mr Willoughby was disappointed. He expected an amusing dinner. He found himself obliged to talk on dull subjects to Higginbotham, who was too much overawed by the company of a Chief Secretary to do more than make respectful replies. Meldon said a word in praise of each dish he tasted, and Father Mulcrone supplemented what he said in the manner of a man who seconds a vote of thanks. Otherwise, neither of the two clergymen talked. They were both hungry. They were both accustomed to take their meals alone. They both regarded the eating of a good dinner as a serious business, demanding undivided attention. Mr Willoughby, tired of Higginbotham, undertook a monologue and kept it going quietly until dinner was over and cigars were lit.

Then Father Mulcrone told a story. Meldon capped it with another. Father Mulcrone replied with a better one. Meldon outwent it. The stories became more and more extravagant. Mr Willoughby looked from one clergyman to the other and laughed heartily. Higginbotham giggled convulsively in a corner. Neither of the clergymen even smiled. With perfectly grave faces, in tones which would have suited a scientific lecture, they narrated absurdity after absurdity. It was Meldon who reached the climax, who told a story so monstrously improbable that Father Mulcrone gave up the attempt to better it.

'For a young man,' said the priest, 'and I wouldn't say you were more than seven-and-twenty——'

'I'll be that in three weeks, if I live so long,' said Meldon.

'You've a deal of experience of this country and the ways of the people.'

'For the matter of that you've seen a thing or two yourself.'

'I have; but when I was your age I didn't know the half of what you do.'

It was a handsome tribute. Meldon appreciated it. He raised his glass of whisky and water, nodded to Father Mulcrone and said—

'May the devil fly away with the roof of the house where you and I aren't welcome.'

'I consider myself fortunate,' said Mr Willoughby, 'in having as my guests tonight two men with the knowledge of Ireland which you possess. I'm learning more from your conversation than from all the Blue Books I ever read.'

'I think we may understand from that remark,' said Father Mulcrone, 'that there's no danger of the slates being taken off the Lodge in the Phœnix while you're in it.'

'You'll be welcome there, either of you,' said Mr Willoughby, 'while I hold office. You'll be all the more welcome if you come together.'

'We'll do it,' said Meldon.

'What are the authorities of your Churches thinking of,' said Mr Willoughby, 'when they leave you a curate, Mr Meldon, and you no more than a parish priest, Father Mulcrone?'

'I'd be well off if I was that itself. It's a C.C. I am, and so far as I know it's a C.C. I'm likely to remain.'

'You ought,' said Mr Willoughby, 'to be bishops at least, both of you. If I had the arranging of these things you'd be archbishops. Why aren't you?'

'I haven't reached the canonical age,' said Meldon. 'You can't be a bishop till you're thirty. I've three years more to wait.'

'I went very near being a bishop once,' said Father Mulcrone, 'and it's my sincere hope I'll never be as near it again. It wasn't in this diocese, but another, and I won't tell you where for fear of an action for libel. The old man that was the bishop died. The night after they buried him I happened to be going along the road in the dark. It might have been ten o'clock or half-past. Who did I see coming along towards me but the dead man, dressed up in his robes, and his episcopal ring on his thumb. When he caught sight of me he took off the ring and held it out to me as much as to say, 'It's yourself, Father Mulcrone, that's to succeed me.' I was pleased, I can tell you. I stuck out my thumb for him to put the ring on, seeing that was what he seemed to be wanting to do. Would you believe it, gentlemen? The ring was red hot!'

'And is that,' said Meldon, 'the place bishops go to when they're dead?'

'It's the only place ever I heard of,' said Father Mulcrone, 'where a ring could get into such a state as that.'

'On the whole, then, I think I'll stick to my curacy. It's safer.'

'You're right. It's what I've done myself.'

There was a silence for a minute or two, broken only by half-suppressed sniggers from Higginbotham. Then Meldon rose with a sigh.

'You have me beat, Father Mulcrone. I give in to you. The equal of the experience you've just narrated never came my way. I think I'll be saying good-night, Mr Willoughby. If you'll send a boat to the pier with me and Higginbotham, I'll get my punt there and go off to the *Spindrift*.'

The *Granuaile's* boat landed Meldon and Higginbotham at about eleven o'clock. A change in the weather was certainly coming. Great masses of clouds were piled up over the western half of the sky. Broken fragments, the advance guard of their army, rushed eastwards. The little wind there had been earlier in the afternoon was gone. The air was ominously still. From the far side of the island came the roar of waves. The sea was dashing sullenly against the rocks and dragging at the stones on the beaches. Not yet lashed by the storm, it already felt a premonition of the storm's coming. Even the water in the sheltered bay was affected with a vague uneasiness. Dark lumps rose here and there on its surface and sank again. Silent surges crept unexpectedly up the smooth sides of the pier, mouthing at the stones, slipping down again unsatisfied, eddying in hungry circles.

Meldon looked round him uncomfortably.

'I'll take the punt on board tonight,' he said, 'and I'll pay out a few extra fathoms of anchor chain. There'll be a blow before morning. If I were you, Higginbotham, I'd stuff an old towel or something into that broken window. It's going to rain and rain heavy. Good-night.'

'Good-night. What a pleasant man Mr Willoughby is! I am so glad there was no trouble between you and him. Good-night.'

Meldon struck a match and lit his pipe. Then he stooped down to loose the painter of the punt. As he did so he heard footsteps on the granite surface of the pier. The footsteps of some one who approached him. He supposed that Higginbotham had returned again to say some forgotten word. With the rope he had cast loose in his hand he stood and waited. It was not Higginbotham who approached. Whoever it was stopped about ten yards away from him. Meldon could dimly discern the figure of a man much taller than Higginbotham. A voice, raised very little above a whisper, reached him—

'Master.'

Meldon stooped and refastened the painter. He heard the voice again but did not recognise it.

'Master.'

He approached the tall figure, peering eagerly through the darkness.

'I'm blessed,' he said, 'if it isn't old Thomas O'Flaherty Pat! So you've got one word of English, have you? Maybe now if you searched in the corner of your mind you might find a little more.'

'I have plenty,' said the old man. 'There's few have more English nor better English than myself.'

'I always thought you had,' said Meldon. 'I'd have laid long odds on it if I'd been a betting man, which, of course, I'm not. Now what is it you want?'

'It's yourself, Master.'

'Is it, then? And what would you do with me supposing you had me? Tell me that. Is it wanting me to speak a word for you to the Chief Secretary you are, to get back your house and land?'

'It is not.'

'If it is, I'll do it, of course; but I tell you straight that it won't be the smallest bit of use. The whole might of the British Empire is against you. They'll get your land out of you if they have to send a man-of-war round to do it. Besides, you know, you gave yourself away badly in that interview with Father Mulcrone today. I don't blame you. I knew very well you were done for when they fetched the priest to you. It was a mean trick, that. No real sportsman would have done it. It was a sort of sitting shot. You didn't have the ghost of a chance. Now if you'd been treated fairly and left to worry it out with nobody but Mary Kate to come between you and the Board, you might have kept them arguing till either they or you were dead.'

'It isn't wanting you to speak for me I am. Neither to himself, nor his reverence, nor to any other man.'

'Is it a writing, then?'

'It is not.'

'Well, I'm glad to hear that any way, for I haven't brought my fountain pen with me on this cruise, and I'm thinking it's poorly I'd write with any pen and ink that you are likely to have. But if it isn't to speak nor yet to write I don't quite see what it is you do want.'

'It's yourself.'

'That's all very fine. I owe you a good turn for giving me that crab, and I admire the plucky way in which you've stood up to Higginbotham and the Board, but I'm not going to hand myself over body and soul to a man I've only known for three days without finding out what he wants me for. Has anything gone wrong with Mary Kate or Michael Pat?'

'I'd be thankful to you if you'd step up to my little houseen, the place that they're going to take from me.'

'What for?' said Meldon. 'I declare to goodness it's very

near as hard to make out what you want now you're talking English as it was before.'

'There's that there that I'd be glad to show you. Maybe you'd tell me what would be the best to be done. It's what I never expected to show to any man, let alone a stranger like yourself. But my mind's made up, and I'll show it to you.'

Meldon gripped the old man by the arm.

'Is it the treasure you have hid there?'

'Treasure?'

'Treasure; yes. Gold. Do you understand? Is it gold you have up in your house?'

'It might, then.'

'Is there much of it? How much is there?'

'There's a power. Glory be to God, there's a mighty deal of it! More, maybe, then ever you saw in one place together in all your life.'

'Come on, then,' said Meldon. 'Let me set eyes on it. I dare say you guessed—I always said you weren't such a fool as you tried to make out to Higginbotham—I dare say you guessed that the Major and I were after that treasure ourselves.'

'I did.'

'I thought you did. And the gentlemen from the other yacht were after it too. You guessed that, I suppose?'

'Didn't I see them going down the Poll-na-phuca? What else would the likes of them be after in such a place?'

'Well, I'll say this. If I wasn't to get it myself, I'd sooner you had it than another. I hope you'll make a good use of it and not be wasting it on drink and foolishness. Give Mary Kate a good fortune when the time comes and marry her to a decent man.'

'Sure, what's the use of talking?' said the old man in a tone of despair. 'It'll be took from me along with the house. The Board will take it and never a penny will the little lady be the better of it, no more than myself or any other one.'

'Maybe they won't get taking it,' said Meldon, 'though indeed for all the good you're getting out of it at present they might as well. I don't see that it's any use to you if you don't so much as buy yourself a decent suit of clothes and spend sixpence on getting your hair cut. It's a shame for a rich man like you to be going about the way you are.'

'What good would grand clothes be to the likes of me?'

'I'm beginning to understand things a bit,' said Meldon, whose thoughts had passed away from the use to be made of the money. 'I see the reason now why you wouldn't give up the house and land to Higginbotham. You're certainly no fool. That dodge of yours, pretending you couldn't speak a word of any language except Irish was uncommonly nippy. I doubt if I could have hit on anything better myself, and I've had some experience in disguises. Only for the priest you might have kept them all at bay. I don't see what they could have done to you, even if they took to asking questions in Parliament.'

'What was the good? They have it taken off me now at the latter end.'

'They have the house and land,' said Meldon. 'There's no doubt of that. But I wouldn't say they have the treasure yet. You came to the right man when you came to me. If that treasure can be saved, I'll save it. What would you say now if we carried it down tonight to Mrs O'Flaherty's, Michael Pat's mother, and hid it under the old woman's bed?'

'I wouldn't trust her. She'd steal it on me.'

'I don't believe she would. Not if you gave her a bit for herself and bought a silver mug or something for Michael Pat. But if you don't like the notion of her, what about Mary Kate's mother? She's your own daughter.'

'She'd steal it on me as quick as another.'

'Would she, then? I declare to goodness you have a pretty low opinion of your relatives and friends. I don't believe they'd touch a penny of it. Have you any plan in your own head?'

'Let you be coming up and taking a look at it.'

'I will, of course; I'm most anxious to see it. But tell me what it is you think of doing with it?'

'I thought maybe——' the old man paused and laid his hand on Meldon's arm.

'Well?'

'I thought maybe you and the other gentleman would take it with you in the yacht and put it in the savings bank beyond in the big town.'

'That beats all,' said Meldon. 'And what would hinder us from making off with it and never coming next or nigh you again?'

'You wouldn't do the like.'

'Well, as a matter of fact I wouldn't. No more would the Major. But how do you know that? It's a queer thing that a man who wouldn't trust his own daughter, and her living under his very eye, would hand over a lot of money like that to two strangers.'

'Sure, I could see by the face of you the minute you first set foot on the pier that you were as simple and innocent and harmless as could be. Anybody could tell by the talk of you that you couldn't get the better of a child, let alone a grown man like myself, begging your honour's pardon for thinking that ever you'd want to do the like.'

'You're quite wrong about that,' said Meldon, irritated by this compliment to his integrity, 'and if you dare to say such a thing again I'll not help you with your treasure. Mind what I say. Another word of that sort out of your head and I'll go straight down to Higginbotham and tell him what you've got.'

'Let you be coming along now,' said Thomas O'Flaherty in an indulgent tone, 'and don't be wasting the night talking. Walk easy. It's a rough way from this on to my houseen, and there's stones on it would break the leg of a bullock, let alone yours or mine.'

19

They reached the cabin. Old O'Flaherty fumbled at the latch and opened the door. Inside, the place was almost quite dark. A few sparks glowed faintly on the hearth. The small square window looked like a grey patch on the black wall. Meldon paused at the threshold, unwilling to advance without light towards unknown furniture, over a pitted and hilly earthen floor. O'Flaherty disappeared into a corner and could be heard breaking sticks. The fragments were flung on the hearth. The old man went down on his knees and blew the embers.

'I have the end of a candle on the dresser beyond,' he said, 'if I could come by as much fire as would light it.'

'If that's what you're after,' said Meldon, 'I have a box of matches in my pocket.'

He drew out the box and struck one. O'Flaherty pounced on his candle, lit it, and set it on the stone seat which filled an angle of the wide hearth.

'Let you give me a hand now, and we'll shift the dresser,' he said. 'I could do it myself, but it'll be done quicker if you take the near end of it.'

Meldon caught hold of the dresser and pulled it over to the far side of the room. O'Flaherty stood on a wooden stool and took down a shovel which rested among the rafters of the roof. He scooped away loose earth from the place where the dresser had stood. At the depth of about an inch he came upon a number of boards laid close together. He prized up one of them with the edge of the shovel and lifted the others out. A hole lay open. Meldon peered into it, but could see nothing. He fumbled for his matches. O'Flaherty fetched the candle from the stone seat in the hearth. He lay flat and, stretching his hand into the hole, held the candle far down. Meldon saw piles of coins standing in neat rows. He, too, lay down on the floor, reached into the hole, and, touching them with his fingers, counted the piles. There were ninety-eight of them. He lifted one and counted the coins in it. There were twenty.

'Hold the candle here,' he said.

Thomas O'Flaherty, rising to his knees, set the candle on the floor at the edge of the hole.

'They're all gold, every single one of them,' said Meldon. 'If those were no more than just ordinary sovereigns you'd have pretty near two thousand pounds. But by the weight of them I'd say that they're worth two or three sovereigns each. You're a rich man, Thomas O'Flaherty Pat. There may be richer men in the province of Connacht, but I don't believe there's one with the same command of ready cash. I declare to goodness if it wasn't for Gladys Muriel, I'd wait a few years on the chance of getting Mary Kate. However did you get all that money up out of the cave?'

'I did have a bit of rope fixed to a big stone the way it wouldn't shift on me and me going up and down. The lids of the iron boxes gave me my 'nough of work before I got them lifted, and them rusty with the damp there was in it. But, with the help of God, I got them lifted at the latter end. Then I'd be putting the gold into a bit of a bag that I had on me. It was very little I could take at the one time, for it would surprise you how heavy it is, and me having to climb the rope and not one at the top to give me a hand. Maybe it wouldn't be more than once in the day and often not that much itself that I'd go down. I did be in dread that some of the boys would discover what I was after. From first to last I wasn't less than a whole year at the job.'

'You would be all that,' said Meldon. 'It's a mortal pity I wasn't here at the time. We'd have rigged up some sort of pulley at the top of the hole, and with me filling at the bottom and you taking the stuff at the top we'd have had it out in a single day. But there's no use talking about that now. The gold's here, right enough, however you got it.'

Meldon turned the coins over and over in his hand, held one to the light and then another, felt the weight of them singly and then two or three at a time.

'What put you on to it?' he said. 'What made you think of looking in that hole?'

'Sure the people always had it that there was a deal of gold on the island somewhere. My father knew it and his father before him, and everybody had heard tell of it. Long ago they did be searching for it. There was two of the gentry once came to look after it. But people got tired, finding nothing, and at the latter end they gave it up. It's maybe a hundred years since anybody laid down his mind to look for it. But there was one place that I knew nobody ever searched, and that was the Poll-na-phuca.'

'Why not?'

'They'd be in dread on account of them that do be in it.'

'Them that—oh, the fairies, of course!'

'Well, I used to be turning it over and over in my mind and me no more than a gossure. And I said to myself that seeing the gold was somewhere and that there was just one place that nobody would be caring to look for it, it was there it must surely be. It came into my mind, too, that the like of them that hid it first wouldn't be in dread of who might be in the hole or who might not. I've heard them say that the gentry doesn't give much heed to them tales. Indeed, they might choose out the Poll-na-phuca just by reason of there being many another that wouldn't go next or nigh it.'

'That was a fine piece of deductive reasoning,' said Meldon. 'I couldn't have argued the thing out better myself. I say, Tom—you won't mind my calling you Tom, will you? I'll say Pat if you like, but your whole name is too long for frequent use—the wind's rising. Did you hear that last gust? It's going to be a nasty night.'

'It was long enough,' said old O'Flaherty, shading the candle from the draught, 'before I could get my mind laid down to go into the Poll-na-phuca. I'd be saying to myself in the daytime that I'd go and thinking maybe I'd better not when it was dark. Or it would be the storms in the winter and the noises there'd be coming out of it would make me think it would be wiser to leave that sort of people to themselves and not be meddling with them. But in the latter end, when I was getting used to living near it and no harm coming to me, I went down.'

'And did you ever come across a leprechaun or anything of that sort? Tell me the truth now.'

'I might, then. Believe you me there's queer things that nobody, not the clergy themselves, knows about, down in the depths of the bowels of the earth where the sun doesn't be shining. There's queer things there.'

'Higginbotham says there's pliocene clay.'

'There might. I wouldn't say but there is. The likes of him would surely know. But there's more.'

'I wouldn't wonder,' said Meldon. 'I didn't come across anything of the sort myself; but then I was only there once, and besides, I'm not the sort of man that a fairy would come near. But we can't afford to spend the night in gossiping. Are you still bent on my taking the gold away with me in the yacht?'

'I am.'

'It'll take the best part of the night to get it on board. For one thing I'm bound to waken Major Kent the first trip and then I'll have to give him some sort of an explanation of what I'm doing. You don't know the Major and so you can hardly realise the length of time it takes to explain anything to him. He'll want to argue, and he's always in a bad temper when you first wake him. The morning will hardly see us through the job. Luckily the only person with any sort of right to interfere is Higginbotham. He's frightfully officious, and you never can tell what his Board might regard as coming under the head of mining rights. But it's easy to put Higginbotham off the scent. Do you happen to have that bag anywhere about, the one you used to take down into the cave?'

O'Flaherty rose, climbed on his stool again, and grubbed among some dirty sails and nets which hung on a beam above the hearth. He descended with an ancient flour sack in his hand.

'That's not such a small bag as you led me to believe,' said Meldon. 'I wouldn't care to go off in our punt with that bag full of gold. You may have noticed that ours is one of those patent collapsible punts, and you have to be uncommonly careful what you take in them. The best thing we can do is put a few hundred of your doubloons in the bottom of the sack, ferry them off, and then come back for more. My goodness, listen to that! There must be half a gale of wind blowing this minute and that won't make the job of navigating the Major's beastly hat of a punt any easier. Still, if nothing else will do you except to get the stuff on to the *Spindrift*, we'll—— Hallo! What on earth are you doing with the candle?'

Old O'Flaherty rose suddenly to his knees as Meldon spoke, held the light aloft, gave an inarticulate cry, and then dropped the candle. As he did so Meldon was struck on the head from behind and rolled over senselessly on the floor.

'I've settled the curate,' said Sir Giles Buckley. 'Have you got a hold of the old man?'

Euseby Langton had not got hold of O'Flaherty. His nerve had failed him at the moment of assault and he stood helpless in the door. Thomas O'Flaherty realised his position at once. He rose from his knees and began to move silently through the hut. It was quite dark.

'No,' said Langton. 'I—I missed him.'

'Damn it!' said Sir Giles; 'we must get him or he'll raise hell all over the island. I can't see a stim.'

O'Flaherty guessed from the sound of his voice that Langton was in the door and that his way of escape was barred. He moved through the hut in the hope that Langton might be tempted to pursue him. Sir Giles felt after him in the dark; but the place, familiar to O'Flaherty, was strange to him.

'Stay in the door, Langton,' he cried. 'Don't let him pass you.'

He struck a match and caught sight of O'Flaherty standing a few yards in front of him. But the old man was ready for the manœuvre and had his wits about him. He struck at the match with his hand and extinguished it. Sir Giles made an effort to grapple him, failed, and dropped his match-box. O'Flaherty moved away from him, felt the shovel with his feet, stooped and picked it up.

'Strike a match, Langton,' said Sir Giles.

The moment the first sparkle of light shone O'Flaherty struck at Sir Giles with the shovel. He brought the flat of the blade down on the arm which Sir Giles stretched out to guard his head. Then, with a call to Langton for help, Sir Giles flung himself on the old man. O'Flaherty was feeble, but he fought desperately. Sir Giles's right arm was numbed from the blow of the shovel. He called again for help. Langton seized O'Flaherty round the neck and pulled him backwards. Between them they overpowered the old man and laid him on the floor. They had come well provided with what they were likely to want. Ropes were produced. O'Flaherty was securely bound and gagged. Sir Giles drew a candle from his pocket and lit it.

'Now for the curate,' he said. 'I've knocked the senses out of him anyway. It's a good job I hit hard. I wouldn't care to be scrapping in the dark with him. The old fellow gave me enough to do, and you're nothing but a damned coward, Langton. Now, we'll tie up the Rev. J. J. Meldon and gag him, so that he won't stir even if he comes to. When there's light enough we'll lower the two of them into the cave and leave them there.'

'That'll be murder,' said Langton, 'and I told you I'd have nothing to do with murder.'

'Don't be an infernal ass. There's no murder. Some fool or other will find them tomorrow or the day after, and they'll be alive all right. We must get a clear start out of this. Don't you know that the steamer would overtake us at once if she started after us? And she will if those two fellows are found and tell their story. Come and give me a hand.'

Meldon's legs were tied together. His hands were lashed to his sides. A gag was forced into his mouth and secured.

'Now we have him safe,' said Sir Giles, 'even if he does come to. Let's get at the gold. We've no time to waste.'

Meldon's head was a hard one. Very shortly after he was bound he recovered consciousness. He recognised Sir Giles and Langton and saw that they were stooping over the hole where the treasure lay. He saw them lifting out the coins and putting them into a leather hand-bag which lay beside them on the floor. He could recollect nothing of what had happened, but he grasped at once the obvious fact that old O'Flaherty was being robbed. He struggled at the ropes which bound his hands and feet, but found that he could not stir them. The gag prevented him from either speaking or crying. One form of activity alone remained possible for him. He rolled across the floor of the hut.

It is not easy to roll in a straight line towards any given object. The human body, like a biassed bowl, has a tendency to turn on the hips as on an axle, and arrive ultimately somewhere near the place from which it started. But the distance which Meldon had to travel was not great. He succeeded, after convulsive efforts, in cannoning with some force against Langton. Taken completely unawares, Langton toppled forwards, extinguishing the candle in his fall. A further effort upset the bag into the hole, and then Meldon followed it and fell, doubled up, on top of the treasure.

Sir Giles cursed vehemently. He stood up in order that he might curse with better emphasis. As a further relief to his feelings he kicked Langton, who still sprawled beside the hole. Then he went down on his hands and knees and felt about for the candle. The search drew from him other expressions of annoyance. Meldon, though his position in the hole was extremely uncomfortable, found a good deal of pleasure in listening to Sir Giles. At last the candle was retrieved and lit again.

'I'd better knock that infernal parson on the head again,' said Sir Giles. 'It's the only possible way of keeping him quiet.'

'Don't; you'll most likely kill him.'

'Nothing would kill that fellow. He wouldn't die if you hanged him.'

'I won't have you smashing his skull anyway. Can't you take him outside the door and leave him there?'

Meldon was pulled out of the hole, dragged across the floor of the hut, and deposited on a bank of grass opposite the door. It was raining heavily.

'Cool yourself there awhile,' said Sir Giles. 'When it's light enough I'm going to drop you down into the cave that the treasure came out of. You and that damned old ragman can lie at the bottom of it and look at each other till somebody comes to rescue you.'

Meldon received a good many bruises and scratches, but he retained his consciousness. He knew where he was. Below him was the end of the bohireen and the door of the hut. His mind was filled with a vehement rage against Sir Giles. He was totally indifferent to anything that might happen to himself. He desired intensely to do something which would obstruct, annoy, and, if possible, injure the man whom he regarded as a personal enemy. He hit upon a plan which seemed hopeful.

He writhed to and fro until he succeeded in rolling down the bank to the bohireen. By much wriggling he arranged himself across the path. His head was on the grass at one side, his feet on the grass at the other. He lay on his side with his face towards the door of the hut. He was extremely uncomfortable. A stream of water was running down the stony track. His body dammed it, and it mounted up against him, soaking him through. The wind blew more water against the part of his clothes which the stream did not reach. A sharp-pointed stone stuck into his right shoulder. His face was cut and plastered with mud. His body seemed to be bruised all over. His head ached violently. But all this mattered nothing to him for the moment. His faculties were absorbed in watching the door of the hut.

Sir Giles and Langton appeared. They carried between them the leather bag, full almost to the bursting-point. Langton held the candle in one hand, but it was almost immediately extinguished by a gust of wind. Their eyes were not yet accustomed to the darkness. They took the first few steps cautiously. Meldon turned over on his face and waited, lying quite flat. He felt a foot touch him. He drew his knees up under him and arched his back suddenly. The stratagem was entirely successful. Sir Giles pitched forward and fell, dragging the bag from Langton's hand. It burst open and the contents were scattered broadcast over the muddy lane. Meldon, highly delighted, waited for the volley of oaths which was to be expected. He was disappointed. Sir Giles rose in silence. His anger this time was too fierce for blasphemy. He stood over Meldon and kicked him savagely on arms and legs and body. He was wearing rubber-soled yachting shoes, and his vengeance was not as ferocious as it looked. Missing Meldon once or twice owing to the darkness and his rage, he kicked stones and hurt his own toes greatly. Langton, who failed to realise the feebleness of the assault, protested.

'Drop that. Drop it, I say. Do you want to let yourself and me in for being hanged? If you leave the man in the middle of the path you've no one to blame but yourself when you trip over him. What's the use of behaving like a madman?'

'I didn't leave him here. He crawled here himself.'

'Rot,' said Langton. 'He couldn't crawl.'

'I'll put him somewhere this time that he won't get away from so easy.'

He gripped Meldon by the feet and hauled him up the bank. He dragged him along the grass till he came to a wall. He called Langton to his assistance and between them they lifted Meldon over it and deposited him in a ditch at the far side.

'Get back over that if you can,' said Sir Giles.

He kicked Meldon again. 'So far,' he said, 'I've just had one solid piece of satisfaction this evening. I've stopped your talking with that gag. If I did right I'd cut your tongue out now I have you tied, so that you'd never be able to talk again.'

Meldon listened. It annoyed him very much that he could not speak. He wanted to refer Sir Giles to the case, discussed by the historian Gibbon, of certain Christian martyrs, who spoke fluently and well after being deprived of their tongues by an executioner. He also wanted to say, that so far, working against long odds, he had got the better of the struggle and had annoyed Sir Giles more than Sir Giles had annoyed him. He tried to give expression to his feelings by winking first with one eye and then with the other. But it was so dark that the winks could not be seen, and Sir Giles departed without knowing what Meldon thought of him.

20

Sir Giles and Langton went back to the lane and set about the task of hunting for the gold which had been scattered. They found the bag at once and in a corner of it a couple of dozen coins. The rest were strewed about among the mud, the pools, the running water, and the loose stones. The wind tore across the island in violent gusts. The rain beat furiously upon them. The candle which Langton had put in his pocket was lighted and promptly extinguished. Sir Giles made a kind of shelter for it with his coat and tried to keep it burning. He succeeded for a minute or two. Then a gust of wind whirled over the coat and the candle was blown out again.

'Let's give it up,' said Langton. 'Let's go back and get another load.'

'I will not give it up. Do you suppose I'm going to leave a small fortune lying in this lane when I might have it for the gathering? Go back to the hut and try if you can find any kind of a lantern.'

Langton searched in vain, for old O'Flaherty owned no lantern. He returned to report his ill-success.

'I'll go down to the yacht,' said Sir Giles, 'and get one of her lamps. You can wait for me here and pick up what you can in the meanwhile.'

But Langton had no taste for crawling about on his hands and knees feeling for coins in mud and water. He was chilled and dispirited. When Sir Giles left him he stumbled back into the hut, wrung the water out of his coat, and waited in shelter. In about three-quarters of an hour Sir Giles returned with the *Aureole's* riding light in his hand. The search began again. After half an hour's hard work the bag was nearly filled, and, carrying it between them, the two men set out for the *Aureole*.

'Two more trips will be enough,' said Sir Giles. 'If we haven't got it all we shall have to leave the rest behind us. Thank the gods, the rain is stopping. The wind will go down now. If it doesn't, Langton, you may say your prayers. We'd never fetch Ballymoy or anywhere else in this gale.'

Meldon lay in his ditch. The ropes with which he was bound began to cut into his flesh. He was more bruised than ever. But he found a real satisfaction in picturing to himself Sir Giles as he searched for the coins in the dark. He was determined to try and free himself. A few efforts convinced him that he could do nothing with the ropes on his arms and legs. The gag seemed more hopeful. It was a woollen scarf. It was forced between his teeth, pulled tight from behind so as to drag his lips out into a kind of grin and knotted firmly at the back of his neck. He tried to gnaw it through with his teeth, but only succeeded in biting the insides of his cheeks until they bled. He wriggled along the ditch and got the side of his head against a stone with a sharp edge. He worked his head up and down, rubbing the woollen gag against the stone. He hoped in this way to wear the stuff through. The work was tedious and painful. But he persevered and in the end reaped his reward. The last strands of the wool parted. His mouth was free.

He looked round him and took stock of his position. At first he could see nothing but the stone wall, the grassy side of the ditch, and the sky. He noticed that it was beginning to get light. The rain had ceased. The clouds were being blown apart. Meldon guessed that it must be nearly three o'clock. He remembered that Sir Giles intended to lower him into the Poll-na-phuca as soon as there was light enough. He had no intention of being buried alive there if he could help it. He set to work to writhe and wriggle himself out of the ditch. He found himself at last in the field below O'Flaherty's house. He had a clear view of the bay and saw Sir Giles rowing out to the *Aureole*. The light increased and he noticed with great satisfaction that there was a heavy sea running outside the bay. He reflected that it would be totally impossible for the *Aureole* to leave her sheltered anchorage. But the wind was falling. In a couple of hours a venturous man might attempt to run for the mainland with three or four reefs tied down in his sail.

Sir Giles and Langton left the yacht again and pulled for the pier. Meldon decided that they must still have another load of treasure to ship. They had, as he calculated, an hour and a half's work before them. He saw below him, two fields off, the house in which Mary Kate and her parents lived. He made up his mind that he must get near enough to waken somebody in it before Sir Giles came to him again. There was only one possible way of getting there. He must roll down the hill.

He made up his mind to act at once. Having the use of his mouth he shouted a word of encouragement to Thomas O'Flaherty before he started:

'Hullo! Thomas O'Flaherty Pat! Hullo! I expect you're gagged and tied somewhere and can't answer. But I've got the beastly thing worked out of my mouth and I'm going to get the better of those two blackguards yet. It'll all depend on my being able to get hold of Mary Kate. Goodbye. I'll see that this business pans out all right in the end.'

The field in which he lay sloped even more steeply than most fields in the island. At the bottom of it was a wall and in the middle of the wall a gap. Beyond the gap was another steep field and at the bottom of it was the house. Meldon aimed for the gap. He congratulated himself that Higginbotham's philanthropic plans for the bettering of the islanders' system of land tenure had not yet been carried out. In the fences that were to be erected there would not be gaps and no man could roll over a six-foot Congested Districts Board bank.

He wriggled himself into position and started rolling down the hill. He advanced rapidly for a few yards and then came to a dead stop, lying up and down the hill. He wriggled again, rolled again, and was again brought up short by the impossibility of keeping his body parallel to the slope of the hill. Still he advanced and at length actually arrived at the gap. He lay still, giddy and breathless. He saw Sir Giles and Langton go into the hut. He started, as soon as he could, to roll across the second field. There were four bullocks in it which were lying together in a group when Meldon rolled suddenly among them. They were startled, struggled to their feet and galloped off in four different directions. After a while curiosity conquered their terror. They returned cautiously and slowly, sniffing and pawing, starting now and then in fresh alarm. Convinced at last that Meldon was harmless they gathered close round him and eyed him with wonder. He lay quite still because he could see Sir Giles and Langton coming out of the hut and suspected that they would search for him. He realised that the cattle hid him effectually.

Having lowered O'Flaherty into the cave Sir Giles and Langton went to the ditch in which they had left Meldon. They were surprised to find that he had disappeared.

'Can he have got loose?' said Langton nervously.

'If he'd got so much as his tongue loose,' said Sir Giles, 'he'd have raised the hell of a row by this time. That fellow would no more keep quiet than a corncrake would stop making the vile row it does make in the middle of the night. He can't have gone far. We must look for him.'

'No. Let's get out of this at once. The people will be awake and about soon.'

'We ought to have been off two hours ago,' said Sir Giles. 'Only for that cursed parson we would have been. First we had to waste time dragging him out of the hut, and then his infernal practical jokes cost us another hour and a half. We'll have to leave him now and chance it. We can only hope he's lying dead somewhere.'

Meldon watched them tramp down the bohireen and realised that he was safe. He understood also that he had very little time to spare. In half an hour Sir Giles would be on board the yacht again.

'He'll have to tie down three reefs,' said Meldon to the nearest bullock, 'if he doesn't want to be drowned. And that'll take him some time with nobody but Langton to help him.'

The remark caused the bullocks to edge away a little. Meldon started rolling again towards the cottage. Now and then as he drew nearer to it he shouted. At length, when he had got within about twenty yards of it the door opened and Mary Kate peered out. Meldon shouted to her:

'Mary Kate! I say, Mary Kate! Come here as quick as you can.'

The child approached him cautiously. Like the bullocks, she had never before seen anything exactly like Meldon as he lay in the field.

'Mary Kate,' he said, in tones meant to be reassuring, 'do you go to bed in your clothes?'

The question was reasonable. The child was dressed just as usual in her red petticoat and flannel bodice.

'I do not,' said Mary Kate. 'I dressed myself when I heard the shouts of you.'

'Very well, then. Go and get a knife.'

'A knife, is it?'

'It is,' said Meldon. 'A knife.'

'What sort of a knife?'

'Any sort of a knife you like, from a scythe down to a lancet, will do. In fact, I dare say we could manage with your mother's scissors. But run now and get something that will cut.'

Mary Kate went back into the house and returned with a sickle.

'My da will be wanting the scythe today,' she said, 'but if this will do you, you can have the loan of it.'

'I don't want the loan of it. I want you to cut the rope that's round my arms, and be quick about it.'

'The Lord save us and help us! Is it tied you are? Who's after doing the like of that to you?'

'I am tied. But if you'd stop standing there staring like a stuck pig, and come over here with the sickle, I'd soon be loose.'

Mary Kate approached him grinning.

'Don't grin,' said Meldon. 'I've said that to you before. Look here, Mary Kate, I've been cracking you up all over the island the last three days for one of the most intelligent children I ever met. It was only last night I offered your grandfather to marry you if he liked. But I'll not marry you. And I'll never say another good word for you, and what's more I'll take the half-crown and the three sixpences away from you unless you come here and cut the rope.'

'You couldn't,' said Mary Kate.

But the threat produced its effect on her. She stopped grinning and began sawing at the rope. The sickle was blunt, but Mary Kate worked vigorously. One strand after another parted. Meldon got his arms free.

'Give me the sickle,' he said.

His hands were numb and he was obliged to rub them up and down against his legs before he could take a firm grip of it. At last he managed to hold it, and set to work at the rope that bound his ankles.

'Mary Kate,' he said, 'go back to your da. Is he in bed?'

'He might, then.'

'Well, if he is, get him out and tell him to go up to the Poll-na-phuca with a rope and a ladder, and he'll find your grandda at the bottom of it if he isn't dead.'

'The Lord save us! They've took him at the latter end.'

'Don't,' said Meldon, 'get any rotten idea about fairies into your head. This isn't a fairy matter at all. Tell your father that if he doesn't go at once the old man will be dead, and as sure as ever he is I'll have your father hanged for murdering him. Do you understand me now?'

'I do,' said Mary Kate.

Meldon found it difficult to stand, and was only able to totter down towards the pier. He saw Sir Giles and Langton reach the *Aureole* and board her. He quickened his pace as much as his numbed, stiff limbs would allow. He watched the mainsail being hoisted, and noticed that the gaff was pulled little more than three-quarters way up the mast.

'Thank God!' he muttered, 'they see that they must tie down some reefs. I'll do them yet.'

He reached the pier. Realising that the water was still rough, he turned from the Major's punt and went along the beach to Jamesy O'Flaherty's curragh. He launched it and took the oars. There was no need for him to row. The wind drifted him rapidly from the shore. Sir Giles and Langton were tying down reef-points in the flapping mainsail of the *Aureole* and did not see him. He headed the curragh for the *Granuaile* and climbed on to the steamer's deck. Everybody on board was asleep. As the readiest way of attracting attention Meldon began to ring the bell which hung amidships and to shout 'Fire!' at the top of his voice.

A couple of sailors ran on deck and stood staring at him. Others followed them and began to ask questions. Meldon continued shouting 'Fire!' and ringing the bell. He saw that Sir Giles had stopped tying reef-points and was hoisting the sail as quickly as he could. The Chief Secretary emerged in his pyjamas. Father Mulcrone followed him in a white cotton night-shirt and a pair of trousers.

'What's on fire?' said Mr Willoughby.

'Nothing,' said Meldon. 'I wanted to wake you up, that's all. Send a boat at once and stop that yacht sailing.'

'Why?'

Meldon's mind worked quickly. He realised that long before he could tell the story of the treasure and reply to all the questions which would necessarily be asked, Sir Giles would have got off. Already he could see that the *Aureole's* jib was being hoisted.

'Never mind why,' he said. 'Do it.'

'I can't possibly,' said Mr Willoughby, 'send a boat to capture a gentleman's yacht without rhyme or reason. It would, I imagine, amount to an act of piracy on the high seas. I'd do a good deal for you, Mr Meldon; but, after all, I have to recollect that I am Chief Secretary for Ireland. Just fancy—the House of Commons—the newspapers——'

Meldon turned without listening to the end of the apology. He appealed to the crew of the *Granuaile*.

'Will any of you lower a boat and come with me?'

The men hung back, some grinning, some open-mouthed in blank astonishment. One glance at them convinced Meldon of the hopelessness of his appeal. He looked round him and caught sight of Father Mulcrone.

'Come along, Father Mulcrone. You're the only man in the whole crowd. Hop into the curragh as quick as you can.'

'Give me time to tuck my night-shirt into my trousers and I'm with you,' said the priest.

He crossed the deck and dropped into the curragh. Meldon followed him. Mr Willoughby peered over the bulwarks of the *Granuaile*.

'Stop!' he shouted. 'Wait! Hold on!'

The curragh shot out from the steamer's side.

'It's no good,' said Mr Willoughby, 'they're off. I have always heard that the clergy did queer things here in the West of Ireland, but—I'm hanged if the other fellows don't seem as anxious to get off as the priest and the parson are to catch them.'

Sir Giles and Langton, one at each side of the winch in the bow of the *Aureole*, were working with frenzied vigour to get the anchor up.

'He can't cut the cable,' said Meldon to the priest. 'Thank God, it's chain; the only thing on board the *Aureole* that isn't absolutely rotten.'

'Pull away,' said Father Mulcrone. 'She's over her anchor now. He'll have it off the bottom in a minute.'

Meldon pulled hard.

'He has it,' said the priest. 'Now he's hauling the jib across her to get the head round. Shove the stern of the curragh in, and I'll grab her before she gets way on.'

The *Aureole's* head paid slowly round and the mainsail began to draw. In obedience to a violent tug at the oars the curragh spun round and her stern struck the yacht amidships. Father Mulcrone gripped the weather bulwarks with both hands. The curragh swung alongside and was dragged stern first through the water as the yacht gathered way. Sir Giles left the tiller, sprang across the deck and began hammering at the priest's hands with his clenched fists.

'Let go,' he yelled; 'let go.'

He stood up and kicked at the priest's hands. Then he trampled on them, still yelling, 'Let go.' Father Mulcrone held on. Sir Giles kicked at his face, holding on to the weather runner to preserve his balance.

'Let go or I'll brain you.'

Father Mulcrone held on. He was not the kind of man who lets go. Mr Willoughby had discovered this about him when dealing with the question of seed potatoes for Inishmore. Meldon scrambled on board the yacht. He came on Sir Giles from behind, seized him by the shoulders, swung him round, rushed him across the sharply sloping deck, and flung him overboard.

'Let go now,' he shouted to Father Mulcrone, 'and pick up the fellow I've pitched into the sea. He may be able to swim or he may not. In any case you'd better look after him. I'll manage the other man and the yacht.'

Langton sat dazed and helpless in the cockpit, holding the end of the mainsheet in his hand. Meldon snatched it from him and seized the tiller.

'Loose the jib sheet,' he shouted, 'and let me get her sailing.'

Langton did not stir. Meldon dropped the tiller, ran forward and loosened the sheet himself. Then he got the yacht under command and set her racing to windward across the bay.

'If you stir hand or foot,' he said to Langton, 'I'll pitch you into the sea. I don't believe you can swim, whatever Sir Giles can do. Ready about now, and mind yourself.'

The yacht swung round and flew off on the new tack. The half-reefed mainsail bellied ridiculously. The water rushed green along the deck and foamed over the coaming of the cockpit. Meldon, a light of triumph on his face, stood up and looked round him.

Father Mulcrone had Sir Giles in tow behind the curragh and was pulling for the shore. It is difficult to get a swimmer into any small boat. It is totally impossible to get one into a canvas curragh. The priest had gone as near rescuing Sir Giles as was possible under the circumstances. A boat was lowered hastily from the *Granuaile* and the Chief Secretary, still in his pyjamas, got into her. She was pulled towards the curragh. A small group of islanders, men and women, stood on the end of the pier. Major Kent was awake and watched the exciting scene from the deck of the *Spindrift*. The *Aureole* ran under her lee. Meldon threw his boat into the wind and hailed the Major.

'Hullo! Everything's all right. I've got the treasure safe here. I always said I would and I have. I'll send Father Mulcrone off for you as soon as he's done rescuing Sir Giles.'

The *Granuaile's* boat reached the curragh. Sir Giles, spluttering sea-water and curses, was hauled on board. Meldon, having got the *Aureole* on the third tack, flew past them and shouted—

'I say, Father Mulcrone, just put back to the *Spindrift* and bring Major Kent ashore. It's a pity for him to be missing all the fun.'

A little group of men came down the hill towards the pier. Among them, supported by his son-in-law and a nephew, was old Thomas O'Flaherty Pat. In front of him, dancing with delight and excitement, her hair blown wild with the wind, went Mary Kate.

Meldon's tacks became shorter as he neared the land. The men on the pier cheered him each time he passed them. He waved his hand in response, and, when that seemed an inadequate acknowledgment of the enthusiasm, took Langton's cap and waved it. The *Granuaile's* boat reached the pier and was greeted with more cheers. The people of Inishgowlan, not yet aware of what had happened, were ready to cheer anybody. The Chief Secretary, stepping daintily, for he was barefooted, went on shore. Sir Giles, dripping and dismal, followed him. Meldon made his last tack and beached the *Aureole* close alongside the pier. The islanders and the men from the *Granuaile's* boat ran to him with offers of help. Meldon gripped Langton by the collar of the coat and lifted him over the side of the yacht into the water.

'Take him,' he said, 'and stand him up on the pier beside the other blackguard.'

He stepped over the side himself.

'I expect the boat has a hole in her,' he said to three of the men who still waited. 'You had better get the anchor on shore and make it fast. If she goes adrift on us now, she'll sink.'

He waded ashore, went to the pier and greeted Mr Willoughby.

'Sorry I hustled you this morning,' he said. 'It seemed the only thing to do at the time.'

'I don't mind being hustled in the least,' said Mr Willoughby. 'Living the kind of quiet, monotonous life a Chief Secretary does live, I'm sure a hustle now and then is good for me.'

'It's very kind of you to say so. Sure you don't mind coming ashore in your pyjamas?'

'Not a bit. I rather enjoy it for a change. But I'd greatly like to know what this is all about.'

'I never,' said Meldon, 'saw pyjamas just that particular shade of pink before. Where do you get them?'

'They're Irish manufacture, if that's what you're driving at. I daren't wear anything else even at night. But you haven't told me yet——'

'Oh, that's a long story.'

'I'm sure it must be. Perhaps you'd rather put off telling it till after breakfast?'

'Not at all,' said Meldon. 'It's not so long as that. Oh, here's Father Mulcrone. Didn't you get the Major?'

'He wouldn't come ashore,' said Father Mulcrone. 'He didn't seem to care about meeting the Chief Secretary.'

'Oh, the geological survey, I suppose,' said Meldon. 'That's all over and done with; isn't it, Mr Willoughby?'

'Quite,' said Mr Willoughby. 'It lies buried in a remote past. Things move so rapidly on this island that the affairs of yesterday are prehistoric before we are dressed this morning. Besides, a geological survey is nothing compared to the—the pragmatist method by which you roused us from our berths. Why did you give us the idea that something was on fire?'

'Because I wanted you to prevent Sir Giles Buckley from sailing off in the *Aureole*.'

'I gathered that from the way you spoke at the time. But please tell me why you wanted to stop him.'

Meldon glanced at the dripping Sir Giles. He was most unwilling to tell the story of the gold which lay in the *Aureole's* cabin. He wondered whether Sir Giles could be counted on to back up a version of the morning's adventure in which no mention of the treasure appeared.

'You may not know that that boat'—he indicated the *Aureole* with his thumb—'is rotten. Everything in her is rotten except the anchor chain.'

'Yes?' said Mr Willoughby.

'Well,' said Meldon, 'that explains what you want to know, doesn't it?'

'Not quite. I'm stupid, I suppose; but as a matter of fact it doesn't explain anything to me.'

'Don't you see that if Sir Giles had gone to sea in a rotten boat with the wind that's blowing today, he'd have been drowned to a certainty?'

'Oh,' said Mr Willoughby, 'you wanted to save him from drowning.'

'Him and his friend.'

'But, as well as I could make out, you flung him into the sea.'

'Quite so,' said Meldon. 'There wasn't anything else to do. Was there, Father Mulcrone?'

'There was not,' said the priest. 'The man was dancing on my knuckles and trying to kick my face.'

'I suppose he must have very much wanted to be drowned,' said Mr Willoughby.

'Well, I wouldn't go as far as that,' said Meldon. 'But there's no use taking up these speculative questions. Where's Higginbotham?'

'He must be asleep still,' said Mr Willoughby.

'Dear me,' said Meldon; 'that's a pity now. Higginbotham is just the man who might have helped to clear things up.'

'I don't know if it interests any of you'—it was Sir Giles Buckley who spoke—'but you're listening to a pack of damned lies.'

'I wish,' said Meldon, 'that you'd try and break yourself of that habit of swearing, Sir Giles. I think I've mentioned it to you before.'

'Of course,' said Mr Willoughby, 'it's no business of mine. Still, I should like very much to understand what all this fuss has been about. Perhaps, Father Mulcrone, you may be able to throw a little light on it.'

'Not a bit,' said the priest. 'All I know is that the gentleman there who seems to be catching his death of cold——'

'So am I, for that matter,' said Mr Willoughby.

'I see,' said the priest, 'that the men have come up from your boat, Mr Meldon. They seem rather angry about something. Old Thomas O'Flaherty is talking to them hot and strong and he's pointing this way. Perhaps we'd better go somewhere else before entering on an explanation.'

'Right,' said Meldon. 'Higginbotham's tin house is handy. Let's go there. It would do Higginbotham good to be made to get out of bed.'

'I should prefer the *Granuaile* myself,' said Mr Willoughby. 'I'd like to get into a suit of clothes.'

'Right,' said Meldon. 'It's all the same to me. In fact, of the two I rather prefer the *Granuaile*. I don't expect Higginbotham could rise to much in the way of breakfast for this party. We'd better take Sir Giles and Langton with us. Those fellows at the other end of the pier are looking rather nasty, and I happen to know that I'm not the man they want to kill.'

'It can't be me,' said Mr Willoughby.

'It is not you,' said Meldon. 'Nor it's not Father Mulcrone. It's Sir Giles. That's the reason I said we ought to take him with us. But before we start I think you should make the men a speech, Mr Willoughby. It might quiet them down.'

'A speech! Good gracious! What about?'

'Oh, anything. The University question, or the intentions of the Government about the land, or Devolution. Yes, Devolution would be the proper thing. It would turn their minds away from Sir Giles and Langton. Try them with Devolution.'

'Get into the boat,' said Mr Willoughby. 'I can't stand on this pier and make a speech in my pyjamas.'

'No? Perhaps not. Well, you have a go at them, Father Mulcrone. You won't? I suppose we'd better not turn on Sir Giles. He might make them more irritable. I'll have to do it myself, though I must say it's rather hard on me. I'm the one of the party who has worked hardest during the night. I can't tell you how trying it is to have to roll about in the dark with your hands and feet tied.'

The Chief Secretary and Father Mulcrone remonstrated with him vigorously. He yielded to them so far as to forbear making a speech, but he insisted on having a word in private with Mary Kate.

Taking the child out of earshot, he said to her—

'Mary Kate, go you to your grandda and tell him this from me: if there's anything that belongs to him in that yacht let him get it out of her and away with it before we come on shore again. Do you understand me now?'

Mary Kate nodded, grinning. Meldon joined Mr Willoughby and Father Mulcrone in the *Granuaile's* boat. Sir Giles and Langton eyed the men who were standing in a group at the far end of the pier and then followed Meldon.

'You're right to come with us,' said Meldon. 'Old Thomas

O'Flaherty is looking uncommon wicked, and you can't altogether blame him. He's working the rest of them up. I don't think that Inishgowlan will be exactly a safe island for you to picnic on, Sir Giles; not for a few weeks anyhow.'

'I'm becoming more and more curious,' said Mr Willoughby. 'I want a key to the mysteries which surround me. I'm a little anxious, too. If ever we get back to civilisation we may find ourselves in a police-court. Don't mix me up in anything criminal if you can help it, Mr Meldon. Consider my position as Chief Secretary.'

'You're pledged,' said Father Mulcrone with a grin, 'to the preservation of law and order in Ireland.'

'It's all right,' said Meldon. 'I'll keep your name out of the business as far as I can. Father Mulcrone and I will take whatever blame there is.'

'I won't take any blame,' said the priest. 'I know nothing about what's going on, either good or bad.'

'You'll have to,' said Meldon, 'whether you like it or not. It's your parish, so of course you're responsible if anything goes wrong.'

21

'I COULD do with a wash,' said Meldon when the party reached the *Granuaile*.

'You shall have it,' said Mr Willoughby. 'You shall have my bath.'

'Oh, don't bother about a bath. There's no use running into extremes. I'm a moderate man in every way, politically and otherwise.'

'Better have the bath.'

'All right, then, I will. But if I do, somebody'll have to go over to the *Spindrift* and get me another suit of clothes. Father Mulcrone, perhaps you wouldn't mind——'

'I'll send a boat,' said Mr Willoughby. 'Father Mulcrone wants to dress like the rest of us.'

'All right,' said Meldon. 'I don't care who goes. But I wouldn't like to get into these things again if once I took them off. By the way, have you any sticking-plaster?'

'I think I have a bit in my dressing-case,' said Mr Willoughby.

'I'll want a good big bit—yards of it, I expect. I'm not sure till I get my clothes off, but I fancy there are very few parts of me just this minute with the skin on.'

'I'll send you what I have. And now, Sir Giles, I must get a dry suit of clothes for you.'

In about half an hour the party reassembled for breakfast. Mr Willoughby made another appeal for an explanation of the morning's events.

'I told you my story,' said Meldon, 'and Sir Giles contradicted me flat—not that I mind being contradicted. I'm accustomed to it. But I think it's his turn to speak now. Anyway I want to eat my breakfast.'

Sir Giles was not eating heartily, but he seemed unwilling to speak.

'You hinted,' said Mr Willoughby to Sir Giles, 'that the account which Mr Meldon gave us of his actions was—er—perhaps exaggerated.'

'"Damned lies" was his expression,' said Meldon. 'I don't know if that's your idea of a hint that I exaggerated.'

'You appeared to think,' said Mr Willoughby, 'that Mr Meldon omitted from his statement some points of interest.'

Meldon, whose mouth was full, got into difficulties in suppressing a laugh. Sir Giles stared sulkily at Mr Willoughby.

'Come, now,' said Father Mulcrone, 'let's have your story. You'll feel easier when it's off your mind.'

'I'm not in your confessional,' said Sir Giles, 'and I'm damned if I'll speak unless I choose.'

'Come, gentlemen,' said Mr Willoughby, 'we needn't any of us lose our tempers. I think, Sir Giles, that you are bound either to substantiate or withdraw the very offensive statement that you made on the pier this morning. You called Mr Meldon a liar.'

'So far as I'm concerned,' said Meldon, 'I don't mind that in the least. I'm quite accustomed to it. There's hardly a man on this island who hasn't called me a liar. I quite recognise that Sir Giles' temper wasn't altogether under control when he spoke. He has a hot temper. I've had to speak to him about it before.'

'I suppose that you think it good fun,' said Sir Giles, 'to sit there bating me and setting that cursed curate on to sling insults at me. But I've stood all I'm going to stand of it. I'll stay here no longer. Come, Langton.'

The whole party, with the exception of Meldon, stood up.

'Don't go away like this,' said Mr Willoughby to Sir Giles. 'Sit down again and talk things over. I am sure we can come to some understanding if we can only find out what all this trouble is about.'

'Make your mind easy,' said Meldon, 'he can't go just yet.'

'Can't go!' said Sir Giles furiously. 'Why not? Who's going to stop me? So far as I know, nobody has a warrant out for my arrest.'

'You can't go yet,' said Meldon, 'because you've got on the Chief Secretary's Sunday clothes.'

Father Mulcrone burst into a loud laugh.

'That's easily remedied,' said Sir Giles. 'I'll change.'

'Please don't worry about the clothes,' said Mr Willoughby. 'You're welcome to them. I wouldn't like you to put on your own things yet. They can't be dry.'

'Lend him your pink pyjamas,' said Meldon.

For a moment it seemed likely that Sir Giles would make a violent assault on Meldon. His hands twitched. His face was deeply flushed. But he restrained himself and went into the cabin where his own clothes lay.

'This is an extraordinary business,' said Mr Willoughby. 'Surely, Mr Meldon, you'll tell me what it all means.'

'He can't go far,' said Meldon. 'I'm prepared to bet my best hat that there's a hole in the bottom of the *Aureole* and the Major won't take him in the *Spindrift*.'

'I don't like it at all,' said Mr Willoughby plaintively. 'I hate being kept in the dark.'

He took Father Mulcrone aside and spoke to him.

'What do you advise?' he said. 'What do you think of all this?'

'I think,' said the priest, 'that you and I had better go ashore with Sir Giles and the other man. I expect the people on the island know the ins and outs of the whole story by this time, and I'll be able to get it from some of them. There's been some rough work during the night. You saw the state Mr Meldon was in when he came on board. I expect that Sir Giles whoever he may be, has been up to some mischief. I don't like that man.'

'Still, it's an awkward affair. It seems to me that we're aiding and abetting Mr Meldon in robbery, and something like an attempt at murder. He threw Sir Giles into the sea, you know.'

'I expect Mr Meldon's all right. But we can't say anything till we get on shore and hear the whole story.'

Mr Willoughby turned to Meldon.

'Father Mulcrone and I,' he said, 'have decided to go—— Dear me, he's fast asleep!'

Meldon had fallen forward. His head lay among the crumbs beside his plate on the breakfast-table. His arms sprawled among the cups and dishes. A half-smoked cigar burned a hole in the tablecloth. Meldon slumbered profoundly.

'He's done up,' said Father Mulcrone. 'Let the poor fellow have his sleep out.'

'We'll make him more comfortable anyhow.'

Meldon lay like a log while they lifted him, laid him down,

and put a cushion under his head. Sir Giles Buckley and Langton entered the cabin.

'Hush!' said Father Mulcrone, pointing to Meldon. 'Don't wake him.'

Sir Giles spoke in a tone likely to waken any sleeper.

'Let me have a boat at once. I demand to be put on shore.'

'Will you whisht?' said the priest. 'Can't you see the man's asleep?'

'I warn you that if you attempt to detain me I shall take an action against you for illegal imprisonment.'

'Nobody has the least intention of detaining you,' said Mr Willoughby. 'The boat which brought us on board is still alongside.'

He led the way on deck, and the four men got into the boat.

'You're not bringing the curate with you, then?' said Sir Giles.

'Mr Meldon,' said the Chief Secretary, 'is asleep, as you saw for yourselves.'

'It's a good job he doesn't talk in his sleep. He never stops when he's awake.'

'He gave you credit for a hot temper,' said Father Mulcrone. 'I should call it a sulky temper if I was giving my opinion.'

Mr Willoughby interfered as peacemaker. The priest did not like Sir Giles, and was at no pains to conceal his feelings. Without the good offices of Mr Willoughby Sir Giles might easily have come to dislike Father Mulcrone as heartily as he did Meldon.

22

Two hours later Mr Willoughby and Father Mulcrone returned to the *Granuaile*. The Chief Secretary's face wore an expression of delight, tempered by anxiety. Father Mulcrone was jubilant and triumphant. They descended at once to the cabin where Meldon still slept on the sofa. Father Mulcrone shook him vigorously.

'Mr Meldon, wake up; wake up at once.'

Meldon opened his eyes, and saw the Chief Secretary and the priest standing over him.

'Hullo!' he said. 'I believe I must have had a nap. Breakfast has been cleared away, I see. I wonder what they did with my cigar. I had a cigar, I know, and I don't believe I finished it.'

'Here's the box,' said Mr Willoughby, 'take another.'

'Thanks, I will. Where are Sir Giles and Langton? They were here at breakfast, weren't they?'

'They're on shore,' said Mr Willoughby.

'Oh, are they? They haven't gone off in the *Aureole* by any chance?'

The priest smiled. 'They have not,' he said.

'I told you they wouldn't—couldn't in fact. Nobody but me knows how rotten that boat is and what a little bump would knock a hole in her.'

'We've been on shore,' said Mr Willoughby.

'Have you? Pleasant spot that island. I wonder more people don't come here in the summer.'

'We heard the whole story,' said Mr Willoughby, 'and we both want to congratulate you on the way you behaved.'

'Now, who did you hear it from?'

'Well, partly from Thomas O'Flaherty and——'

'I didn't think the old boy was such a fool.'

'And partly,' went on Mr Willoughby, 'from a little girl.'

'Mary Kate O'Flaherty,' said the priest.

'I thought better of Mary Kate,' said Meldon. 'She ought to have had a keener eye to her own interest than to tell that story. I suppose you've grabbed the treasure in the name of the Government.'

'He has not, then,' said Father Mulcrone grinning.

'No,' said Mr Willoughby. 'There was no treasure to grab. At least we couldn't find any. To put the matter plainly, the *Aureole* has been looted.'

'That's all right,' said Meldon. 'I wouldn't have liked to see poor old Thomas O'Flaherty Pat robbed by the Government any more than by Sir Giles. But how did you get the story? As far as I know Thomas O'Flaherty he's not the sort of man to talk more than he need, and I never got more than half a dozen words and a grin out of Mary Kate at one time.'

'The way of it was this,' said Father Mulcrone. 'No sooner did Sir Giles and Langton leave us to go down to the *Aureole* than all the children on the island, seven or eight of them, began to boo at them and throw stones. Mary Kate O'Flaherty was at the head of the crowd.'

'She would,' said Meldon. 'I always said she was a high-spirited little thing besides being intelligent. I expect, now, she hit them with as many as three out of every four stones she threw.'

'I shouldn't wonder,' said the priest. 'Anyhow, Sir Giles lost his temper.'

'He's always doing that. I hope he didn't hurt Mary Kate in any way or use language that a little girl oughtn't to listen to.'

'The language,' said Mr Willoughby, 'so far as I could hear it—I was some way off—was pretty bad. But he didn't do the children any bodily harm.'

'It wasn't for want of wishing to if he didn't,' said the priest. 'He looked as if he'd have been glad to skin the lot of them alive and pickle them afterwards.'

'They ran for their lives, I suppose?'

'No, then, they did not. But the fathers and the mothers of them came at Sir Giles with scythes and pitchforks and hayrakes and all sorts. It was then we thought we'd better interfere. Well, I'm not a coward exactly. You'll give me credit for that. But I give you my word I didn't fancy running into that crowd at all. I could have faced the men right enough, but the women——! Did ever you notice, Mr Meldon, that a woman when she gets her blood up is twice as reckless as any man? She doesn't care who she hits or where she hits him. I tell you I thought twice about facing the women. But the Chief Secretary is a hero, a regular hero.'

'It was nothing,' said Mr Willoughby modestly. 'I'm accustomed to women. A Cabinet Minister must be nowadays. If he didn't get hardened to it he would be dead in a year.'

'Anyway you went for them like an hero,' said Father Mulcrone. 'I never admired a man more.'

'I'll tell you what it is,' said Meldon to the priest, 'you ought to let him off those seed potatoes as a token of your respect and esteem.'

'I will,' said the priest. 'I'll do that. I wish you'd seen young Mrs O'Flaherty brandishing a flail and looking as if she'd skelp an archbishop if he came her way.'

'Had she Michael Pat with her?'

'She had not.'

'Well, if nobody was left at home to mind Michael Pat I expect the old woman's dead by now. But that can't be helped. Go on with the story.'

'We got them quietened down after a bit,' said Father Mulcrone, 'and then Mr Willoughby made them a short speech.'

'Was it Devolution, land, or universities?' asked Meldon.

'I can't for the moment recollect which it was, but I know it was a soothing sort of speech,' said Mr Willoughby.

'I expect it was Devolution, then,' said Meldon, 'not that it matters, of course, so long as you pacified the people. But I'd like to know where Higginbotham was all the while. You don't mean to tell me he slept through a battle of that kind, and it raging in front of his hall door.'

'I understand,' said Mr Willoughby, 'that the people locked Mr Higginbotham into his hut earlier in the day. He wasn't able to do anything except give us good advice through the window.'

'The fact is,' said Father Mulcrone, 'that when they started to pillage your yacht——'

'I expect Thomas O'Flaherty Pat was in the thick of that work,' said Meldon.

'He might,' said the priest. 'Anyhow, when they started at the yacht—that was while we were at breakfast on board here —Mr Higginbotham came out of his hut and tried to stop them. Of course they weren't going to put up with any interference from him. They ran him back into the hut and locked him up.'

'They didn't hurt him,' said Mr Willoughby. 'They seem rather to like Higginbotham.'

'Are you sure Mary Kate didn't fling a stone at him?' said Meldon.

'Not that I heard of.'

'I shouldn't have wondered a bit if she had. She had a grudge against him on account of a misunderstanding about some sugar-candy, and she might have considered it a good opportunity of paying him out. However, you say she didn't, so I suppose that's all right. Go on with the story. You left off just where you had made a soothing speech.'

'After that,' said Mr Willoughby, 'everybody began to talk at once. I imagine that most of them spoke in Irish. I couldn't understand a word anybody said. Fortunately, Father Mulcrone kept his head. He got old O'Flaherty away from the crowd and dragged the truth out of him somehow. Then he took the little girl and got the rest of the story out of her. There's just one thing we can't any of us understand, and that is how you managed to get down the hill from the old man's house to the place where the child found you.'

'Oh, that was simple enough. I rolled.'

'Rolled!'

'Yes. Rolled. That's the reason I asked you for sticking-plaster this morning. I haven't rolled as much for years and years, and it's a kind of exercise that requires preliminary training. But what have you done with Sir Giles and Langton? If you've left them unprotected on the island Mary Kate will have at them again and Michael Pat's mother will back her up. She has it in for Sir Giles ever since the day he wouldn't give the bottle to the old woman.'

'What bottle?' asked Mr Willoughby. 'I heard nothing about a bottle. It seems to me that this affair is even more complicated than I thought. You alluded casually a moment ago to sugar-candy, and now you speak of a bottle.'

'The sugar-candy and the bottle are side-issues. I strongly recommend you not to go into them at all. You'll gain nothing by it if you do, and you'll get yourself confused. But you haven't told me what you did with Sir Giles.'

'He's quite safe. We locked him and Mr Langton into Higginbotham's hut. It was Father Mulcrone's suggestion.'

'I hope you let Higginbotham out first.'

'Oh, yes. We let him out. In fact, we left him on guard outside the door.'

'And did old O'Flaherty get his treasure back safe?'

'I didn't get any very definite information about the treasure,' said Mr Willoughby.

'If you ask me,' said Father Mulcrone, 'I should say that every man on the island has his own whack of that treasure by this time. If half old O'Flaherty says is true, they have money enough among them now to buy out the island without asking a penny from the Board.'

'Then poor Higginbotham will be out of his job. I'm sorry for Higginbotham. I intended to give him a trifle if I got the treasure, to make up for not taking him entirely into my confidence at the start, and on account of the tuberculosis business.'

'That, I suppose, is another side-issue,' said Mr Willoughby, 'and perhaps of a pragmatist kind.'

'It is,' said Meldon with a grin. 'It's both. But I think you might stop rubbing that pragmatist philosophy into me now. It's not my philosophy, you know, any more than it's yours. I'm not continually throwing it in your teeth that you're a politician, although you are. Why can't you let the dead past bury its dead? It's not good form to be for ever dragging skeletons out of cupboards. I see that I've forgotten to wind up my watch and it's stopped. Would you mind telling me what time it is?'

'It's half-past twelve.'

'I dare say you'll be lunching early today. I may as well stay where I am till after that. Then I'll ask you to have me rowed across to the *Spindrift*. The Major will be getting anxious about me if I stay away too long. In fact, I expect he's rather worried now. I wonder if you'd mind going over to him, Father Mulcrone, and reassuring him a bit. He'll be delighted to see you. You'll get sardines and biscuits for lunch. He hadn't any bread when I left him, and I don't see how he can have got any since.'

'Take a loaf with you if you go,' said Mr Willoughby, 'and the remains of the ham we had at breakfast.'

'Are you sure we can spare the ham?' said Meldon. 'It was a very good ham.'

'There's another on board,' said Mr Willoughby.

'Very well, then, Father Mulcrone, take the loaf and the ham and give them to him with the Chief Secretary's compliments. That will reassure him. As you will be spending some time with him, you may as well tell him the whole story. It'll give you something to talk about. If you don't tell him I shall have to, and I hate telling stories to the Major.'

'Isn't he interested in stories?' said Mr Willoughby.

'He's too interested,' said Meldon. 'He keeps on asking questions, questions about details; and any one who has ever told a story knows that the details won't always bear working out. It's awfully good of you, Father Mulcrone, going like this just to oblige me. You're sure you don't mind?'

'Not a bit,' said the priest. 'I shall enjoy telling the story, as much as I know of it.'

'You're doing a kind act,' said Meldon. 'The Major's a lonely man at the best of times, and he's been shut up on the *Spindrift* ever since the *Granuaile* came into the bay.'

'Mr Meldon,' said the Chief Secretary after the priest had left them, 'I should like to say that I think you behaved uncommonly——'

'Oh, don't start that,' said Meldon. 'You wouldn't expect me to join in robbing old Thomas O'Flaherty Pat, would you? Besides, if I'd wanted to itself I couldn't have done it. They didn't give me a chance. Sir Giles knocked me on the head without any preliminary negotiations.'

'It isn't simply about last night's work that I wanted to speak. The fact is that I've got something rather important to say to you, and I'm very glad of this opportunity of speaking privately.'

'Is it the geological survey again?'

'No, no, not that.'

'It can't be the tuberculosis business, or the national school. Surely to goodness old O'Flaherty hasn't raked up the *Athalonia miserabilis*?'

'It's nothing of that sort. It's something quite different. Just before I left Dublin I had a letter from my friend Lord Cumberley.'

'I don't know him,' said Meldon. 'Is he an Irish peer?'

'No. He's an Englishman.'

'That wouldn't prevent his being an Irish peer.'

'Do listen to me,' said Mr Willoughby. 'What I have to say is really rather important, and I can't get on with it if you keep interrupting me.'

'Go ahead,' said Meldon. 'I won't open my lips till you give me leave.'

'Lord Cumberley is a man with a large property in Nottinghamshire and he is the patron of several livings there. One of them is now vacant, and he writes to me to know if I can recommend a man to him whom he might nominate. He wants an Irishman because he thinks that only the Irish

Church now produces genuine evangelicals.' Mr Willoughby paused.

'Am I to say anything yet?' asked Meldon.

'Perhaps not yet. Let me tell you a little more. The value of this particular living has been largely increased lately by the opening of a coal mine. It used to be a quiet country parish. Now it's becoming a small town, a town inhabited by colliers. I understand that from an ecclesiastical point of view colliers are not pleasant parishioners. Lord Cumberley writes that he wants an energetic man, not thin-skinned, resourceful, determined, and capable of making some impression on a rather rough class of people. From what I've seen of you since I came to Inishgowlan I think you'd suit the work very well. By the way, are you married?'

'Not at present, but I have a little girl—Gladys Muriel is her name—who is engaged to be married to me. I have her photograph in my coat pocket. I'll just get it. Where is my coat?'

'Don't trouble to get it. Lord Cumberley is anxious to get a married man; but the lady's personal appearance is not of any importance.'

'It is to me,' said Meldon, 'and I think you'd like to see the photo.'

'I should. But not just now. Would you mind telling me, are you an evangelical?'

'Now that,' said Meldon, 'is a difficult question. I may say at once that I'm not a ritualist; but it doesn't quite follow that I'm what your friend would call an evangelical. Some time ago there was rather a row about a sermon I preached.'

'I can quite understand that there might be. In fact, I'm surprised if there's only been one row.'

'A dear old sheep went bleating to the bishop——'

'Had you been preaching in its field?'

'I was speaking figuratively,' said Meldon severely. 'When I said a sheep I meant an elderly country gentleman. You know what they are, Mr Willoughby. Excellent old fellows, every one of them, with a kind of Mrs Hemans' way of looking at things.'

'I've come across them at times,' said Mr Willoughby. 'They form an interesting class. But why do you speak of them as sheep? Is it the prevailing type of countenance which suggests the comparison?'

'Partly, and partly their habit of following each other through gaps. Also they're all so respectable, and they let themselves be driven in flocks by people who bark at them. But I needn't go on working out the idea. If your friend, Lord Cumberley, is the kind of man who expects a parson always to say precisely the usual thing he'd better not get me into one of his parishes.'

'I respect your wish to make your position clear,' said Mr Willoughby. 'How did the—the bleat to the bishop end?'

'The bishop was asked to excommunicate me, or haul me up before all the rest of the bishops, or something, that's all.'

'But what happened?'

'Nothing happened. Father Mulcrone may say what he likes about bishops, but they aren't absolute fools.'

'If nothing happened, I suppose we may take it that the incident is of no real importance?'

'Not the least bit in the world. Only, if Lord Cumberley happens, as I said before, to be that kind of man, there might be unpleasantness—unpleasantness for him, I mean. I shan't mind.'

'I think we may risk it,' said Mr Willoughby. 'He never goes near the parish himself. He lives miles away and detests the place.'

'Goodbye,' said Meldon. 'I think I must be getting back to the *Spindrift* at once.'

'But you said you would stay for luncheon.'

'Can't possibly. If we're to get home tonight we must start at once.'

'But need you get home tonight?'

'Of course I must. I have to telegraph to my little girl to tell her to get ready to be married at once. If Lord Cumberley insists on a married man there's no time to be lost.'

'But I'm sure Lord Cumberley wouldn't wish to hurry Miss—Miss Gladys Muriel in any way. '

'Oh, she won't mind. She's just as keen on getting married as I am. By the way, now that the *Aureole's* wrecked, what's going to happen to Sir Giles and Euseby Langton? You can't leave them here marooned on the island. It would be rough on Higginbotham.'

'I can't well take them in the *Granuaile*,' said the Chief Secretary. 'I wonder if Father Mulcrone would keep them on Inishmore till I send off a hooker for them from the mainland.'

'I should think not. They wouldn't get on with him a bit, and I don't think he likes them. If you've no other plans for disposing of them I'll persuade Major Kent to bring them back in the *Spindrift*.'

'But won't that be rather unpleasant for you and Major Kent?'

'It will. But I'd put up with more than that to do you a good turn. I owe it to you on account of the parish. And you are in rather a hole about those two thieves, aren't you?'

'I suppose I am, though I confess the difficulty hadn't occurred to me till you suggested it. I'm greatly obliged to you for helping me out.'

'Don't mention it. Apart altogether from my feelings of gratitude to you personally, I enjoy helping people out of difficulties. If ever you find yourself in any kind of fix——'

'I'm never out of a fix,' said Mr Willoughby. 'The position of Chief Secretary for Ireland is one which involves a man in a continual series of fixes.'

'Well,' said Meldon, 'you've nothing to do when you're stuck but wire to me. I'll go to you at once. But I haven't time to go into any more of your difficulties just now. I must be off at once.'

'I'm inclined to think,' said Mr Willoughby meditatively, 'that you ought to be Chief Secretary and let me go to Lord Cumberley's parish. You would get on admirably.'

'I'm sure I should. But how would you suit the parish?'

'I'm afraid I should be a failure.'

'That's it. We can't risk that. A man at your time of life, with a reputation to keep up, can't run the risk of coming a bad cropper. It will be better to leave things as they are. You stick to Ireland. I'll go and hammer the fear of God into those colliers.'

23

Two years later Major Kent took another cruise in the *Spindrift*, this time with a hired man to assist him in managing the boat. He anchored for an hour in the bay at Inishgowlan, and then, not feeling inclined to go ashore alone, sailed on to Inishmore. He found Father Mulcrone in the presbytery and invited him to spend the evening in the cabin of the *Spindrift*. There had been a change of government some months before, and Mr Willoughby had left Ireland. The priest lamented his loss.

'The new man's not his equal,' he said. 'I don't say but what he means well. Only it's my belief that he'll never understand this country. I met him when he was round seeing the West. I told him the way the treasure was found on Inishgowlan, and what do you think he said to me?'

'I don't know,' said the Major. 'What was it?'

'He said, "That's a good story, Father Mulcrone." Now that was as much as to tell me to my face that the story wasn't one an honest man would take his oath to in a court of justice. There's unbelief for you. A fellow that starts off by thinking himself clever enough to know what's true and what isn't will do no good in Ireland. A simple-hearted, innocent kind of man has a better chance.'

'One like Higginbotham?' said the Major.

'I hear he's high up now, earning a good salary. He deserves it. How's Mr Meldon getting along with his parish?'

'I was over there last summer,' said the Major. 'I was standing godfather to the baby. She had another godfather, too, which is unusual with a girl. It was Mr Willoughby stood along with me.'

'And what did they call her?'

'Cecily May was the name the mother chose.'

'But what about the parish? I heard the men in it were a rough lot and disrespectful to their clergy.'

'They're cured of that now. There was a man there, a sort of leader among the colliers, who set up to be an agnostic or something of that kind, and was for ever talking to the rest of them about the folly of believing what the clergy said.'

'A fellow like that would turn the milk with his blasphemies. I've heard of such.'

'Well, the Rev. J. J. used to go to that man's house two evenings in the week and argue with him. The rest of the people took to coming to listen until they had to move into the schoolroom to accommodate the congregation. By the time I got over there that agnostic was singing in the choir with a surplice on him.'

'He was convinced in the end, then?'

'I'm not sure that he was convinced. I was talking to him one day and he told me, privately, that he wasn't any more persuaded than ever he was. He said he'd lost his taste for arguing. My own belief is that the man was cowed, and that if J. J. had wanted him to swear publicly to the truth of all the confessions of faith of all the Churches in Christendom he'd have done it for fear of having to argue any more. And he wasn't the only man in the place that changed his way of living. There was more than one that gave up beating his wife on account of the amount of talk he got from J. J. whenever he was caught at it. The very worst of them mended their language. You'd see a man looking round him and up and down the road before he'd venture on a simple "damn".

I needn't tell you, Father Mulcrone, that the necessity for that sort of precaution takes all the pleasure out of a swear. And as for drink——'

'What did he do about the drink? I've had my own trouble over that. Since ever the people of Inishgowlan got the gold out of the yacht I've been administering the temperance pledge to them in batches of half a dozen at a time, and often to the same lot twice in six months. I'd like to hear what Mr Meldon did about the drink.'

'I don't quite know how he did it,' said the Major, 'but I'm told that whenever a man in that parish feels that he must have a burst he goes off somewhere else and doesn't come back till there isn't a sign left on him of what he's been doing. And even so he's generally made to feel sorry for himself.'

'I'd like to have a talk with Mr Meldon about the way he manages.'

'He's coming over to Dublin next Christmas,' said the Major, 'and I mean to get him down to spend a few days with me. If you'll come too, I'll give you a room in my house with pleasure. J. J. is going to take out his M.A. degree. He thinks it's time for him to be wearing a blue silk hood in his church. I had a letter from him just before I left home. He says he's going to make his old rabbit-skin hood into a cot quilt for Mary Kate.'

'For Mary Kate, is it?'

'That's the baby. They christened her Cecily May to please the mother, but I never heard J. J. speak of her by any other name except Mary Kate.'

THE HOGARTH PRESS

This is a paperback list for today's readers – but it holds to a tradition of adventurous and original publishing set by Leonard and Virginia Woolf when they founded The Hogarth Press in 1917 and started their first paperback series in 1924.

Some of the books are light-hearted, some serious, and include Fiction, Lives and Letters, Travel, Critics, Poetry, History and Hogarth Crime and Gaslight Crime.

A list of our books already published, together with some of our forthcoming titles, follows. If you would like more information about Hogarth Press books, write to us for a catalogue:

30 Bedford Square, London WC1B 3RP

Please send a large stamped addressed envelope

Frank O'Connor
Irish Miles

New Introduction by Brendan Kennelly

Scouring the byways of Ireland on their bicycles, the famous story-teller Frank O'Connor, his wife and a friend set off in search of their country's buried past. O'Connor's discoveries range from the windswept headlands of Kerry to the mountains of Connemara, from country pubs to Cistercian abbeys – a magical journey, packed with anecdotes, strange meetings and curious characters and salted with his inimitable wit, tenderness and pungent opinions. *Irish Miles* is an enduring pleasure and an invaluable guide to an Ireland hidden from the tourist trail.

E. Œ. Somerville & Martin Ross
The Real Charlotte

New Introduction by Molly Keane

'A masterpiece, a classic' – *Lord David Cecil*

The Irish cousins Somerville and Ross have won many hearts with *Some Experiences of an Irish R.M.*, but their greatest work, and their own favourite, was *The Real Charlotte*, which tells of the rivalry between sunny Francie Fitzpatrick and her older cousin Charlotte, proud and ambitious, driven by secret desires – a sparkling portrait of the golden summer of Irish society, loved by generations of readers.

Neil Jordan
Night in Tunisia

Introduced by Sean O'Faolain

'One of the most memorable pieces of fiction to be published in recent years' – *Time Out*

The title story of Neil Jordan's stunning collection was described by Sean O'Faolain as 'one of the most remarkable stories that I have read in Irish storytelling since, or indeed before, Joyce'. Neil Jordan's powerful, distinctive voice has established him as one of the most important and original of contemporary writers. *Night in Tunisia* was awarded the *Guardian* Fiction Prize.

E.F. Benson
Paying Guests

New Introduction Stephen Pile

Bolton Spa is infamous for its nauseating brine and parsimonious boarding-houses. Exceptional is the Wentworth. Every summer this luxurious establishment is full of paying guests come to sample the waters and happy family atmosphere. But life in the house is far from a rest-cure. Acrimony and arthritis are the order of the day: battles are fought with pedometer, walking stick and paintbrush, at the bridge table, the town concert and afternoon tea. The trials and tribulations of the Wentworth will be relished in drawing-rooms throughout the land for years to come.

E.F. Benson
Mrs Ames

New Introduction by Stephen Pile

Mrs Ames is Queen of Riseborough society. Sceptre firmly grasped in her podgy little hand, she reigns supreme in a world of strawberry teas, high street gossip, and riotous insurrections by misguided pretenders such as Mrs Altham, Miss Brooks and dear cousin Millie. But her rule is threatened when, to the delight of her subjects, her husband's attentions stray from home and Mrs Ames, feeling all of her fifty-seven autumns, goes on the warpath. The series of restorative treatments – Shakespearian, feminist, but mostly out of a jar – with which she sets out to rewoo her gardening major are exquisitely chronicled in this comic masterpiece of provincial life.

E. F. Benson
The Freaks of Mayfair
New Introduction by Christopher Hawtree

Impaled on the pin of Benson's genius are prime specimens of Edwardian society: inveterate snobs and vicious gossips rolling up to receptions in Belgravia; young men with a taste for embroidery; health-cult devotees playing badminton in parquetted ballrooms; fossilised dowagers off to séances in Chesterfield Square. Here, in a fictional extravaganza, illustrated with the marvellous original line-drawings, are the bizarre, the great and the good E. F. Benson knew so well and all the forerunners of the unforgettable characters in his novels.

J. F. Powers
Morte D'Urban
New Introduction by Mary Gordon

'This is the book for which his many admirers have long been waiting' – *Evelyn Waugh*

Father Urban Roche is a formidable golfer, raconteur and star of the preaching circuit – no ordinary priest he. Hardly surprising that he harbours less-than-meek ambitions of inheriting the highest of posts, Father Provincial to his Order. Then, banished to a deserted retreat in the wastes of Minnesota, this man for all seasons is forced to confront the realities of life on earth which, through a sequence of events at once uproarious and moving, he triumphantly does. A novel about a priest, a special priest, *Morte D'Urban* is a parable of the straitened role of belief in a secular age. It is also one of the comic masterpieces of our time.

Caryl Brahms and S.J. Simon
Casino for Sale
New Introduction by Ned Sherrin

'Witty and elegant fantasies' – John Mortimer

The hilarious misadventures of the Ballet Stoganoff continue...

Hoping to break the bank, they buy a casino on the Riviera, only to see their reckless impresario arrested for murder. Place your bets here, *mesdames* and *messieurs*, for the funniest book you're ever likely to read on backstage ballet life, gambling and other foul deeds.